UNTANGLED

KENNEDY RHODES

Untangled

Editor: Sandra Wissinger

Cover design by Dana Isaly Instalove Graphics

ISBN: 979-8995160106

First Edition: 2026

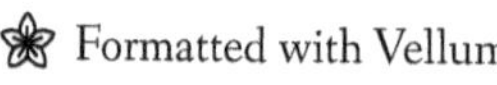 Formatted with Vellum

CONTENT WARNING

Mild Violence
Insinuated Harm to Animals
Unwanted Sexual Advances
Childhood Trauma

ALSO BY KENNEDY RHODES

Uprooted

This book is for anyone who has decided to live unapologetically.
Let's get weird.

PROLOGUE

Tai

"**Y**OU!" It's not the first time Bri has greeted me as if she is offended by my very existence. I laugh.

Critical mistake.

Technically, I am laughing *at* her, but really, I'm laughing at the memory of the first time she addressed me the same exact way. Aro had dragged me along so he could flirt with Bri's friend, Elowen, the human that had caught his attention.

Apparently, Bri has been holding a grudge for the way I treated her since then. She'd puked when she landed. How was I supposed to know she was trying to find a place to dispose of the bag? I honestly thought she was keeping it for some weird human custom.

The angry, blotchy red look on her face promptly dries up my laughter. The words "retreat," "danger," and "volatile" run through my brain as she tears into me. I'm so focused on our argument, it doesn't fully register that the warnings are coming from the waysta- tion's intercom, not my inner monologue. It takes being knocked over by a Pyrrian rushing past to realize the station is being evacuated.

I've been here less than ten minutes, and I'm being evacuated already? At least I got what I came here for, and she's standing in front of me furious and determined to make my job difficult.

"What's happening?" she asks while I drag her toward the cargo bay.

"Evacuation. How should I know?"

"I dunno, aren't soldiers supposed to know things?"

Every word out of this female is aimed at shrinking my confidence. Now I'm expected to know the inner workings of a space station I've never seen before?

The evacuation port is utter chaos. Aliens of all sorts run in every direction. I place Bri in an empty lifepod and plant her in the seat with my hands on her shoulders.

"If I'm not back in five minutes, close the airlock and hit the button right there." I point at the big red blinking light on the control panel.

"Where are you going?!" she yells through the frenzy.

"I'll be back in five." I sprint for the main hub. Everyone is moving toward the evac port. I'm the only one stupid enough to run in the opposite direction. I arrive at the empty hub and look around for anyone left behind.

"Zone isolation in 60 seconds," the overhead speaker announces. I run to the maintenance halls next. Luckily, they are empty as well. I go to retail then to dining. I search behind the garbage chutes and storage units. Nothing.

"Prepare for airlock in 20 seconds," the speaker blasts. I spin around one last time looking for anyone who might need my help.

The countdown for airlock initiates and time is up. I sprint through the now empty halls back to Bri. She leans the top half of her body out of the lifepod, her white-knuckle grip keeping her in place. She's biting her lower lip, anxiety written all over her face.

All the other occupied lifepods have already deployed and she's alone in the echoing evac port. Relief floods her face when she sees me come through the tunnel. Relief that is quickly replaced with rage.

"What the fuck, Tai? What could possibly have been so important?"

"I needed to double-check something."

I step over the threshold to join her when she stops me.

"Just what the fuck do you think you're doing?" she asks with fire in her eyes and a firm hand on my chest.

"Evacuating."

"Not with me you aren't. I told you, I'm not going anywhere with you."

I take a calming breath and ball my fists to stop myself from shaking some sense into her. It's impossible to think straight with the screaming alarm and commotion swirling around us.

"Bri, I can't argue with you about this. We need to get out of here. Now," I say, my jaw painfully clenched.

"Get your own lifepod." She shoves me out and slams her fist on the control panel, activating the airlock and effectively ending our conversation. Her lifepod is halfway down the ejection port when I realize I didn't remind her to override the autopilot.

It's fine—she should know how to override coordinates. It's mandatory training on every station.

Damn it. I *really* hope she paid attention during the course. From what Elowen mentioned about Bri's patience during training at the muraDome, I'm not so sure the module *Navigational Systems Trajectory Modification* would have kept her full attention. In hindsight, I would have petitioned to have it renamed *BRI, PAY ATTENTION! THIS IS IMPORTANT!*

Now it's on me to make sure she's safe.

Fuck.

I jump into the empty lifepod closest to me, strap myself in and link my location to hers. This conversation isn't over—and whether she likes it or not, I'm bringing her back to j'Tilak.

ONE

Bri

I pull off my boots for the millionth time and dump out the sand. It was a struggle to get up this dune. I wipe the sweat out of my eyes so I can get my bearings. My wrecked lifepod is down below me nestled deep between two dunes. It's hot. I'm sweaty. And there is sand everywhere. *Everywhere* everywhere.

The crash keeps replaying on a loop in my head. The feeling of dead weight dropping through the atmosphere. The deafening roar followed by the absence of noise, which now I know is different from silence.

The console was dead by the time I came to. A pounding headache was the only confirmation I was alive. I felt around in the darkness for toggles or buttons to reboot the lifepod when my fingers snagged on the emergency survival pack under the cockpit.

The shape of the portable respirator was unmistakable when I pulled it out. Every space traveler knows to secure the air mask first. I haven't traveled much, but I can recite the instructional video from memory. The clear face mask formed a tight seal around my nose and mouth. With a hiss, sterile oxygen flooded into my lungs. The bitter air from the respirator was beyond gross. It took everything in me to keep it on so I wouldn't suffocate.

The hatch opened and my ears popped, stoking my blinding headache. The respirator flashed green, indicating the air was safe. At least I had that going for me. I pulled off the mask and took a deep breath. The atmosphere smelled like dust. Not great, but better than the canned alternative.

Perched on top of the dune, I watch little avalanches of sand rush down and come to a stop against my lifepod from the impact of my tread. It's a strange sensation, watching the ground literally fall out from under me.

From up here, dunes spread out in every direction except one, so that is exactly where I will be heading. Is it north? South? Who the hell knows? But the flat, cracked ground riddled with dried-up bushes is more appealing than the alternative.

This is all Tai's fault. If he would've minded his own damn business, I wouldn't be here right now. The overbearing alien maybe *possibly* saved my life, but I will never admit that to him.

I should have been happy to see him. After all, he was there to take me back to j'Tilak. Which is what I wanted, but when I saw him across the room—tall, blue, and surly—my baser instincts took over, and I picked a fight. A normal person might have cooled off after those few weeks, but it seems my issue with him only festered and grew. His calm, cool demeanor sent me through the roof, and our entire convoluted past flashed through my mind. Every time I thought he was redeemable, he would swiftly remind me that he wasn't. Now it's hardwired in me to get mad the instant I lay eyes on him. It's damn near Pavlovian at this point.

More sand falls down the dune, the unsteady ground getting more precarious by the second. I plop down and anchor myself to the ridge. My khaki coveralls are doing a shit job keeping me clean. Handfuls of sand weigh down every pocket and scratch against my skin underneath my clothes.

I hate sand. I hate it so much. I avoid the beach because of it.

The only redeeming quality of the beach is the water. It's absolutely my luck that I've crashed on a planet covered in sand with no water in sight. As fate would have it, there are no waves crashing against the shore making me forget the itch of the sand in my underwear. No cold water lapping at my feet. The rough grains between my toes are already forming painful blisters. And there is a distinct lack of ice-cold beverages with tiny umbrellas to quench my thirst.

What I wouldn't do for one of those drinks right now. I'd order a pink one with a slice of fruit or pretty flower on the rim. Every summer, I trudged along the beach delivering those kinds of drinks to rich assholes on loungers.

I see it so clearly, me balancing tray after tray of glasses with condensation dripping down the sides. A refreshing drink of blended colors to take the edge off. I'd stare longingly when I'd hand one over to a guest.

It's crazy to think how far I've come from being that girl in Myrtle Beach. I finally got my wish to leave Earth and travel to a distant planet. All with the added benefit of playing a part in solving the food crisis on Earth.

Sure, things have gone a little off course, but what's an intergalactic adventure if nothing goes wrong? It all happened so fast. A classic case of "hurry up and wait." It gives me whiplash each time the thought comes back around.

Between classes on molecular biology and working on my genetic model, I worked shifts at the bougiest resort on the other side of the city. When I wasn't tits-deep in sand delivering cocktails, I dreamed about getting me and my family out of our miserable apartment in our miserable town, and out of working miserable jobs.

Fuck the beach—and fuck Earth, for that matter.

I lace up my boots and cinch them tight. It won't keep the sand out, but hopefully I won't have to stop so often to empty them. I rifle through my pack one last time, taking inventory. The contents haven't changed the last three times I've checked. A little reassurance goes a long way.

Don't think about food.

"Hello, my old friend," I say to the nutrigels as I push them to the side. I haven't had one of these since I traveled to j'Tilak from Earth. I was so hungry when I woke up from stasis, I pounded the gel and tore into a bowl of noodles. I ended up puking for hours.

I've got my air supply canister, some hydropacks, a foil blanket, liquid sutures, and a tiny graphite translator patch the size of my fingernail. There's also a flat disc and a tightly sealed pouch. I have no idea what those are for.

Whoever thought of including the translator did me a solid. I'm not in the mood to play charades to get myself home. The chances are slim that someone way out here will speak the universal language.

I step down on the opposite side of the dune ready to tackle the sprawling desert to find salvation. My foot sinks down into the soft sand, and before I can catch myself, I'm rolling ass over tea kettle all the way down. I land with a thud at the bottom. It's as solid as I had hoped—the air punched out of my lungs can attest to that.

"That's one way to do it."

Great, Bri. You're talking to yourself. It's only been a few hours, and you're already losing it.

I tighten the straps on my pack and stagger forward. My shirt is drenched. Fluid pours down my back and legs. Two thoughts flash at the same time: Is that pee? Or did I just destroy my emergency provisions?

"Fuck!" My scream evaporates into the hot ground. I drop to my knees and flip the pack open. Most of the hydropacks broke along with half of the nutrigels. I slurp the ooze off my fingers, trying to get anything I can from the ruined supplies. It would have been better if I had peed myself. Something I never thought I'd wish for. A hollow laugh starts in my chest. Wow, context really is everything.

Now is not the time to freak out. I take a slow and steadying breath. Calm and focused, calm and focused. Panicking now could mean the difference between life and death. And I refuse—absolutely refuse—to die on a goddamn oceanless beach.

I secure the straps on my shoulders again with the same determination and start walking, one limping awkward foot in front of the other.

"This is nothing but a little recreational hike," I say out loud to myself.

Whenever I'm in a terrible situation, I play this game. I picture myself retelling the story of the event I'm experiencing. I think of ways to make it funny and maybe even embellish a tiny bit to raise the stakes.

This is definitely going to be a hilarious story I'll tell over ice-cold cocktails, regaling a crowd with my survival skills. Impressing my brothers with my prowess.

The terror at realizing I've lost half my supplies is nothing compared to the horror rippling through my body when I realize my shirt and pants are bone-dry already. I grit my teeth and dig deep into the stubborn part of me that refuses to give up. There is only one outcome, and it's where I conquer this desolate planet and get back to my life, surrounded by cold air and even colder drinks.

The toe on my good side catches a rock, and I'm pitched through the air again, landing on my face. Again.

"Jesus titty-fucking Christ."

It takes all my mental energy to not list everything against me right now. Dwelling on all the negatives won't do me any good. I'm fine. Everything's fine.

I pull my arms out of my dirty coveralls and tie the sleeves off at my waist. If this is the adventure I get, then I will damn well enjoy it. I tighten my ponytail, ignore my swollen ankles, and set off.

This is going to make one hell of a story someday.

TWO

Tai

Crash-landing is not the way these fucking pods are supposed to work. I'm alive, but this thing is dead. I kick the hatch open and immediately know where I am when the sand pours in. The one place in the entire universe I swore I'd never return to. I fling the respirator back into the lifepod. It would *almost* be better if I needed to use it because then it would mean I wasn't on Sabaak. At least I've got my blaster this time.

This is all Bri's fault.

Once things calmed down back home, Aro gave me a simple mission: get Bri back to j'Tilak. But things are never that simple with her. Silly me for expecting her to be happy when I showed up. Instead of gratitude and cooperation, she radiated disdain and fury. It still doesn't quite make sense to me. A few weeks ago, Bri was on my home planet doing anything she could to stay. Then, she wouldn't let me take her back.

I guess I shouldn't be surprised by any of this. Come to think of it, every interaction with Bri has sent me on a collision course with ruin.

I don't know which is more irritating: Bri refusing my help, which she obviously needs, or the sand grinding between my teeth.

The thing I hate most about Sabaak is the bad memories it brings up. I'm a completely different Tilak now—those memories belong to someone else.

First things first: I need to get to higher ground and locate Bri. She can't be far. Hopefully she's still with her pod. Anyone with the smallest amount of self-preservation knows to stay with the lifepod after a crash landing. It's a lot easier to find a lifepod than a lone figure wandering the desert.

We'll probably be stuck here a day or two—max. Then we should be picked up. The locator beacons in the lifepods these days are pretty reliable. Any competent recovery operator should find us easily.

But then again, there are multitudes of travelers who get marooned on random planets and have to make it their home. Not me, though. I'll get back to j'Tilak—or die trying.

I double-time it up the hill, moving fast so the sand doesn't fill up my boots. From the top of the dune the howling wind lashes my face. I put on my visor, and it gets to work gathering data on my surroundings. Neon green glyphs leap across the screen and blink, rubbing in the bad news, as if I needed a reminder.

Inoperable lifepod.
Boiling temperatures.
Limited emergency supplies.
No known way off the planet.

The visor pinpoints my location relative to local civilizations—useful information. I prefer not to interact with anyone on this planet.

There is a Sabaaki village to the south and an Oo'rahim colony to the north. Now I know exactly where to avoid. The only person on this planet that matters is Bri. The instant I find her, I'll drag her ass back home and never think about this place again.

Seventy percent probability of survival flickers across my field of vision. I thought I had better odds than that. My bionic arm is already reacting poorly to the environment. Sand has worked its way into the joints. The gears hitch when I move the arm.

Fuck. Every second on this planet increases the likelihood of permanent damage. These things are hard to come by, and I'd rather not have to deal with the hassle. As it stands, it's going to take me weeks to get my arm working properly again.

My visor locks on the horizon. It takes a second for my eyes to adjust to the distance, but very clearly I can make out a trail of footprints through the sand.

Fuck. Fuck. Fuck.

The visor shows what my own vision can't: the green outline of another lifepod on the backside of a distant hill and farther in the distance a tiny bright red dot.

Biosignature Identified: Human
Identity: Brisa Mitchell

This is bad. Worse than bad—it's annoying.

My objective hasn't changed, but it is getting more complicated by the second. Why can't that female stay where she's supposed to?

It shouldn't be a problem to get to her. I'm bigger and faster and should be able to catch up in less than a day.

She should not be out here alone. These desolate planets are the perfect place for outlaws and criminals to hide out. I should know.

THREE

Bri

The blinding sun makes it hard to keep my head up, and watching my clumsy feet is extremely discouraging. So, I do my best to aim for the blurry space between the hot ground and the scorching sky. The view hasn't changed in hours, so I have to trick my brain into thinking I've made progress.

You've got this, Bri. Keep going. You're almost there.

I'm nearly swept away by a gust of hot wind that does nothing to cool me down. It only blows more dust into my parched mouth. I try to draw saliva to wet my throat and come up empty-handed. Even my sweat dried up hours ago.

Every night on j'Tilak, I imagined all the great adventures out in the universe waiting for me. This is not what I had in mind. But it *is* a new planet, and it's pushing me to my limits. I would prefer less sand and heat. Whatever—this is exciting and an opportunity to test my survival skills.

I reach into the bag and pull out one of the few remaining hydropacks. This fist-sized pouch holds the key to my survival. Shaky hands unscrew the cap, and I carefully raise it to my mouth. All it takes is a few small sips and I'm a new woman.

"See? It's not that bad. All you needed was a little water," I assure myself out loud. A list is forming in my mind of things I want to do when I get out of here. I add *See a psychiatrist about talking to myself* and carefully cap the water and store it away.

The solitary sun baking me alive confirms my suspicion that I am not on the beautiful and temperate j'Tilak with its two suns. I wonder what Elowen is doing there right now. She's probably in the lab trying to focus while Aro hovers around, trying to be useful, but getting in the way.

Way before Aro hulked out because of the whole mate thing, I knew they were made for each other. There is nothing more obnoxious than two people in love, so I'm surprised I miss them already.

I pin my hopes to the spindly bushes dotting the landscape. They've got to be a sign of water. I try to remember all the survival skills I learned as a kid. Finding water is the first and most important step.

With no comms and no sign of civilization, I have no choice but to keep moving forward. Jamison's voice echoes in my head: *No retreat, no going back—only forward.*

Being out in the wild is nothing new. There was never money for actual vacations growing up, so instead we would grab our packs and head out into the wilderness. Sitting around at home drove my dad crazy. He would announce it was time for an adventure, and the entire house would jump into action. Jamison would plan the route, Nate would double-check the supplies, and Hollis and I did our best to keep up. I inherited our father's restless streak—it doesn't let me stay in one place for too long.

Hollis would turn this into some game if he were here. He'd find some rock or stick and give it a name, personality, and backstory. It's his way of distracting me from miserable conditions. Playfulness always annoys Nate and Jamie, but it keeps us younger kids going.

Nate and Jamie prefer a battle for dominance to silly distractions.

All they care about is beating each other at anything and everything. Something as simple as a leisurely walk home or a friendly game of Cubes turns into a fight with those two.

One night we were all helping Mom bring in groceries. Nate and Jamie grabbed as many bags as they could and were racing up the seven stories to our apartment. I can't remember who swung first, but there was more than one black eye that night. By morning, they were back to being best friends.

I wish they were here with me, and not just because they would have insisted on carrying the survival pack. They definitely wouldn't have tripped on their way down a dune and destroyed half of our supplies. I miss their laughter and constant joking. After our dad left and Mom fell apart, they made sure Hollis and I had everything we needed.

I scan the horizon one last time before I strap on the pack and limp forward with my two swollen ankles. The right is worse than the left. But when I'm moving, the throbbing isn't as bad, so that is what I'm going to do: move.

It's been a while since I've let myself think about my brothers. I didn't think I'd be so homesick when I left Earth. *Stop complaining about them being overbearing dickheads* is added to the list of things to do when I'm back home.

Somehow, they are overbearing dickheads *and* extremely generous and supportive at the same time. The boys all take after our mom. They'd do anything for our family. I fear I take after my dad: restless and selfish.

"Come on, Bri! Get out of the bathroom! Nothing's going to hide the giant zit on your forehead." I can hear Nate now—the way he would yell as he banged on the bathroom door in the mornings before school. I felt justified in taking my time in there. As the only sister, it was my right.

"Zits come and go, but needle dicks are forever!" I remember saying back. I was particularly proud of that insult.

I always gave him shit right back, but I never had to worry about injuring Nate's self-esteem. He had a long line of women and men on standby. We'd hear giggling coming from his bedroom at all hours of the night. Horny laughter was my sign to make myself scarce because I knew what came next, and I didn't want to hear it.

The time Hollis finally snapped on him makes me giggle.

"Hey Nate, next time you have friends over, don't forget the walls are thin. I don't need to hear you prematurely ejaculate all night!" Hollis snatched the apple out of Nate's hands. Nate grabbed it back and took a giant bite, reclaiming the fruit for himself.

"Don't be jealous, baby brother. Someday you'll find someone desperate enough to let you disappoint them."

The burn on my skin brings me back to the present. My shoulders are red and painful. I untie the sleeves from my waist and ease them back on me, the stiff fabric scraping my skin all the way up.

Don't think about that, Bri. Think about nice things. Think about your family back on Earth. For some reason talking to myself helps.

I couldn't ask for better brothers, especially when it came time for college. It was quickly made clear that my mom's humble earnings wouldn't cover the costs of the schools I was being accepted into. I hid the notifications after I saw the look on Mom's face that first time. She tried her best, but there was no hiding the teary eyes overpowering her smile. I soon resigned myself to attending a local university and working my way through when my brothers sat me down and told me that was not going to happen.

"You are going away to the best school possible. We are going to make sure of it," Nate said.

"We talked. We're all going to pick up a third shift. We have what we need to live. Anything extra goes for your education. Period. End of story," Jamie declared.

No one stood a chance once Jamie made up his mind. He took it upon himself to be the authority in the house after Dad left without warning, and most of the time we accepted it. "Stubborn as hell" is basically the family motto, and it has served us well.

The power of my family's generosity has fueled me through

everything. Their unrelenting belief in me carries me through when things are hard. Every time I was underestimated or looked over, my family's support kept that determined fire in my belly burning. Even now, trudging through the heat and sand, my thoughts turn to them.

As a poor kid growing up in an affluent resort town and going to fancy and expensive universities, I could have given up, and no one would have batted an eye. In times of frustration, my family was my source of strength. I was succeeding for them, for myself, and for anyone left behind by those who cared for nothing other than the bottom line.

Deep in thought, I've walked farther than I realized. The hard-packed dirt comes to an end with yet another steep sand dune. Optimistically, I imagine that it blocks my view from the modern oasis waiting for me on the other side. Never underestimate the power of positive thinking. I'm willing it into existence through sheer determination. Kind locals will take one look at me, gasp with horror at my sunburned face, and insist on leading me to cool water. They'll heal my skin with some miracle elixir, all while feeding me ice-cold fruit.

My ankles complain at the new angle when I begin the climb.

"Just over this hill," I repeat out loud to myself, "Just over this hill."

When I finally crest the top, I blink a few times to make sure my eyes aren't playing tricks on me. Below is a valley of endless sand dunes. With a crashed pod—my crashed pod—half buried at the bottom. Clear as day, my footprints trail up the opposite side.

I walked in one giant circle.

"What the fuck?!" I try to scream, but it comes out as a hoarse whisper. I drop down to my knees. If I had any spare moisture in my body, I would cry.

FOUR

Tai

The sky is fading to dusk when I finally admit I'm not catching up to Bri today. Even though I'm still pissed, the idea of her being out in the desert all night by herself gnaws at me. I'm worried. It took most of the day to reach her footprints and no matter how hard I pushed myself, I couldn't catch up to her.

After the tent is up and I'm mostly satisfied it won't blow away in the middle of the night, I pull the small disc out of my pack, put it in my mouth, and bite down with my back teeth. I swish the minty foam around before spitting the disc into my hand and the cleaner onto the ground. This small act gives me so much relief. Since joining the military, I have become obsessive about my hygiene. Being here in dirty clothes all day is akin to torture.

Today was miserable. There is nothing to do here other than walk and think. A day on Sabaak would make anyone question every single one of their life choices. I prefer to avoid that line of thinking altogether.

I shake out my boots and pants to keep as much sand out as possible. I don't know why I even bother. There is no point in trying to get away from it.

The wind picked up a few hours ago. The sound of it whipping against the tent makes me increasingly agitated. Or worried—maybe a little of both. The image of Bri being buried by the relentless sand weighs heavily on me. No—she's in her tent. Unless she couldn't figure out how to set it up.

She's a grown-ass woman. And let's not forget how she never passes up an opportunity to tell me she doesn't need me. Even though she does. If she would only accept my help, things would be a lot easier for both of us.

When Aro asked me to go get her, I could tell he was tickled by the thought of what she would do to me in the process. He knows my history with Bri, mostly. It began the day I learned the human term "wingman." Bri was amused that Aro needed a wingman to get to know Elowen. Now that I think about it, so was I. That was the only time we agreed on anything. It was fun for both of us to watch him struggle to win her over.

Had anyone else asked me to come get Bri, it would have been an immediate *no*. Not only is Aro my ranking officer. He's also the closest thing to a brother I've got. So here I am, chasing down someone who doesn't even want my help on a planet I never wanted to see again.

The ground is hard and unforgiving. It is impossible to find a comfortable position. I toss back and forth trying to settle in for the night, but I can't stop arguing with Bri in my head. If she had simply followed the most basic survival rules, we'd both be in our respective lifepods waiting for rescue. Instead, I'm here—dead tired, with sand up to my ass—trying to chase her down.

Seared into my brain is the look of pure disgust on her face when I stepped onto the waystation.

"I hope you're here to apologize," she growled at me.

"Better. I'm here to take you home." I acted unaffected by her. I wish it were the case.

"Ha! I'm not going anywhere with you." Her eyes narrowed on me.

"Go get your stuff. We're leaving as soon as I get fuel." The anger flowing from her grew stronger the closer I got.

I'm ashamed to admit I loomed over her, aiming to use my size to intimidate. Maybe I should've tried talking to her instead. But at the time, all rational thought was light-years away.

She pointed an angry finger at me. *"I'll say it again. I'm not going anywhere with you."* Each word was punctuated with a jab to my chest.

Another step closer had me looking straight down at her furious face. *"You want to stay here and rot on a station? Fine. I'm simply following orders."*

She flinched, and I knew my comment hit its mark. The only thing that stopped me from tossing her over my shoulder and dragging her back was the guilt I still carry from doing that very thing a few weeks ago. It was simply too dangerous on j'Tilak at the time for me to let her stay like she was trying to do.

I was following orders. *I* was doing what I was supposed to do. *She* is the one who can't follow a rule to save her life. So, why am I the one who feels guilty now?

FUCK.

My irritation at Bri—compounded by the sand stuck to my back—makes sleep impossible.

The tent takes a beating from the wind. It sounds exactly as it did six years ago. Might as well have been a lifetime. Back then I was a scared, stupid kid with nothing to lose. I've been pretty good at not thinking about him. That kid is gone. He died on Sabaak. What grew in his place is all that matters.

FIVE

Bri

The silver lining to walking all day in one giant circle and ending up right back where I started is that at least I have a place to sleep. The temperature dropped along with the sun. The sharp change prompted me to go down to the crashed pod. I took more care this time going downhill. I don't have any ankles left to fuck up, but there is no shortage of other body parts I could injure.

I turn the latch to lock the hefty pod door and breathe a heavy sigh. It was rough there for a minute, sitting on top of the dune, realizing what I had done. It's a mystery to me how people walk in circles when they get lost. I still don't understand how it happened. Jamie would've lectured me. I ought to be better at this—at surviving in the wild. Today I wasn't thinking straight and made a rookie mistake.

Tomorrow is a new day. I'll rest and wake up ready to get myself out of here.

As I settle into the seat with the foil blanket pulled up to my chin, my stomach grumbles loudly. I only ate two nutrigels today. I'm rationing my supplies should things not go to plan. In the dark I rummage around for my bag and take out another, hoping something in my belly will help me sleep.

The blanket crinkles every time I move on the uncomfortable captain's chair. I'm exhausted, but between the world's loudest blanket and the sand pelting the pod, sleep doesn't come. Eventually, I give up on the seat and lie down on the floor, using my survival pack as a pillow.

At least I'm protected from the elements. From the sound of it, if I were sleeping outside, I wouldn't have any skin left in the morning.

In the darkness of the pod, my mind wanders. I think back to those few weeks on the waystation when I was waiting to return to j'Tilak. When I was forced to evacuate j'Tilak because of the Atorum, I was determined to return as soon as possible.

Elowen had been trying to reach me for weeks, but I was salty she got to stay behind. Not my finest moment. I avoided her attempts at reaching me. At first, I told myself that I was just busy getting settled on the station. After I settled in, I had to admit to myself the truth: I was punishing her for something that wasn't her fault.

I'll be the first to admit that I've been throwing a fit since being sent off j'Tilak. I've had plenty of time to rehearse my apology to clear the air. It certainly won't be the last time I'll have to apologize for my behavior.

When Tai showed up bossing me around, something snapped. It hurt when he said he was only following orders. After everything we had been through, he wasn't there because he wanted to be.

Of course I wanted to go back. But not with him. Something about him made me rebel at the idea of agreeing to anything he suggested. We didn't even have time to finish our argument. The station's alarms sounded, and I stood there like an idiot with my mouth hanging open, trying to figure out where the blaring sound was coming from when he dragged me to the lifepods.

I can't believe he had the nerve to try and get in with me. In retrospect, I should have let him in. It wouldn't be the worst thing in the world to be here with Tai. He might have even known how to land this damned thing. We could have gotten a signal out for help.

I must have fallen asleep at some point through the night because a small strip of light cuts through the darkness, perfectly aligned with my eyes. Everything hurts. My swollen ankles, my throbbing head, the blistering sunburn, and everything in between. I gently test my cheeks and nose. The light touch shoots pain all over.

Yeah, that's gonna hurt for a while.

"Not your beautiful face!" Hollis would have teased me about my vanity. There's nothing wrong with being concerned with the integrity of my skin while exploring a new planet. It's not an either/or situation.

Today is a good day to discover what else is on this godforsaken sand planet. Months ago, I was desperate to get out of the mura-Dome. The claustrophobic research facility was boring, and all I could think about was getting out and exploring the unknown. I push the hatch open, and a humorless laugh ripples out of me as sand pours in. My mom always said to be careful what I wished for.

The pod is more than half buried in the sand now and appears to be slowly sinking. That's concerning.

"I'll find help today, and everything will be fine," I say, hoisting myself up. "This is an adventure. It's supposed to be a little bit terrifying." I put some force behind the sentiment to convince myself it's the truth.

The hike up the dune is worse than yesterday. I lack the delusional optimism that pushed me up the hill the first time. Now I know exactly what's out there, and I'm not excited about facing it. I weigh my options as I slowly work my way up: go in the same direction as yesterday or take a different way and fight through the sand.

I reach the top of the dune and sit to catch my breath. My instincts tell me to find solid ground. This time I'll take more care to head in one direction.

My first step proves to be just as clumsy as yesterday. For the second time in two days, I fall all the way down to the bottom.

Face down in the dirt, I try to summon the energy and motivation to move. I'm fucked. I'm so deeply fucked. The pack is damp against my shirt, and I already know more of my supplies were destroyed. I confirm my fear that more of the nutrigels have burst, and there are only three hydropacks left.

"It's okay. It's fine. Today is going to be different. I'll get past the sand and dirt to civilization. Yes, civilization is over the horizon, and everything will be okay."

I drag myself up, straighten my ponytail, and head forward.

SIX

Tai

Just as I predicted, the wind erased Bri's footprints over the course of the night. What I wasn't expecting to see was a set of significantly larger, not human, tracks.

They are about twice the size of my feet, made by some four-legged creature with claws. It circled my tent a few times and left me in peace. Whatever it is, I'd like to be far away when it returns.

My visor is malfunctioning and not picking up on Bri's signature. It only registers her crashed pod that's about half a day behind me. I take off the visor and tap it against my palm and try again. Just her crashed pod. With no tracks to follow and no visor to pinpoint her location, this day is fucked.

Yesterday I was mad. Today I'm worried. Constantly being on high alert will keep you alive, but it can also drive you crazy. The presence of footprints isn't the only concern nagging at me.

On Sabaak, there are two main groups of residents. The Sabaaki seem to be a harmless tribe of desert-dwelling folk who keep to themselves. And then there is the Oo'rahim.

The Oo'rahim were banished here about a decade ago. They were granted a remote place to practice their extremist "religion." More like a cult.

They got chased away because of their weird-ass beliefs and bonkers prophecy. In a rare move, their species wanted them off the planet and got them banned, which is not easy to do. If memory serves, it was specifically their hostility toward females that got them booted.

Now they're here, shuffling around the desert unencumbered by decency and social norms.

If Bri encounters the locals, they will be spooked. What if they attack her? And the Oo'rahim—well, who knows how they would react. If their past treatment of women is any indication...

Yeah, I really need to get to her first.

I toss the useless visor into my pack and look around. I guess we are doing this the old-fashioned way. I'm going south until I hit the colony.

I stop for the day even though there are a few hours of daylight left. Dark clouds rolled in not long ago, certainly a sign of rain. The only thing that changed was the systematic lightening of my pack as I depleted more of my survival rations. All this walking, and not a single sign of Bri. Not a footprint or discarded nutrigel pouch, nothing.

The tent practically pitches itself, requiring very little help from me. I double-check the anchors to make sure they're secure when I hear the pitter-pat of raindrops on the nylon material. I look up at the sky and let the multiplying droplets roll over me, washing away the sweat and dust. I twist open the empty hydropacks and set them out to collect the rain.

Before I get completely soaked, I crawl into the tent and settle in for the night. The sound of the rain hitting my tent is relaxing. As my eyes slowly close, my mind drifts to the first time I saw rain. Growing up on space stations meant that the concept of weather was completely new to me. When I landed on j'Tilak, my home planet, for the first time, I felt the wind. Then came the rain. The newness of my surroundings made me feel intoxicated.

That day, I was cleaned up and given my first regulation haircut, the same style I've maintained all these years. Short by the ears, longer on the top and in the back. My belly was full for the first time I could remember, but I was still terrified. Life alone on the space station was hard, but it was all I knew.

That first day, I walked around in a daze. I decided then and there, drenched in the rain, that I was done stringing together bad decisions. My entire perspective changed, and suddenly, the possibilities of the future shined a light on my past. I locked up those shameful memories and put them aside until I forgot they were even there. From then on, it was structure, discipline, and anything that would keep me from ending up back where I started. Things were going to be different. I was going to be different.

SEVEN

Bri

I curl up on my side in the narrow shade of a dried-up husk of a tree. I used the last nutrigel hours ago. A painful emptiness stabs at my stomach. My throat and mouth are so dry it's hard to breathe. I clutch the last hydropack in my dirty hand.

I can't even trust my own eyes anymore. They've been playing tricks on me for hours. Footprints in the sand wind around me, in and out of my vision. The wind carries the sound of tinkling bells. Jagged rocks pop up on the horizon but always stay out of reach.

Bells jingle again. I don't bother to look up—another hallucination. Memories of games and good times have shriveled up and died, along with any hope. Nothing can distract me from reality now. I'm too tired, hot, and thirsty to care what happens next.

A warm drop of water lands squarely on my chest. I blink a few times, trying to clear my head. Did that actually happen, or is my brain messing with me again? Another, then another. Soon, wet marks on the ground begin to connect. I open my mouth to catch some of the rain. Unable to keep my eyes open, I pass out.

A sharp poke to my ribs rouses me. I groan and twist away from the assault. Another poke, harder this time. I blindly swat away in the direction of the intrusion and my hand hits against a long hard stick.

"Brethren! She's alive! Our salvation has arrived," the stick says.

The stick drops to the ground next to my head and calloused fingers grab my face and force my eyes open. Hands pinch my mouth agape and cool water trickles over my dry, cracked lips. It feels foreign in my mouth at first. As it washes away the sand, I'm able to swallow.

A face comes into view. Black round eyes stare down at me. A head tightly wrapped with a scarf casts a shadow across my face. I force my eyes to focus and realize it's not eyes but darkened goggles watching me from above.

"Brethren, lift her carefully. She must be unspoiled," a voice says from outside my periphery.

"The prophecy foretold the rain would come."

"Yes, Brethren. You take her legs. I'll lift her arms." Hands grab my ankles and wrists, and I'm off the ground and moving.

EIGHT

Tai

I'm being hunted. The same tracks surround my tent again. I double-check my blaster and tuck it into my belt. This weapon hasn't left my side in six years, and I've never been more comforted by its presence. Whatever is stalking me, I'll be ready for it.

I'm not thrilled about being prey. If it weren't critical that I find Bri as soon as possible, I'd set a trap for the creature and end this once and for all. But I've lost too much time out here as it is.

Like yesterday, the visor can't locate Bri.

I'm comforted at the thought that Bri is too stubborn to let this place win. Bri is out there somewhere, raising hell and fighting for her life.

The visor registers a spring at the bottom of a crater to the southwest. I adjust my trajectory to head there.

My bionic arm is getting worse by the hour. It doesn't respond half the time, and when it does, it's slow and jerky.

It's funny how it's giving me trouble here. The same place that led to me needing it in the first place.

The circumstances are different, but the planet hasn't changed. The first time I felt solid ground was here on Sabaak. It was brown and miserable, but it didn't bother me. I felt free. Eventually the environment took a toll on me, and I stumbled around in the desert until I reached a small village with painted arches and a water well right in the center.

I wonder how far that village is from here.

I still don't know how I got caught. Maybe it was the Sabaaki. Maybe someone tracked down the stolen ship I arrived on. Either way, I shouldn't have been surprised when the Authority showed up with an ultimatum.

The time has come for me to face the reality of my situation. Bri isn't at the crater. There are, however, several sets of animal footprints. Some large, like the ones surrounding my tent this morning. Some small, all heading in the direction of the stagnant pool of water at the base. I don't bother climbing down. No sense in putting myself in unnecessary danger.

Animals get territorial near water, and my scent is new. I don't trust it here. The swirling wind keeps me from seeing very far, and there is a long list of things that could use the terrain against me down there.

My blaster sits lightly in my belt, a reassurance until it reminds me that Bri doesn't have one. She doesn't have anything to use for protection. If she could defend herself with sharp glares and even sharper words, I wouldn't be worried. But I doubt she would be able to outrun or outmuscle whatever is out here.

Biosignature Identified: Bacteria
Identity: Uncategorized

Looks like I'll have to stick with my hydrogels. Shitting myself to death in the desert is not how I plan to leave this plane of existence.

My visor maps out the surrounding area. I weigh my options. I could keep wandering around out here hoping my visor picks up Bri's signature while my hydropacks dry up and a fucking monster hunts me down, or I could take my chances with the notorious Oo'rahim cult. They'll have food and water, and I can regroup before continuing my search. Beyond the crater is a dry riverbed that will lead me directly to their underground colony. I just hope they don't sacrifice me to their gods.

I need to keep myself hydrated and focused on finding Bri.

The heat alone could kill her. If the local wildlife doesn't do it first. By the size and positioning of those footprints, there is no way the sand creature is an herbivore. The small bushes scattered around the local landscape aren't enough to sustain an animal of that size. Whatever it is, it's big and likely *very* hungry.

It's a miracle I survived this planet when I was here before. I didn't know shit about surviving anywhere but grimy stations. Now, I can read the terrain and assess risk. It's a blessing and a curse. The experience I have is an advantage for keeping me alive, but it's also a reality check of all the ways Bri could be hurt.

Without any other good options, I sling on my pack and head in the direction of the colony. My visor chirps and lights up green on the edge. It looks happy I'm heading that way. My probability of survival ticks up to 73%.

The riverbed on the other side of the crater will take me right where I need to go. I skirt the edge of the crater and follow the carved-out riverbed. After a while, my visor chirps, notifying me the colony is nearby. I cautiously look around before sliding down the steep slope of the canyon wall. My field of vision is limited down here, and it's disconcerting. But it's worth it if it gets me to the colony without being seen.

Behind me, a few pebbles bounce their way down from ledge to ledge until they settle on the ground. I spin around and scan the rim.

Nothing.

It's eerily quiet down here. I've gotten accustomed to the howling wind. The still air down here feels menacing.

More pebbles tumble down. Without looking behind me, I casually jog. A full-blown run could set off a chase instinct. If I'm going to be something's next meal, I'm putting up a fight. Every sense is on high alert. Over the sound of my running, I hear a hiss. The ground shakes when something drops down.

Now it's time to run. I sprint toward the bend and hope there is something I can climb or hide behind.

Whatever is behind me sounds fast.

NINE

Bri

The hallucinations have taken an interesting turn. I am in a dim room. There are sheets below me on a soft bed. A bed that sits on a platform hovering over the rest of the room.

I step to the edge and look down. Can I fly? I raise my arms in front of me.

Fly, bitch!

Nothing. Damn.

A sharp knock on a door makes my head whip around.

Another knock, and the door creaks open. "Ahem." Someone clears their throat. "Sacred Goddess, are you awake?" they whisper in universal language through the crack in the door.

"What's going on?" My words come out with a croak from a dry and unused throat.

"I'm sorry to have awoken you. I was sent with clothing and a message that your meal is ready." The short, robed figure carefully lays out some clothes on a chair in the corner. A hood hangs low and blocks their face from view.

"Where am I?" I ask.

"You're safe underground now. We found you unconscious on the surface."

I look down at my hands and turn them over. This feels...real. My brain is catching up. This isn't a hallucination! I made it! I'm saved! Take that, you stupid fucking desert.

Now I need to find out who the hell this guy is. The way he talks is awkward and stilted.

"I'm Bri—"

"We know who you are. If you will, please prepare for dinner. You must be famished." He slightly bows as he backs out of the room and closes the door behind him.

I have a million questions, starting with: How could he possibly know who I am? Those can wait. First things first. Where is the food? Because he was right. I am starving.

A pitcher of water sits on a small table across the room. I stumble down three steps and over to it. My hands violently shake as I gulp the fresh water until it pours down my chest.

The reflection in the full-length mirror gives me a jump scare. I look like shit with my sweat-stained coveralls, limp ponytail, and sunburn that is not going away anytime soon.

From here, I get a better look at the clothes laid out for me. They don't look quite right. I tilt my head, trying to make sense of them from a different angle. They must have forgotten the rest of the outfit. This seriously cannot be all of it.

The bottoms, if you can call them that, are no more than a flimsy metal chain waistband holding two sad strips of maroon fabric. One for the front, one for the back. leaving my legs exposed all the way to my hips. This can't be the skirt. This is the thing you wear *under* the skirt. The top is simply a molded leather bra, barely enough to cover my tits. I could punch myself for not wearing panties the last day on the station. I was between laundry days and figured no one would ever know.

I look back and forth between my ruined coveralls and the

skimpy outfit laid out for me. Sand is still leaking from my pockets and the smell is awful.

Okay, iconic sexy captive outfit it is. I'm sure this is a misunderstanding and there is actual clothing down here. Coveralls are universally available. There must be a spare set I can borrow. Less than ideal wardrobe options aside, things are starting to look up.

See? Things always work out. I just needed to keep going. Soon, I'll be on my way quicker than you can say, "Galaxy Far-Far-Away discount rack."

Bath first, then clothes. I shake the sand out of my hair and brush off my skin, making a pile of sand on the clean floor. My mom would throw a fit if she saw the mess I am making. *I'll clean it up later, I promise.*

Sunken into the ground of the adjoining bathroom is a giant steaming bathtub. No, not a bathtub. Better. One of those ancient Roman baths that can fit enough people for an orgy, and it's all mine. The water is going to need to be drained by the time I'm done with it. I sink down in the warm chest-deep water, and all the dirt and sand floats away.

Colorful glass bottles line the edge of the tub. I twist the cork out of the one with a light citrusy scent. This is the one I want to drench myself in.

Starting at the top, I work my way down, not missing an inch of my body in my mission to get clean. I scrub the sand off my scalp and out of my ears. I dig it out from my fingernails and go all the way down to between my toes. When my fingers are wrinkled, I step out and tightly wrap a towel around my chest.

Reluctantly, I pick up the clothes and look them over once more. I set my shoulders back in defiance. I refuse to be intimidated by an outfit. I'll wear it, and I'll rock it.

Putting the bra on is the first challenge. I awkwardly tie it behind my back. It technically fits but doesn't cover much. I dangle the bottoms out in front of me. Once secured, it hangs loosely below my hips, the fabric barely covering the essentials. I braid my faded pink hair back. The strappy sandals tucked under the bed are next. They are tight and cut into my feet. I kick them back under the bed. I don't do uncomfortable shoes.

This time, the reflection in the mirror looks familiar. A little more sideboob than I'd prefer, but I'll take it.

I scoop up my dirty clothes and take them to the sink in the bathroom.

I run water over them and squeeze them out a few times, concentrating my scrubbing on the dirtiest and smelliest parts. It's not perfect, but it will have to do. I hold the dripping clothes in front of me and open my door. I peer out into the dim stone hallway, a tunnel seemingly hand-carved out of rock. Small hash marks speckle the walls and rounded ceiling.

Seeing no one, I push the door wide open and walk straight into an alien, their hooded face landing right between my tits. I jump back and almost drop my clothes.

"Oh, sorry! You scared me!"

Why am I apologizing? Who waits at the door like that?

"Radiant Golden One, it is I who should be apologizing. Please, if you will allow me, the brethren have assembled should you deign to bless us with your glorious presence." He lowers his head and waits for my response. I try not to laugh at his flowery language. Elowen would be elbowing my bare ribs right now reminding me to be respectful of other planets' customs.

"You can call me Bri. And your name is...?" I ask, hoping it's something I can pronounce.

"You may call me Brethren."

"Um, okay. Can I take my clothes to the surface so they can dry out?" I ask, holding up the dripping clothes in my hand.

"Celestial Loveliness, do not concern yourself with such tasks. I will take care of your every need."

I stifle a laugh. If Jamie heard someone call me "celestial loveliness," I'd never live it down.

He takes the sopping mess from me and tucks it under his arm.

"Is there some way I can call home? I need to let people know where I am."

"But...you are home," he says with all sincerity.

My stomach drops. I can't quite figure out who they think I am.

This is the weirdest case of mistaken identity ever.

"Okay, right there." I wave toward his face. "The way you said that was creepy as fuck."

I pause and take a deep breath. Elowen would want me to be diplomatic and respectful of my hosts' culture.

"Probably a cultural difference," I add, training my voice to sound patient, "but it was weird, just so you know. And where is the rest of the outfit? This can't be all of it."

Am I crazy? Or is this legitimately weird?

"My deepest apologies. I would never want to cause displeasure. Your clothing is perfect. You look quite fetching in it."

His apology seems genuine, so I dial it back a notch. Plus, the flattery feels kind of nice. I'm still getting my bearings, and I don't want to seem ungrateful. After all, they did save my life.

There has got to be a comms system around here somewhere. If this weirdo won't help me, I'll find it myself. I'm mildly annoyed he didn't directly answer my question, and it's probably written all over my face.

The robed man turns and beckons me to follow down the hallway. I don't have much choice but to trail after him. He leads me through twisting and turning stone tunnels. It's quiet down here and feels miles away from the brutal surface.

Completely lost, I'm at his mercy to lead me wherever we are going. The tunnels lack any distinction between them. Where's the emergency exit map when you need it? The old-school *You Are Here* sign with a giant red arrow.

"Right this way. The brethren are eager to lavish their praise upon you." He pulls back a heavy curtain, leading me into a large room. Hushed voices go silent when we step in.

"What the fu—" I cut myself off when all the hooded figures in the room turn toward me in unison.

A few dozen sit in circles. My new friend leads me through the crowd to the middle of the room. A spotlight shines down on me when I step into the center.

The long shaft of light narrows to a pinpoint at the top, confirming my suspicion that we are really deep underground. I look back over the crowd and it takes a minute for my eyes to adjust to the dark room again. Everyone in the room has the same robes on with the hoods pulled up, blocking their faces from view. The "brethren" sit quietly. I guess they are waiting for me to say something.

"Uh, thanks for saving me," I say and look around, hoping someone else will fill the silence.

"Luminescence, it is you who has saved us," someone says from the circle closest to me.

"We have awaited your arrival for many turns of the wind. We never gave up hope the prophecy would be fulfilled," another in the smallest circle says.

"I think there has been some misunderstanding. I'm Bri. And my lifepod crashed here. I need—"

"Heavenly Rain-Bringer, please forgive my interruption. We already know who you are. We have been preparing for your arrival."

This feels like a prank. There is no way this is actually happening. Is this some heatstroke-induced fever dream?

"What's going on here?" I ask.

They all jointly lower their hoods.

I catch a glimpse of their faces and notice they each have pale skin and black eyes. Two vertical ridges frame their wide foreheads. In place of a human-like nose, a long slit stretches above their mouths. Big gums and tiny teeth show as some of them smile at me, or bare their teeth. It's impossible to tell.

"Our mighty goddess has at last descended. The brethren welcome you and are ready to do your bidding."

Where the fuck am I?!

TEN

Tai

DANGER! IMMEDIATELY VACATE THE PREMISES! The visor flashes with the bright red warning across my eyes. ***DANGER! IMMEDIATELY VACATE THE PREMISES!*** It repeats the message, as if I could have missed it the first time.

Biosignature Identified: Scoravex Terralis (sand hunter)
Warning: Venomous and Extremely Lethal
Likelihood of Survival: 12%

"Working on it," I grind out between clenched teeth.

At the bend in the riverbed, I get a good long look at what's chasing me. It's also gaining, which is a nice touch. Four thick legs tear into the sand, giving away its camouflaged body. From this distance, I can see a face full of fuck-around-and-find-out teeth. There is no way I can outrun this thing.

I skid to a stop and turn to face it head-on. I make myself as big as possible and hope to scare it off, though I seem to be the only one terrified here.

Its yellow pupils dilate when our eyes lock.

I grab my blaster, point it in the air, and fire off a warning shot. The creature stops and stares me down, unfazed. Its tail whips back and forth, excited to have something to toy around with.

I stare right back, not showing any fear. Crouched low to the ground, it lifts its snout toward me. Six nostrils open up and drag in my scent.

Oh shit.

The thick tail rises up from behind, and a hooked end with a sharp stinger points directly at me. This time, I fire right at it. The beam bounces off its armored body and it doesn't even flinch.

I root myself to the ground, not ceding an inch. In another stroke of bad luck, my bionic arm hangs uselessly at my side. The sand hunter launches itself at me—faster than I thought possible.

It barrels straight into my chest, pinning me to the boulder at my back. I swing at its nose and eyes, anything within reach to get it to loosen its hold on me. It bites the blaster, yanks it out of my hand, and spits it away.

Drool drips out of its mouth. I grab the snout and manage to hold it closed. Its strong jaw slowly overpowers my grip. My bionic arm twitches when I try to get it to do its fucking job.

The sand hunter frantically thrashes against me. Its tail hovers over its scaly back poised for a life-ending strike. My hand slips from around its mouth and the creature seizes its opportunity.

Thwack.

Faster than lightning, it strikes. Somehow, my bionic arm comes alive and blocks the attack. It strikes a second time but doesn't get past my metal arm. On the third strike, I let go of the mouth and grab the stinger with both hands. It sinks its needle-like teeth into my chest and I let out a guttural scream.

With everything I've got, I wrench the stinger off. The sand hunter shrieks in pain and I shove the stinger into the side of its neck. It staggers backward and collapses into a heap at my feet.

My bionic arm once again hangs uselessly at my side. I drop to the ground and assess the damage. I peel off the control panel and it's immediately clear what's broken: the neurochip is cracked right down the center.

Mentally I take inventory of what's in my pack. What else has a neurochip I can use? As if it can read my thoughts, my visor pings, alerting me to the broken component in my arm. I carefully disassemble the visor. Using my fingernail, I pop out the neurochip. It slides right into place, and my arm comes back to life. When it comes to survival, a functioning arm is more important than a visor.

Sticky blue blood spreads across my ripped shirt. My chest throbs and burns from the bite, but I ignore the pain and stagger to my feet.

I really hope I get a friendlier greeting from the Oo'rahim.

ELEVEN

Bri

These "brethren" are making it extremely difficult to enjoy my first interplanetary adventure. A history lesson on their religious beliefs and symbolism is not my idea of a good time. All I know is they are all called brethren, and it's super confusing. They 'shed their identities' to serve the goddess. Whom they presume me to be.

"This alcove symbolizes the..." My mind wanders when one of them explains the closest cavity in the wall. Each one has some significance, and these dudes are all very eager to go into excruciating detail for each one. My stomach is loudly grumbling. The single glass of water I had in my room is not enough.

I steal a glance down the hallway, looking for any sign of a kitchen or comms room. Surrounded by the brethren, they each stare lovingly up at me and their bulging eyes go even wider when I make eye contact.

I muster a smile, but it feels like a grimace. Once this tour is over, I'll explain this misunderstanding and be on my way. Preferably with a full stomach and a canteen full of water.

"Anointed Rain-Bringer, what do you search for?" one of the little guys pops his head up and asks.

"I'm pretty hungry and dehydrated—"

"Yes! Yes, of course! How could we have overlooked this? Please forgive our egregious transgressions! Come this way. We have failed in our true purpose!"

Their groveling takes me by surprise.

"It's really not—"

I'm led into a room with rustic wood tables evenly spaced throughout. My head brushing against the ceiling distracts me, and I bang my knee on the corner of a table while we make our way to where they want me to sit.

"Bring the goddess her sustenance!" a brethren with eyebrows that grow down past his face and merge into a long beard yells down the hall.

This guy is clearly the boss. A few of the others jump into action and hurry out of the room to follow his orders.

"That really isn't necessary. If you'll show me the kitchen, I can make something."

One at a nearby table is about to take a drink of water. Boss snatches the cup out of his hand. He hands me the cup and pushes it up toward my mouth.

What a dick move. I could have waited for my own. The guy who lost his cup to me hangs his head low and cowers away from Boss.

I give the cup back without taking a drink. "Please, take it. It's yours."

He takes it and looks next to me at Boss. The leader shakes his head 'no', and the brethren sets the cup down on the table reluctantly, clearly conflicted as to what he is supposed to do.

"We are but your humble servants, ready to serve your will," the seated brethren says, bowing his head.

Boss disappears down a hallway and takes the tension in the room with him.

All is forgotten when platters of plump berries and steaming bowls of rice and meat are placed in front of me.

It's possible being their goddess for a few days won't be so bad after all. Maybe I can influence these brethren to stand up for themselves while I'm here. Sowing a little discontent for social justice sounds right up my alley.

I settle into my place and one of the brethren, who I now refer to as Bug-Eyes since he's the only one who hasn't removed his goggles underground, reaches out to hand me some grilled meat on a long skewer.

His hand veers up and all of a sudden, he's feeding me. I awkwardly take a bite and pull away as quickly as possible.

"Hmm. Thanks," I mumble with my mouth full.

"It is our duty to provide for you," he says and forces the skewer back into my mouth. "It is our highest calling."

Before I can finish chewing the bite, another brethren dangles a cluster of grapes over my mouth.

Oh, fuck that. I draw the line at being fed grapes. I snatch the cluster out of his hand and feed myself.

I'm not going to be here long. Nonetheless, it's time to establish some boundaries.

"I can feed myself," I say loud enough for the whole room to hear.

"But the prophecy says that you mustn't toil or your displeasure will rain down upon us," Bug-Eyes says.

"I'm not displeased. I prefer to feed myself." It's odd that I have to repeat myself so many times. Can't they let a girl eat in peace?

They murmur amongst each other, shaking their heads. I don't know what's so confusing about me wanting to feed myself. These poor heatstroked little guys have completely lost their minds.

Another leans in closely and lays a cloth napkin across my lap. I give an awkward laugh and inch away from him.

"I'm good, really. You don't need to do all this for me."

They stare back at me with confused looks.

"It is our duty and pleasure to serve you," a brethren says. He holds up a glass of water to my mouth like he didn't hear me tell them to knock it off.

"Really. You need to stop," I tell him and level him with my most serious look.

Boss walks in the room and everyone hunches lower in their seats. He strides through the rows of tables, head held high, dead eyes inspecting everything in the room. They act like this is some egalitarian society, but I'm seeing some signs confirming this is the one pulling the strings around here.

"The goddess has spoken. She must feed herself," Boss says.

I do not appreciate males speaking for me.

I really wish Elowen were here. She would know what to do. I have zero experience outside of Earth and the research lab on j'Tilak. My well-traveled friend would know how to handle this weird situation.

It's quiet. I could cut the tension with a knife.

Looking around, I offer a friendly smile to anyone who makes eye contact with me. I notice the brethren are all eating a grayish mush while Boss and I have a much fancier spread ahead of us. The realization makes the food taste sour in my mouth. They aren't equal here at all.

I stand up from the table and grab my plate, looking to see where the dirty dishes go. The first guy I met back at my room takes the plate from me.

"Thank you...brother?" My voice turns up at the end as I test out what exactly I'm supposed to call him.

"You may call me Brethren, Holy One," he says and bows deeply.

"I'm really supposed to call you all 'brethren'? Wouldn't the singular be 'brother'?" If I really was their goddess, the first thing I'd do is clear up this brother/brethren nonsense.

I am met with blank stares. They seem perplexed by what I said.

Okay, maybe not. I'm going to roll with it.

"If you are finished with your meal, I can return you to your room, Glorious Cloudweaver."

His eyes dart to Boss, who gives him a nod of approval.

Once we are away from the dining room, and away from Boss's prying eyes, I test the waters with this guy.

"So, don't get me wrong, dinner was nice, but you know you don't have to do whatever the boss says," I tell him.

"Boss?" he asks, confused.

"Yeah, the guy in charge. He orders you all around like you're at his beck and call."

"We are all equal here. There is no one in charge." He sounds so sincere. He doesn't seem to know any better.

"I just want everyone to actually *be* equal, ya know?"

"We are all equal in serving our goddess," he says, genuinely confused.

They are damn lucky I crashed here and not some narcissist who would take advantage of their beliefs. The wrong person would relish the opportunity to have these aliens do their bidding. Maybe I can get them to think critically, so next time someone wanders into the colony they'll be more prepared. In the meantime, I need to get a message to Elowen that I'm safe.

"I really need to get a message to my people. Where is your comms system? Do you have those here?"

His face shifts from confusion to intense focus. His wide black eyes zero in on me, all affection and reverence gone.

"That is not possible. There is no way to get a message out. We don't have the technology to communicate off Sabaak. The goddess, I mean...*you* demand we live a humble life."

He opens the door to my room and swiftly closes it behind me.

Getting out of here is proving to be a little more difficult than I thought.

I'm stuck on a Paleolithic planet with a creepy cult. I'm not crazy about any of them, especially Boss. I hate how he treats everyone.

I am so ready to get out of these uncomfortable clothes and back into my coveralls. I search the room for my clothing. I open every drawer, look under the bed, and check the bathroom. They're gone.

A soft knock on my door and a meek throat-clearing rouses me out of the bed. With no windows or daylight, it's impossible to know what time it is.

"Just a sec!" Every muscle in my body screams when I throw the blanket off and hobble across the room. I'm still sore from two days of endless walking, and I don't think my feet will ever fully recover from the blisters. I swing open the door and standing in the hall is another brethren.

"Blessed Goddess, your morning meal has been laid out for you. Might I escort you?" he asks, keeping his eyes trained on my feet. I shift a little, not feeling comfortable with the way his expression shifts. A brethren with a foot fetish is just as alarming as the ones who look me up and down.

Ugh. I guess the "male gaze" exists no matter where you are in the universe.

You little freak. Keep your eyes to yourself.

"Keep it professional, buddy. My eyes are up here." I give him the two-finger point and motion from his eyes to mine.

He blushes and bows his head, clearly embarrassed I called him out.

"Have you seen my clothes anywhere?" I ask.

"Those rags were not fit for a goddess. They were destroyed."

"What? Those were mine. Who told you to get rid of them?"

I suspect I already know the answer. They did not have the right to take away my clothes. I'm pissed.

"Brethren told us that you would be pleased to have your new clothes," he says, sounding defensive.

"Which brethren? Never mind, I already know." I throw my hands up in defeat.

"We all speak as one brethren," he says.

"Sure, you're all the same. Except for when the boss barks orders at you." I'm taking my frustrations out on this guy when they should be directed at Boss.

I really wish I had my coveralls back.

The dining room goes silent when we step in. Their robes rustle when they turn to watch me weave my way through the tightly packed room.

Boss is at the front of the room standing over everyone like a prison warden. I stare him down, trying to get it across that I'm not intimidated by him.

"The goddess is not pleased. You have failed in your one true purpose. Food is only for those loyal to Her Sublimity. Prostrate yourselves, and maybe you can eat next time," he announces.

Now I *really* don't appreciate him speaking for me. He's not going to use me as his bullshit excuse to refuse food to anyone.

That's it. The goddess is coming out.

"Everyone, enjoy your meal. You've all been great brethren." I stare at Boss, daring him to defy me.

A sickening smile stretches across his face, and he bows. "What a gracious and forgiving mistress we have been blessed with."

TWELVE

Tai

It's nightfall by the time the Oo'rahim colony comes into view. I could have easily passed the small sandstone dome if the visor hadn't already shown me what to look for before I harvested its parts.

My legs are weak from running nonstop for the last few hours, but the run cleared my mind. I focus on my objectives: caution, expediency, and if they've got Bri—extraction.

I approach with my hands out so any potential guards can see I'm not a threat. My blaster is safely tucked away, out of sight, under my pant leg. Just because I don't see any guards doesn't mean they aren't here.

My boot lands on something metal and I freeze. It could be a number of things. This is when the visor would have come in handy. My mind goes straight to "land mine" and the possibility of losing another limb to Sabaak.

I take a slow breath and consider my options.

I crouch down and feel around. Barely under the surface, a flat metal plate connects to a wire. I gently tug the wire, and it pops out of the dirt, leading directly to the dome.

"I wouldn't do that if I were you," a voice echoes through the canyon.

Not wanting to make any movements that could make the situation worse, I slowly rise to my full height. The Oo'rahims' scrawny, diminutive stature makes me an imposing figure. Any sudden movement could be mistaken for a threat, and right now I need to de-escalate and take control.

"I don't want any trouble." My eyes dart across the canyon walls. I'm not sure what I'm walking into, but I know Bri well enough to know that if she's down there and being kept against her will, things are not going well for them.

"How did you find us?" the voice asks.

In these situations, it's best to give as little information as possible. Especially with the Oo'rahim. They might appear harmless, but the stories of their violent religious tendencies are widely known.

"I crash-landed here a few days ago. I only need some food and water, and I'll be on my way."

What I actually need is to get down there and see if they are holding Bri hostage—and it's a lot easier to walk in than to try and break in.

"Any movement will mean your immediate death." Heavy metal scrapes through dirt, ratcheting up the suspense.

A short figure, about as high as my chest, in a brown robe emerges from the dome. A bell hanging from their belt dings with every step.

"Who are you?" they ask.

A shaking hand raises a blaster and points it directly at me.

"Just someone unlucky enough to crash here."

These are critical seconds, so I chose my words carefully. I need to know what is happening underground before I start running my mouth.

"Are you here with the others?" he asks, not moving the blaster away from me.

"No, just me," I clarify.

What others? Bri?

My pulse races. I don't respond well to weapons being pointed at me. He's either going to lower it, or I'll lower it for him.

As he closes in, he lowers the blaster, yanks my pack off, and wrenches my arms behind my back. Metal cuffs snap tight around my wrists, and when I strain against them, sharp electricity shoots up both arms. He pats down my body, hesitating on the blaster at my ankle.

So much for taking control.

"No weapons," he says and pulls it from my boot.

It was a long shot, but I was hoping he wouldn't find it.

"You've got a blaster. It's only fair for me to have one as well."

"Go." He pushes me toward the small structure covering the entry to the colony and I lurch, trying to keep my foot in place.

"What are we going to do about this?" I say and nod down at my foot.

"Nothing. It's an alarm," he says with a grotesque smile and shoves me again. I follow without protest, down into the underground colony. I've got to hunch over to fit through the small door and follow my captor down the stairs.

My ear twitches. He's lucky I'm restrained because I might have "helped" him down the stairs for that little laugh he had at my expense.

Orb lights dot the walls, guiding our way down into the darkness. The old tech is a holdover from a distant past, when a ball of tightly packed filaments was the only other option apart from an open flame. The temperature cools with every step. It's a welcome break from the punishing sun, but I won't be relieved until I know Bri is okay.

"This isn't necessary. I'm happy to cooperate," I say.

"Protocol."

I can tell from his one-word answer I'm not going to be able to talk my way out of this.

We reach the bottom of the long staircase, and I look around the open space. The ceiling is raised over the intersection of tunnels and stairs. I step toward the main area, but the guy nudges me to the left to another staircase leading down. This one is dark, not a single orb lighting the way. Walking down stairs with a pushy Oo'rahim at my back is quickly becoming one of my least favorite things.

"Is there someone I can talk to?" I ask, trying to delay going down there.

"Eventually."

He says even less than I do. Aro loves to accuse me of being the surliest motherfucker out there. I can't wait to tell him I found someone worse than me. Hey, we can't all be Aros—with his endless energy and pathological optimism.

The farther down we go, the cooler it gets. I don't mind the temperature, but I'm not getting a good feeling about where he's leading me. A long, dark and narrow tunnel leads to a single light on the wall next to a smooth metal door.

This is a dungeon, if I've ever seen one.

With a shove, I'm in a small, unlit cell. I mark the Oo'rahim's face into my memory. If it comes down to a shoot-out, I'm aiming for him first.

"What brings you to Sabaak?" a voice from the corner of the cell asks. This one has a long beard and eyebrows that go down his robes.

"I told your friend here—"

"Brethren," he barks, sharply interrupting me.

Oh yeah, that's what they call each other. Another odd detail of their ideology.

"I told your *brethren* already, I crashed here."

He narrows his eyes. "How did you find us?"

"I guess I just got lucky." I shrug.

"That's impossible. No one can get past the Halo—"

The bearded Oo'rahim silences the other with a raised hand. He flinches, clearly intimidated.

It all starts to make sense. Somehow, they got their hands on a Halo, a powerful shield that prevents incoming and outgoing electrical pulses. A Halo is capable of bringing down small aircraft, like lifepods, and even blocking signals for rescue. The invisible barrier is impossible to detect, and difficult to come by. They are used by people who don't want to be found.

"Whatever you've got going on here is none of my business," I say, trying to put them at ease.

"How do we know that you aren't here to steal away the Golden One?" he asks.

"Shut up, you imbecile!" The bearded one raises his hand again. This time, it comes down hard across the face of the Oo'rahim who asked the question.

"Not here for your gold. I just need some food and water, and I'll be on my way."

"Yes, you will be leaving shortly."

The way he says it sends a shiver down my spine. There is something about the look in his cold, dead eyes that makes me think I won't be walking out of here. He's got something closer to a body bag in mind for me.

"Good. We are on the same page," I say, faking agreement.

"Page?" the bearded one asks.

"It means we agree."

The Oo'rahim close the cell door behind them. On their way out of the dungeon, I hear muffled voices.

"Keep him away from her until we know what he's doing here."

He said her.

Bingo. Bri is here. I fucking knew it.

THIRTEEN

Bri

These guys hold my survival in their creepy little hands. Today, I'm going to sneak a little food here and there to set aside. That way, when the time is right, I can grab my pack and go.

There has got to be a way off this planet, or at least a way to signal for help. My strategy is to lull them into thinking I have accepted the role as goddess, and I'm going to turn them all against Boss and find my way out of here.

Unfortunately, it also means cozying up to them. It would be less off-putting if they were all each other's boyfriends, but from the lingering looks up and down my body—I don't think that is the case.

The telltale sound of a bell alerts me to approaching brethren. Boss sits down next to me at the low table where I'm currently picking at my breakfast.

"Good morning, Goddess. Today is an auspicious day! As the prophecy foretold, it rained again last night. Your arrival has heralded the return of the lifesaving water we have been waiting for!"

"Rain. Great," I say with a forced smile. Obviously, it's a big deal here, but that's a brethren problem. I'm grumpy and don't feel like playing along with Boss's little games today.

"We are planning a celebration in your honor. We have gathered our finest food and wine for your enjoyment tonight," Boss says. He picks up on my lack of enthusiasm and his smile fades.

I'm not trying to be a jerk. I just don't trust him.

I look over at him and conjure up a more sincere smile. "Thank you. That will be nice."

He smiles back, seemingly satisfied for now. I'm well aware he's manipulating me along with everyone else.

"We have a whole day planned. If you follow me, I will take you to your first experience." He stands up from the ground and offers me his hand. I stare at it. His skin is pale and sickly with long and sharp fingernails. I ignore the offer and push myself up off the ground without his help.

"What's on the agenda for today?" I ask, trying to seem interested in where he's taking me as we wind our way through the tunnels. Their insistence that they take me everywhere doesn't feel like a nice gesture anymore. It feels like they are hovering over me, and the walls are closing in.

There's got to be someone else on this forsaken planet who can help me get home.

"It is a ceremony meant to impart satisfaction and to release all of your burdens. Tonight, we culminate and feast. The first phase is right this way," he says and pulls aside a heavy tapestry from a doorway.

I shudder at his odd phrasing. His words are all nice, but the way he says them creeps me out.

I look around the room, trying to discern what this is all about. The thick pile of pillows in the corner looks suspiciously out of place on the hard stone floor. This room lacks any distinguishable purpose. It's not a bedroom and lacks the religious iconography present in the many prayer rooms.

Boss stands there, watching me take in the room.

"So, where are the females?" I feign nonchalance, but I'm feeling pretty fucking chalant. It feels extremely weird that I haven't seen another woman here, human or otherwise.

"Don't concern yourself with other females. The goddess is the only female who matters," he says.

I want to vomit.

I bet all the women on this planet got the *ick* and got the fuck out. Good for them. Now I need to as well.

He bows at the waist and steps backward out of the room. "Brethren will be with you shortly."

I plop down on the soft pile of cushions. Startled by a throat clearing from behind, I spin to see who it is. One of the brethren stands awkwardly in the doorway. This one wasn't wearing a bell.

"Oh hi, you scared me," I say with a shaky voice. Over the last two days, I've gotten used to the sound of the bell warning me of their presence.

"Glorious One, I am here to give you pleasure to completion through touch," he says and steps forward. I scramble up and take a few steps back to maintain the distance between us.

"What?" There is no way he's saying what I think he's saying.

"Please, make yourself comfortable and I will stroke your cunt until you have achieved orgasm."

"Um, no thanks, I'm good," I say through laughter.

This is not how I thought today was going to go. *Back the fuck off, Brethren Hand Job.*

"It is my duty, nay honor, to satisfy the goddess," he says sounding a little confused by my refusal and takes another step forward.

I dart around him, so he isn't standing between me and the exit.

"No, really, I'm fine. Thanks for the offer," I say and move toward the door. There is no way on this planet I am letting him come near me. I push aside the curtain and stumble into the tunnel right in front of Boss.

"Radiant Mistress, is there a problem?" he asks quizzically, "Has Brethren done something wrong?"

"Oh no, nothing like that. I'm good. I guess we should do that ceremony, huh?"

"It has already begun," he says and walks away without waiting for a reply. Reluctantly, I follow behind, equally curious and concerned by what he could mean.

I pay close attention this time to where he is leading me. We take two lefts then a right. He leads me to another room, sweeps aside the curtain, and motions for me to enter. I step in hesitantly and look around for any creeps offering me an orgasm. This room is identical to the last, the same questionable pile of pillows.

"Please wait here. I will notify Brethren you are ready," he says and disappears without giving me a chance to ask any follow-up questions. Questions like, "What the fuck is going on around here?"

The curtain is pulled aside and another brethren steps in.

"Ethereal Goddess, I am honored to taste your essence until you quiver with release," he says and steps forward.

I belt out a laugh. This is absurd. No one is going to believe me when I tell them about this place.

My mind races to find a way out of this. Isn't it every woman's fantasy to be worshiped like a goddess, with their pleasure being the top priority?

Call me shallow, but there is no getting past their appearance. The slitted noses, the tiny teeth, not to mention the height...

I've never been precious about sex. Consenting adults should explore their sexuality without antiquated perceptions, but this doesn't feel hot. It's weird. In these situations—not that this has ever happened to me before—straightforward communication is best.

"Here's what's going to happen. You're going to back the fuck up and never, *ever* say those words to another living thing for the rest of your life."

Brethren Cunnilingus stands rooted to the spot. "Am I not pleasing to you? I would be honored to find another brethren to lick your cunt," he says so matter-of-factly.

"It's not you. I, uh…" My voice fades out. I don't want to offend these guys, but I'm not going to do anything I don't want to do. I'm the goddess here. I am the decider.

"Then allow me to escort you to the next room." His head hangs low as I reluctantly follow him straight through an intersection, right, then left. I repeat the directions in my head as we walk.

I *almost* feel bad for this weirdo. He's taken my rejection personally. Not my intention, but come on—this is fucking weird!

The next room is well lit, for once. A wave of relief goes through me. Hopefully that awkward part of the ceremony is over and we can move onto something a little less sexual.

A dozen brethren file into the room and sit in tidy rows behind me. They bow their heads and hum a low tune until Boss steps in carrying a weathered tome. I sit down on the ground and wait.

This is fine. It's still super uncomfortable, but at least they aren't coming onto me.

Boss reads from the heavy book.

"The advent of the Sublime Goddess of the Holy Water will signal the arrival of the life-sustaining essence. Upon her satisfaction, the water will flow freely," he reads, dragging his finger across the page.

Oh fuck. This is bad. The word "satisfaction" hangs heavily in the air.

They think getting me off is going to literally keep them alive.

Boss looks up at me. "Follow me to the next station, m'lady," he says, setting the book down on the small table to his side.

"There has been a misunderstanding," I say, trying to soften the blow I'm about to deliver.

"There has been no mistake. The prophecy is quite clear," he says firmly without looking back at me. I hurry to catch up with him. I tug on his sleeve to get him to stop. He looks back at me wide-eyed and gasps.

"You honor me with your touch," he says and deeply bows again.

"Please listen. I am not who you think I am," I blurt out. I don't want to play along anymore.

He brings the sleeve I touched to his mouth. He kisses the spot and rubs it over his face. I school my face into something neutral, but that might have been one of the most repulsive things I've ever seen in my life.

"This robe will forever bear your blessing upon me. Today truly is a special day," he says and continues down the hallway.

Dammit.

The next room is the biggest one of the day, and the entire floor is covered with blankets and pillows. I don't like the look of this at all. I carefully step between the blankets. Before I can turn and try to talk my way out of this, three brethren step in, completely naked except for the thin cord around their waists with bells hanging to the side of their dicks. They are in varying states of arousal, and I force my eyes to stay up.

"Okay. I need to get back to my room." I sidestep my way toward the door, but they are still standing between me and my escape.

"It is our honor to bring you pleasure. You must receive our seed," one of them says.

"Uh, you guys have fun without me." I pause at the door and turn back. "And no one calls it 'seed'! At least call it 'cum' or 'jizz' like normal people!"

Boss steps in front of me and blocks my path.

Great. Now I'm stuck between the horny triplets and the boss.

"What seems to be the problem, Shimmering Brook?" he says.

I don't know why he looks confused. I've been very clear from the beginning. This is not happening. Of all the bizarre cultures and religious fanatics I could've encountered, it seems I found the one with a breeding kink.

"As your deity, I am telling you that I do not wish to receive any... pleasure or *seed*."

The word feels gross on my tongue, and I gag on it. Invoking their goddess and taking advantage of their misunderstanding feels even worse. But at this point I'm desperate to get back to my room and away from these weirdos.

"But the prophecy requires—"

My final thread of patience snaps.

"Am I the goddess or not? I want to go back to my room. Now."

"Yes, Magnificent One." His gaze sharpens, pinning me in place. Sizing me up.

I narrow my eyes right back.

That's it. My mind is made up. Before I get the fuck out of this terrible place, I am going to turn every single one of these brethren against Boss.

FOURTEEN

Tai

Wherever they've got Bri, I hope she's getting better treatment than this. All I've got is a dirty blanket and a rusted bucket. The smell wafting off the bucket makes its purpose unmistakable.

It's not the first time I've been locked up. I've been in my fair share of station brigs growing up. When times were really bad, I'd purposefully get caught breaking some minor rule so I could get tossed in a cell just for the guaranteed bowl of noodles that came with it.

I must have been eight or nine years old the first time. I had run away from the outpost for orphans where I was supposed to learn a trade. We were shipped off to the Star Ash Collection Orbital, "SACO," to do a dangerous and underpaid job nobody wanted. Bots were too valuable. We weren't. The only thing more dangerous than harvesting the collapsed star matter for production was the threat of my fellow wards.

SACO taught me one thing: the weak are at the mercy of the

strong. I was scrawny and underfed and learned very quickly I would rather strike out on my own than stay there.

My first stop was Westgate Orbital IV. That first night the station manager caught me breaking into his office. It was a dumb move, but being tossed in the brig was a mercy compared to what he could have done. Stations are little kingdoms, and managers do whatever they want.

This one happened to be a good one. While we walked to the brig, he talked to me. He asked me about my upbringing and made me an offer I wasn't ready to accept.

"I know what it's like to scrape by. I'm gonna lock you up tonight and give you a hot meal. In the morning you can stay and get a job on the station, or you can move on. It's your choice."

Rather than accept the generosity of someone who wanted to help me, I snuck onto the next freighter and continued the destructive cycle.

I press myself against the far wall, away from the bucket, and slide down to sit on the ground. This far down, the air is cold and quiet. It would be easy to be forgotten here.

I grab the dirty blanket when the cold becomes too much. It's riddled with holes and barely covers my shoulders. The miles in the sand are catching up with me. I fight the urge to close my eyes. I need to stay alert and figure out how to get out of here when the time is right.

I wake up at eye level with the rusted metal bucket and scramble back at the realization of how close it is. I kick the bucket across the room with a loud clang.

"What was that?" I hear outside the door. Fuck.

"Just having a problem with my arm," I yell back through the thick metal.

"He's awake! Go get Brethren," another voice says. Fuck—there's two of them.

"Which brethren?" the first one asks.

"The brethren who told us to get him when the prisoner wakes up."

I can't help but laugh at the back-and-forth. They must have these conversations constantly. It's a ridiculous notion that they're all the same. Any religion that makes you give up your identity to conform is beyond problematic. Plus, it's completely impractical and ripe for misunderstandings.

"Oh yes, *that* brethren."

Moments later, the door swings open and the Oo'rahim with the long beard steps in with a metal tray. He presses his hand to the panel lock, and the door rattles closed behind him.

"Here," he says, pushing the tray toward me, the metal scraping harshly against the stone floor of the cell.

He signals for me to turn around so he can remove the cuffs. A few minutes of respite from the warning shocks are as welcomed as the tray of food on the floor.

I drink the small cup of water in one swallow. The thin slices of dried meat are barely edible—tough, tasteless, and a step below food for livestock. It's not enough to fill my stomach, but it does help clear my head.

"Thank you. You don't need to keep me down here. I'm just passing through," I say between swallows. "You could send me on my way with a fresh canteen."

"We will determine that ourselves," he grumbles while he slaps the cuffs back on, but this time in front of me. My stoic face doesn't betray my excitement.

He made a big mistake.

I relax my body to avoid the shock that comes with any resistance.

"We were unaware Tilaks were here with the Others," he says, watching me closely.

This is the second time they've mentioned "the Others." The visor only listed the Sabaaki and the Oo'rahim as inhabitants on this small planet. If there's anyone else here, they have cloaking tech, which is not something the average citizen would have.

"I told you, I crashed here and am trying to get home."

"If you aren't here with the Others, then it is up to us to decide your fate," he says.

He scans his palm on the panel next to the metal door. It slides open and he is gone. The sound of the bell and his mocking laughter fades as he climbs the stairs.

Left alone for a second time, I methodically scan every inch of the cell. The stone walls are carved right out of the ground. Air circulates through the fist-sized holes at the top of the wall.

The only way out is through that door.

With my wrists cuffed together, I work the panel away from the wall. It breaks loose and hangs from exposed wires. I assess what I've got to work with.

It's old tech.

I shove my hands into the wires, doing my best to get the cuffs as deep into the mechanism as possible. With a deep breath, I tense every muscle in my body, activating the shock.

Everything goes black.

* * *

I wake up on the ground with a pool of bile next to my face. I groggily get up and check the door.

It swings open with a nudge. I take the stairs three at a time, keeping close to the wall and shadows.

I'll grab Bri, figure out how to get these cuffs off, and get the fuck out of here.

At the top of the stairs, an Oo'rahim sits on a bench to the left. The sad excuse for a guard is dozing off. His head bobs up and down as he loses the battle to stay awake. I patiently wait until his chin slumps to his chest. I shuffle my feet from the shadows to see if that rouses him. He doesn't even twitch—completely knocked out.

I edge along the wall, moving from one shadowed alcove to the next. The distant sound of bells gives me the confidence to move without fear of running into anybody.

I turn left at the first tunnel and duck into a shadowed doorway. The door is cracked open. I look through the narrow space before stepping in and close myself in. Through the complete darkness my hand brushes against the rough material of robes hanging in a long line. I pull on a robe—not an easy task with my hands cuffed—and get a few warning shocks in the process.

It's tight across my shoulders and hangs above my knees.

I must look ridiculous. No Oo'rahim would ever mistake me for one of their own.

I catch the sound of mumbling outside of the door. I shove my way behind the robes, crouch down, and lean my back against the cold wall. An Oo'rahim walks in with a flickering light.

I freeze. My pulse hammers in my ears so loudly it could give me away. The feet stop, turn, and face me.

I don't breathe. I don't move. Every second stretches on for a lifetime.

Then—finally—the light shifts. He turns back toward the door and slips out, taking the glow with him and plunging me into darkness once more.

I move swiftly and press my ear against the door. Through the hard wood I strain to hear the muffled voices.

"Where is she now?"

"She demanded to go back to her quarters. What were we supposed to do? Deny the goddess?"

Goddess? Did Bri convince these fucking idiots to worship her? In some way, I'm not surprised.

"She was not satisfied by our offers. We have failed her," another voice says.

"We will try again, Brethren. Do not be dismayed."
The bells trail off in the distance.
What is going on down here?

FIFTEEN

Bri

"But the prophecy—"

"Your prophecy said I needed to be satisfied. I am. I'm totally satisfied. No need for anymore...whatever that was." I cut him off, desperate to end this conversation.

"Yes, Your Radiance," he says and bows.

"Please take me to my room." I put some force behind my words. I'm tired of repeating myself and want to be left alone. This ludicrous situation was funny at first, but that wore off a while ago.

"Yes, Your Greatness. Please forgive us for our transgressions," Boss says.

I pay close attention to the turns through the tunnels back to my room. There is so much going on here, and I'm getting the feeling that I only know half of it. The situation with Boss, the vague prophecy, and where the hell are all the women?

"Where are all the women? Are they in a different colony?" I ask again, trying to sound casual.

"Please, Goddess. Do not worry yourself with such things," Boss says.

I let out a slow exhale through my nose to calm my frustration with this asshole. I hate it when people brush off my questions. It's so patronizing.

I'm more determined than ever to turn the brethren against him. Once that's done, I can leave with a clear conscience.

"It seems strange there aren't any females here. And why can't anyone answer a goddamn question every once in a while?" I take a breath, trying to cool my rising temper.

"Our ways are different from the rest of the universe," he says cryptically.

Yeah, no shit, Sherlock.

He talks the entire way back to my room about the day-to-day operations of the colony, never pausing long enough for me to say a single word. I get the feeling he's filibustering, so I don't ask any more inconvenient questions.

If they are telling the truth and they don't have any comms systems, I'll gather some food and water and leave on my own.

Alone in my room, I rest my tense back against the closed door. It's where I hold my stress, and there has been plenty of it lately. What I need is a good soak in that giant tub, not some creep with chafing hands offering to get me off.

On my way to the bathroom, I leave a trail of clothes behind me. Using my only hair tie, a prized possession, I fashion a loose bun on the top of my head. Next time there's an emergency evacuation, I'm grabbing a backup.

I picture Tai's face if I'd sprinted back to my sleeping unit for a spare hair tie while the station evacuated around me. It might have been worth it to put myself in a little bit of danger to get a reaction out of the gorgeous overbearing alien.

It's the first time I've thought about him in a while. I wonder what he's doing right now. Probably trying to explain to Aro how he lost me.

The tension leaves my body as I step into the warm water. I uncap the bottles along the edge and test each substance on my hand. One smells like jasmine in the summertime and reminds me of a moisturizer I used to steal from the resort I worked at, a perfect treatment for my sunburn. I pour a generous amount into my hands and gently rub it all over my face.

I lean back on the edge and let the cream work its magic.

My eyes fly open with the quiet snick of my bedroom door closing. A bell tinkles, giving away the pervert who is moving around my room. Dude, seriously? I thought they had finally given up. These are some persistent little freaks.

I frantically look around for my towel. It's just out of reach, neatly folded across the room. I would have to run past the wide-open door to get to it. I wade deeper into the tub and hope the water obscures my naked body.

"Hello?" I call out.

No response.

"Um, hi, I'm busy right now. Please go away," I say loudly to the peeping tom.

The bell hesitates then continues its approach.

"Really. I appreciate the offer, but no orgasm necessary," I call out.

"Who said anything about an orgasm?" a deep and familiar voice says.

Relief and anger crash over me all at once.

"You!" I snap at him.

Of all the people in all the universe, it's Tai. How is it every time I turn around, this giant blue alien is underfoot and driving me crazy?

Tai stands at the edge of the bathtub. "When I said this conversation isn't over, I didn't think it would pick back up word for word. You need to think of another way to say, 'Thank you, Tai, for coming to save me'." He mimics me in a high-pitched obnoxious voice that sounds nothing like mine.

A hood covers half his face, unfortunately not the half with a wide cocky smile. I want to smack the smirk off his annoyingly hand-some face. Without anything else being in arm's reach, I opt to splash him with the bathwater.

"If you want me to get in with you, you just have to ask," he says.

Prick.

"So, what's this about orgasms? I've been out searching for you in the desert, and you've been down here getting serviced by a bunch of lonely outcasts?"

"No one is getting *serviced*. It's a little misunderstanding. How the fuck did you find me?" Technically he's sort of correct, but I'm trying to do a good deed down here! Not treat them like my own personal harem.

"You're quite the talk of the colony. I didn't have to slink around in the shadows long before I put together that you are their 'Golden Goddess of Majestic Whatever.' There are only so many places a goddess can be locked up down here."

"I'm not locked up, and I already said there's been a little mix-up. They think I'm...their...you know...goddess," I say the final word under my breath, hesitant to even utter the word because it sounds absolutely insane.

"Okay, well, whatever they think you are, playtime is over. Get out and get dressed. We're leaving," he orders and goes back to my bedroom, closing the door behind him.

His tone activates a part of me that has been dormant since the last time I saw him. I want to stomp my feet like a petulant child and refuse to cooperate. As soon as I'm dressed, I can tell him to get fucked.

I scramble up the edge and tightly wrap the towel around my body. My reflection in the mirror startles me. The face mask dried and cracked, making me look 200 years old. I'm sure Tai loved this.

If he were a gentleman, which he is not, he could have announced himself from the bedroom. He's trying to aggravate me. I scrub the mask off and look around the bathroom for my clothes, but every stitch of clothing is in my bedroom, with him.

"My clothes are out there. Turn around and close your eyes," I tell him from behind the closed door.

"Isn't that a little redundant? Turn around *and* close my eyes?"

"Ugh. Just do it!"

We've been in the same room for a whole thirty seconds, and he's already tried to pick two fights with me.

I run to my clothes on the floor and get dressed as quickly as possible, my wet feet catching on my skirt while I try to pull it up. I lose my balance and teeter over trying to work my foot free.

"You okay back there?" he asks over his shoulder.

"Fine, everything's fine. Give me a minute." I grab the top next, burning with irritation. What I wouldn't give for my coveralls right now. He better not comment on the goddess outfit. I tug everything into place, throw my shoulders back, and straighten my spine. I hate this outfit. It's meant to be a spectacle and reduce me to a sexual object, but I refuse to give it power over me.

"I'm decent," I say, summoning my most dignified tone. The skimpy outfit doesn't cover much, and I'm the tiniest bit nervous about him seeing me in this. Even though he has seen me in much less.

He slowly turns. His eyes wander all the way up my body. The chemistry between us is palpable, but it doesn't change that I'm still mad at him.

"What the fuck are you doing here?" It didn't even occur to me until now he could have ended up on the same planet as me after the evacuation. Even though he's annoying, and his sudden appearance complicates my plans, I'm glad he's okay.

"I'm here to save your ass. You're welcome," he says irritably. "Where are your clothes?"

As though I had a choice.

So much for the warm feelings. They disappear as quickly as they show up.

"You can't come in here and act like this isn't your fault!" I cross my arms in front of me, hoping it looks obstinate and not self-conscious.

"My fault?" He smolders with anger and takes a step closer. "How in the universe could this be my fault?" His face is tightly controlled. A ripple of self-righteous disdain simmering under the surface.

"You forced me off j'Tilak. If you would have *just* minded your own damn business, none of this would have happened!" I let my temper get the best of me and the words are loud and harsh.

"Shut up! Someone is going to hear you," he whisper-shouts. His eyes dart around the room and he takes another step closer to me. "If you would have *just* stayed with the escape pod, we wouldn't be down here with these nutjobs."

I stop myself from complimenting his correct usage of the word "nutjob." But I make it a rule to not flatter alien men like Tai, even if they are incredibly hot when they are mad.

"I'm not going anywhere with you. In fact, I think I'll stay here." Whatever he says, I want the opposite. "I don't know if you had a chance to meet any of...my followers...but I am needed here," I say, doing my best to sound regal and unbothered.

"PUH-LEASE. If by 'followers' you mean the brethren, yeah. I met them and they are all certifiable. Get your bag. We need to leave. You aren't safe here with them." Tai paces across my room. I assume he's looking for my pack. My eyes flicker to the bottom drawer of the only cabinet in the room. Tai picks up on the movement and walks toward the drawer.

"I'll be fine. They'd never hurt me. They worship me." I look him up and down, sizing him up. It just now occurs to me that his arms are under the ill-fitting robe, and not through the sleeves.

"What's going on there?" I pull up the robe to see what's underneath.

"I'm cuffed," he mumbles.

Laughter bubbles out of me. "The great soldier, Tai fucking pt'Alquon, got captured by a couple of harmless religious aliens?"

His face turns deadly serious. "They aren't as harmless as you think. They got kicked off their planet for trying to eradicate all the females."

"There is no way that's true. You can't believe everything you see on the newsfeed." They wouldn't do something so awful. They're horny, not homicidal.

"Believe me or don't—it doesn't matter. Because we are leaving *now*."

"Where's your ship?" I ask.

"About that."

"You crashed here too? What's the play? You think we can sneak out and what? Wander around in the desert? No thank you."

"You've got to be kidding me." He seethes and it feeds my inner rebel. I've already set my sights on Boss, and I'm not leaving until the brethren are free from him. The sudden appearance of this grumpy Tilak changes nothing.

"I'd rather not be cooked alive on the surface of this awful planet. I'm good right here, for now. I'm not leaving until I know I'll survive up there." I don't want to tell him my plan to lead an uprising against Boss. It's none of his business what I do with my free time.

"We are leaving."

I clear the laughter from my throat.

"I don't think it's up to you. In fact, I think you should sneak back to where it is you came from, and I'll come up with a plan to get us out of here." I wave my hand at the door, a dismissal I know will piss him off.

Tai's nostrils flair. His ear twitches, and a thrill shoots through my veins. I'll admit, sometimes I mess with people, but there is something especially delicious about pushing Tai's buttons.

"I am not spending another second in that dungeon—"

"We have a dungeon?" I interrupt. "Just when I think this place can't get any more awesome." A villainous cackle erupts out of me, but Tai isn't amused.

"Bri—" His voice drops an octave, and his rebuke is meant to scold, but it has a different effect on my body. His growly deep voice stokes something reckless in me. It's totally normal to have moments of weakness around handsome assholes, right?

"What's the plan for those?" I point to his cuffed hands, trying to get back on topic instead of letting my traitorous, sex-deprived body distract me.

"I don't know. I'll figure out how to break them." He shifts his arms and a wince of pain crosses his face.

"What if we could get the brethren to take the cuffs off willingly?" I ask, a devious plan forming in my mind. Tai would never agree to it, which makes me love it even more.

"You're scaring me. I don't like that look in your eye," he says, scrutinizing me.

"Don't underestimate my powers of persuasion. But for my plan to work...you're going to have to go back to the dungeon." I bite my lips to stifle my laughter.

"No."

"Okay, I can always call the brethren in here and see what happens after that." I glare at him in a silent challenge.

"You wouldn't dare."

"Wouldn't I?"

"If you leave me down there."

"I'll get you out of the dungeon. Go back down, and I'll get you out—*without* the cuffs."

"You better do it quickly. If I have to wait down there while you are doing, whatever it is you're doing up here, so help me. I broke out once, I'll break out again, but next time I'm leaving your ass here." His ear twitches again. Aro told me it's the Tilak equivalent of the middle finger.

"You can twitch that ear all you like, but if you want out of the dungeon, you'd better be nice."

"Quickly." With the last word, Tai cracks open the door and peers out. He's about to slip out when I remember something.

"Tai, don't let your pants out of your sight."

"What's that supposed to mean?" he asks.

"Just trust me on this, and never say I didn't do something nice for you." I wave him out of the room, anxious to enact my plan.

He slips out the door while I collapse into hysterical laughter.

SIXTEEN

Tai

I wind my way back down to the dungeon, keeping to the shadows and quiet tunnels. It's a perfect opportunity to get a sense of the layout of the colony. The dungeon appears to be the lowest level. It's unclear how many levels there are in total, but each one has a similar layout with random offshoots, and each room is either a bedroom or a prayer room. The main level, the one where Bri is currently, also has the dining room and kitchen. On one of the lower levels, I find a dark tunnel that dead-ends with a wide shaft down in the center of the floor. The smell of decomposing food hits me when I lean over to look in. It's a garbage chute going straight down to a smelly pit.

A bell approaches, and I've got nowhere to go. I climb down into the chute and hold myself up by pushing my back against one wall and feet against the other. A steady stream of electricity runs through my arms, vibrating my entire body. I squeeze my eyes shut and wait.

A handful of wilted vegetables drops on my lap. I hold my breath to save myself from the smell and to stay completely silent. The electric current from the cuffs radiates hot electricity and gets worse the longer I hold myself there. The bell recedes, and I shimmy my way up and out.

That was close. The Oo'rahim are already suspicious that I've got plans for their goddess. If they caught me slinking around in the shadows, it'd be over for me.

The sleeping guard at the top of the final set of stairs snores lightly, unmoved from his spot earlier. He snorts and shifts when I step into the light. I bolt down the stairs. No point in standing there waiting to get caught.

I wrestle off the robe awkwardly with my hands bound together and earn a few extra shocks. I kick it into a closet for safekeeping—who knows if I'll need to use it again.

Something on the bottom shelf catches my eye. I shake my head and laugh. Amateurs put my pack and my blaster unsecured in the closet next to my cell. This is going to be easier than I thought.

It goes against every instinct, but I lock myself back in the cell. The control panel hangs uselessly from a few wires. The drive is irreparable. I push it back into place and hope no one notices.

Hours drag by. My mind races, trying to think of every possible way Bri and I can get out of the colony. Which route we would take, how far we could get before they realize we are gone.

Every minute ticking by brings me closer to losing my shit. Why did I agree to come back down here and wait for her to get me out? I know better than to put my survival in the hands of another. I resolve to break back out of my cell when the door swings open and an Oo'rahim steps in.

"You lied to the brethren," he says while removing the cuffs.

"What's going on?" I sound confused—because I am. He didn't seem to notice the control panel was broken.

"The Goddess told us she was separated from her Tilak servant in the desert. She asked us to find him."

I inwardly groan. Of course she would make me her servant. I finally understand why humans say, "Always read the fine print."

"Follow us. Her Eminence awaits."

He leads me to a crowded dining hall where everyone's attention is fixed in the same direction. On a platform at the other end of the room Bri lounges on a cushion while an Oo'rahim drops fucking grapes into her mouth. What kind of bullshit is this? I've been down in the dungeon pissing in a rusty bucket and huddled under a dirty blanket for hours while she's being hand-fed grapes?

An Oo'rahim fans Bri with a giant palm frond. She finally notices me, and when our eyes meet, I can see laughter in them. She bites her cheeks and waves away the brethren.

As I walk over to her my eyes drift to the smallest shirt ever made. In the dimly lit bedroom, I only got a hint of her clothes. Now I get the full effect—in a room full of strange little brethren. Bri always looks good, but this outfit is next level.

"My eyes are up here, creep," she says and glares at me. The laughter is gone. Her eyes are now full of fire and brimstone—and I've never wanted to be burned until now.

"I'm sorry, I, uh..." I shove my greasy hair back away from my face, suddenly aware of how dirty I am from the last few days. I hate this feeling.

A voice carries through the room. "Magnificence, is this the servant that abandoned you in your time of need?"

I snort at the ridiculous title, and her scowl deepens.

"Yes, dear Brethren. This is him."

You have got to be fucking kidding me.

"M'lady, he will pay for his transgressions. Never trust a Tilak. They are not allowed on Sabaak, after the *incident*," he says solemnly.

"Inci—"

"I humbly apologize for not being there when you needed me," I cut in with. That's enough of that. I'll agree to this preposterous plan —for the sole purpose of stopping this conversation.

Bri mouths the words "What incident?" and I pretend to not notice. She looks me over. Her eyes linger on the bite from the sand hunter.

"You're hurt!" she says.

"I'm fine. I just need to clean up."

"It looks pretty bad."

"I said, I'm fine," I grit out between my teeth

"Tai, tell me right now. Did they do this to you?" she asks, tilting her head toward the brethren.

"It was a sand hunter, and I'm fine."

She lets it go, thankfully. Arguing with Bri in front of the brethren is not my idea of a good time.

"Alright then—it's your funeral. Brethren, please take my servant," she says—choking back laughter at the word servant— "to get a bath and food before he begins his duties."

They direct me to a side room with a dripping faucet and a clean rag. I peel off my shirt, careful to avoid the wound. The blood has crusted over, and it feels warm and swollen. I dab the wet rag against it, sucking air between my teeth.

"Hurry up," one of the Oo'rahim barks at me. "Do not keep the Goddess of Sunlight waiting."

Here I was, worried she was being mistreated, and they made her a goddess. I grudgingly put on the robe they shove towards me. The Oo'rahim motions for me to hand over my pants, but I hold them in my clenched fist. I surmise Bri left her dirty clothes somewhere and they disappeared, leaving her with the current clothing option, which I'm not going to complain about.

My former jailor hands me a string belt with a bell hanging down. "Put this on."

"What's this for?" The robe is itchy and tight around my neck. I pull the collar back with a finger and try to make some space, but the thick, rough fabric is unforgiving.

"It's so when you get lost in the desert, we can find you before the sand hunters do."

Too late for that.

"We are watching you, Tilak. Get out of line, and we will return you to the gods."

"Got it." I don't plan on giving them an opportunity to follow through on the threat.

Back in the dining room, I grab a few flatbreads and a cup of water while I make my way toward Bri.

"Today we honor the Sublime Goddess of the Holy Water," the Oo'rahim with the long beard who I met in the dungeon says with his booming voice.

Behind her hand, Bri whispers, "That one I call Boss. They pretend they're equal, but he calls the shots around here."

Another Oo'rahim steps up to the slightly elevated platform Bri is on in the front of the room. "Brethren, please accept my rectification —she is the Divine Radiant Golden One, not the Sublime Goddess of the Holy Water."

"Our prophecy clearly states the arrival of the goddess will herald the rains that will wash away our indiscretions and begin the cycle of prosperity anew. There is only one goddess," the one Bri calls Boss says impatiently.

Oh, this is getting good. Nothing compares to a little disagreement between cult members to keep me entertained.

I lean back on my elbows, settling in for the show. She tenses next to me and shifts uncomfortably on the pillows. I can't tell if it's my proximity or the arguing brethren that has her agitated. Part of me hopes it's the brethren and not me. Our history is complicated, but attraction has never been a problem.

"Our prophecy speaks of two distinct goddesses," the other brethren argues.

"That one is Hot-Breath. Don't get too close. His breath is vile," Bri whispers into my ear again. Goddammit—I wish she would stop leaning in, pushing her tits against my shoulder. I look down to avoid her chest and see the slit on her skirt has opened slightly, giving me a view all the way up to her hip.

"I beseech you both to return to your seat, and do not bother the Magnificence of the Crystal Water with your nonsense," a third brethren says, trying to keep the peace. Boss seethes at him and he quickly sits down and lowers his head.

Hot-Breath refuses to step down. "Do not denigrate the Goddess of Light with your silly ideas."

This is way too confusing. There seems to be an endless number of ridiculous titles they will give Bri. Will anyone notice if I start eating? This could go on all night. I raise the food to my mouth and Bri slaps my hand away. A growl rumbles in my chest and goosebumps erupt all over her arms.

"Brethren, please, do not argue," Bri says with a sickly-sweet tone I've never heard her use before.

"Of course, Gracious One," Hot-Breath says with a bow. Boss glares at him for speaking first. These idiots are lining up to kiss her ass, and it's getting under my skin.

"Everyone, eat. This is supposed to be a celebration," she announces to the room. I dredge the flatbread through some paste and shove it in my mouth before she can stop me.

I earn a withering look for not waiting, but running through the desert the last two days on nothing but a handful of nutrigels is making me grumpy. Well, more grumpy than usual.

"What?" I ask with a mouth full of food.

"Nothing." She shakes her head and takes some veg and pops it into her mouth.

Boss approaches our table reverently. He's the same brethren who interrogated me and left me in the dungeon to rot.

He looks over at me and inspects my face. "You look familiar," he says.

"I don't see how that's possible."

There *is* a very good chance he has seen me before. Everyone on Sabaak knew what happened the last time I was here. I'm sure a holographic image was sent all over after everything went down.

"When Her Holiness is done with you, report back to your previous accommodations," he hisses at me.

I open my mouth to reply and tell him where he can shove the previous accommodations when Bri cuts in.

"No, he'll stay with me."

I gape at her, shocked she would offer that. I'll stay *where*? If it's between Bri's room and a dungeon, I'll take the room.

"Hm," he says slowly and steps down from the platform. He sits at the table closest to us. No doubt to keep a close eye on me.

"What was that all about?" Bri asks under her breath.

"Don't worry about it." I look at her with an obnoxiously large smile, one that's meant to provoke her. Bri's smile turns sharp and she grabs my knee and digs in her blunt nails. It's so easy to get a reaction out of her.

"Be a good boy and go find me something to drink."

For everything I've gone through to get to Bri and save her, I decide I'm going to throttle her instead.

SEVENTEEN

Bri

Something is off with Tai. He was way too quick to agree to my plan. If I didn't know any better, I'd say he did it to shut that brethren down.

Their faces go from adoration to sneers when Tai returns with a glass of water for me. Clearly, they don't approve of this new arrangement. I could cut the tension with a knife.

Tai drops down on the ground next to me. He shoves more food in his mouth like a barbarian, completely unaware the brethren are all glaring at him. Tai's arrival seems to have disturbed the delicate balance. The harmless brethren appear to have sharper edges than I believed.

Their debate continues in heated whispers a few tables away. The bullshit prophecy can be interpreted in a million different ways, so it's not shocking they might form into factions. I'd rather not get caught in the middle of their religious debate.

"Brethren, we may not agree on everything, but the prophecy is clear: the goddess must bless the holy water of the Wahadi. Perhaps then her true purpose will be revealed to us," Boss says. His announcement is met with a low rumble throughout the room. Something about the way he says "true purpose" sends a cold shiver down my spine.

I might not like the guy, but his suggestion works in my favor. A little time on the surface will give me a chance to get the lay of the land and the chance to get through to some of the brethren. Once I'm convinced they will stop bowing down to Boss, Tai and I can make a run for it.

"On the way, we must stop by Table Mountain for a sky reading, to fulfill the requirements of the prophecy," Hot-Breath says.

"The blessing of the Wahadi is what will bring back the life-saving water and transform Sabaak into paradise for all of eternity, not your silly sky reading," someone else says. The menacing look in Boss's eye shuts down any further discussion.

The room goes unnervingly quiet. The only sound is Tai's open mouth chomping next to me. I dig my elbow into his ribs.

"Ouch! What the fu—" He stops himself when he sees fury in my eyes. Tai looks around the room, finally observing the situation around him.

Boss also takes note of the mood. "Brethren, of course we will go to Table Mountain on our way to the Wahadi. Our merciful goddess would never neglect one of her sacred duties." Another one of his sickening smiles spreads across his face. A face that is asking to be punched.

Keep speaking for me and see what happens.

A brethren I haven't nicknamed yet leans down to place more food in front of me. I use the opportunity to ask the questions I need answers to before I agree to any of this.

"What's a wahadi?" I whisper into his flat ear.

Without looking away from his task, he responds. "It is the sacred oasis." The way he picked up on my need for subtlety makes him my favorite so far.

"And what's sky reading?" I follow up with.

He looks down at me, baffled. "It's when the shapes in the clouds answer our most important questions. It's how we knew our goddess would be our salvation."

I feel caught in a lie, and the only way to get out of it is more lies. "Oh yeah, that. We used to call it something else."

Tai laughs and tries to disguise it as a cough. I slap him roughly on the back, a playful punishment.

Boss's eyes narrow on me, and the brethren shrinks away out of his field of vision. I stare back, daring him to say something. Boss is the first to break eye contact and stands stiffly to leave, his robes sweeping behind him.

I glance at Tai. "Road trip!"

"What the fuck do you mean we can't leave?" Tai paces around our small room, roughly combing his hands through his hair.

Our room. I had to think quickly when Boss suggested Tai go back down to the dungeon.

There is something going on here, and Tai seems to know more than he led me to believe. I don't feel like I can trust anyone at the moment.

"I can't go yet! You heard them out there—they need me to bless the water and read the clouds or whatever for their cult. I'll play goddess a little bit longer, and then we can leave." The lie comes so easily. What I really need is a chance to help get rid of Boss so these guys can live out their lives in peace.

"It's the perfect opportunity for us to leave!" His fingers curl up like claws. I bite my lips to keep from smiling. Messing with Tai is the most fun I've had in months.

"Tai, have some compassion. These poor guys are stuck here, with only their religion to cling to. They think I'm going to save them. It's the least we can do." Another easy lie. I'm impressed with how convincing I sound.

"This isn't our problem, Bri," he says through clenched teeth.

"I hate to do this, but you should probably call me something like Goddess Divine or something." I quickly turn my back to him and pretend to straighten my pile of blankets to hide my smirk from him, but my shoulders shake from the effort of keeping it in.

"You've got to be shitting me," he says, clearly annoyed. The laughter bubbles up out of me.

"I'm taking a bath. When I get out, you better have a damn good reason why we can't leave tomorrow, and playing goddess for their sake doesn't count." He slams the bathroom door behind him, and I shove my face into a pillow to stifle my laughter. The look on his face was priceless. To think, when I was bored all those months in the muraDome, I could have been torturing Tai the entire time. Such a wasted opportunity.

He's clearly not buying my excuses to stay. It won't be forever. Only a few days. Maybe a week. That's all the time I'll need to poke a few holes in Boss's authority and help lay the first stone of the egalitarian society they think they have. Unfortunately, it appears I'll need Tai's cooperation.

Why does he have to complicate everything?

I loosely braid my hair back for the night and undress as quickly as possible. I jump into bed and pull the blankets up to my chin. I'm going to ask the brethren for some pajamas tomorrow. Sleeping naked with Tai across the room is not a good idea.

The source of my discomfort walks back in a few minutes later. He's dripping wet, with the towel wrapped around his waist. I look away as quickly as possible, but I can't escape the soft padding of his feet on the ground reminding me of our mutual state of undress.

"Are you ready to tell me the real reason you want to stay here and not get home as soon as possible and never touch sand again?" he asks. Clearly the bath did nothing to ease his bad mood.

"I don't like Boss. I don't like the way he runs this place and treats everyone terribly. They all live under this fantasy of being equal, but he's clearly abusing his authority."

Tai runs his hands through his damp hair. It's short by his ears and a little longer on top and in the back. It looks good on him. I don't know many who can pull off that haircut.

Stop it. Stay focused.

"How long is your little religious reformation going to take?" he asks, sounding exhausted.

His question gives him away. He's actually considering it.

"A few days. A week max." I try to suppress my smile.

Victory.

"I'm only agreeing to this because I know how dangerous leaders like Boss can be."

I kick my feet under my blankets and free the smile I've been trying to rein in.

"I'm not doing this for you. I'm doing it because it's the right thing to do, so don't get too excited." He sounds so gruff and serious. I was able to convince one of the most stubborn aliens I know to go along with my plans for the second time in one day. Now I have a few brethren to get through to and we can be on our way.

"What's with the orgasm thing?" he asks, changing the subject abruptly.

"You want to talk about that now?" I hoped he had already forgotten about the awkward greeting.

"Yes, I do."

"This is going to sound crazy." I stop right there and search for the words to describe what happened earlier.

"Try me."

"So, before you got here. Well, I guess it began with some prophecy about their goddess needing satisfaction—"

I stop myself when a laugh bursts out of him. It's a nice laugh. Even though it's at my expense.

"I told you it's crazy."

His laughter is contagious, and soon I'm laughing so hard I'm clutching at my side trying to get the rest of the story out. It's been a while since I've had a good hard laugh. Tai's laughter softens. He inhales deeply and wipes a tear from his eye.

"Go on. I can't wait to hear what happened next." He watches me with a persistently wide grin on his face. The orb light near the door casts a warm light across the room. His bright eyes watch me with amusement. It's a nice smile to go with his nice laugh.

"Well, they kept propositioning me in different ways. I had to pull the goddess card to get them to stop offering to eat me out."

He chokes and coughs. "Eat you out?"

"Go down on me," I explain.

"Yeah, I know what it means. I just can't imagine the brethren doing that."

"I'll have you know I am a very desirable person, and an extremely capable lover," I blurt out, instantly cringing from embarrassment. I don't need to defend myself to him of all people.

"Capable lover?"

"Whatever—you know what I mean." I punch my pillow and try to beat it down so it's more comfortable. I huff and turn my back on him to face the wall so he can't see me blushing. My face is hot and I want the ground to swallow me up. Memories of *that* night back at the muraDome flood in. The night I can't seem to forget.

We had both been drinking just enough to let down our guards. My face got hot and red every time we made eye contact. We were all celebrating the breakthrough in our research which would end the food crisis on Earth. Our mission on j'Tilak was a success—the unique environment held the key to ensuring crops could be grown on Earth. There was hope in the air, which felt even more intoxicating than the drinks.

Over the course of the night, I had forgotten why he was so annoying and why I was holding a grudge. He was smiley and kept laughing at all my jokes. Our shoulders brushed when I went to refill my drink. I remember that feeling of static electricity when our arms touched.

I woke up curled up against him on a couch that was too small for the both of us. His arms around me. It was the closest thing to home I'd felt in months. He climbed over and effortlessly scooped me up and started walking.

"I can walk." I pushed against his chest, and he tightened his arms around me, holding me close.

"I know. Let me do this."

Call it temporary insanity, but when we got to my room, I dragged him in with me.

Before the door had fully closed, we were already ripping at each other's clothes. I pulled his shirt over his head while he fumbled with the buttons on my coveralls.

I ran my hands over his smooth blue body, feeling his muscles bunch under my touch. His skin was too tempting, and I kissed across his chest. I was rewarded with a growl and buttons flying across the room. It sent a shiver straight between my legs and my body ached for more.

"You got the shot, right?" I asked, needing to confirm his birth control.

"Of course."

Cha-ching! Let's do this.

His soft lips matched my movement as he went from one nipple to the next. I carded my fingers through his black hair and held him to me.

Without taking his mouth from my body, he toed his boots off and kicked them one by one across the room, hitting the far wall with a thump.

"You think you're pretty talented, huh?" I asked, gasping for breath.

"I know I am," he said against my skin, dragging my coveralls down past my waist.

Not to be outdone, I pulled at his belt. I had to yank hard, the tightness in his pants making the belt difficult to remove. With a thunk, his pants joined the belt on the floor.

I hope whoever was on the other side of the wall found somewhere else to sleep that night, because I couldn't care less about being quiet.

I was less graceful with my boots. I stumbled forward, and Tai caught me before I could recover. His hands moved slow after that, wandering down the length of me and back up like he was memorizing every curve. Then he took my face in both hands and brought us close. Not even an inch between us.

"You're so fucking beautiful, it hurts." His honest words and the vulnerability in his eyes sent me to my normal tough-exterior response.

"Don't tell me you're going soft on me."

"Oh no—not soft." He rolled his hips to mine, pushing his erection against me.

I stumbled backward toward my bed, dragging him with me. Not wanting to miss a single second of his body against mine. At the last minute I spun us around and pushed him down. The headboard hit the wall with another bang.

The view from above had me thoroughly wet. Tai lying on my bed. His thick blue cock pointing straight up in the air. His hooded eyes met mine and I bit my lip, making him wait a second longer, torturing him a bit before I slipped my leg over his hip and straddled him.

His cock rubbed obscenely against my slit, pointing up above his belly button pinned between us. He guided my hips up and down his length. It was pure, agonizing pleasure. Before I could reach down and direct him inside me, Tai reached up and pulled me down to him. Our lips crashed together, his tongue tangling with mine. A hum of approval vibrated his chest against mine.

He dragged his lips from mine and searched my face. "You want to do this?" he asked, his hands fisting my sheets next to his body, holding back from touching me. His silver bionic hand had ripped a hole through my sheets, apparently not knowing his strength. Knowing I'd pushed him to this point transformed me into the most powerful woman in the universe.

I nodded and bent forward to kiss him again.

"No. Words. I need your words," Tai said, letting go of the ruined bedding and holding my shoulders in place.

"Fuck yes." He lifted up my hips and brought me back down, his cock rubbing down my center and spreading my slick all over him. His thumb pushed its way straight to my clit.

"You love this. Having me at your mercy, begging for you," he said as he kissed from my wrist up my arm.

"Tai—"

"Yes. Whatever it is, yes," he groaned into my neck.

"Shut up and fuck me."

I'd never admit it, but being there with him felt right.

"Yes, ma'am." He grabbed his cock and positioned it under me. I lowered and rolled my hips, taking every inch of him. Moans and gasps escaped both of us, and I rode him like my life depended on it.

He flipped us over and flung my ankles over his shoulders. One more stroke of his cock over my clit and he pushed into me. I might have screamed—maybe it was his name or some profanity. The look of pure satisfaction on his face told me what I needed to know. He enjoyed it as much as I did.

The tension built in my core the faster he thrust into me. I watched him inch closer and closer to losing control. My legs shook first, then everything felt like too much and I came, stars blotting my vision. Tai followed me with an erotic moan.

He collapsed next to me and kissed his way down my shoulder. Blindly I fumbled around on the wall next to the bed. My fingers found my towel hanging on a hook past my nightstand. I dragged it over and we cleaned ourselves off.

I was preparing a flimsy excuse about why he needed to get dressed and get out of my room when he dragged me to him, flipped off the light, and snuggled deep into my hair.

It was the best night. Ever.

That is, until the morning and he pushed me off the bed, and I hit the ground, bruising my tailbone.

Fucker.

I have no difficulty remembering all the reasons why I hate him now. That's what I need to remember, the ending. I need to keep that memory at the top of my mind, especially with us sharing a room now.

"Good night, Tai," I say and press my eyes closed. As if that could block the memory.

"Good night, Sunshine."

EIGHTEEN

Bri

"Hi, there." I cautiously approach the h'axom I'll be riding through the desert for the next few days. The enormous animal is twice the size of a horse and covered in short, wiry fur. The long up curled eyelashes and drooping trunk give it a friendly face. Mine looks docile enough as it lazily chews on its lunch of dried grass.

First things first, how am I going to hoist myself on? I size her up, the bottom of her belly level with my shoulders. She's nearly as wide as she is tall.

"Their wide abdomens store water for the long treks across the desert. They are very special animals," Hot-Breath says from behind me. I jump in surprise. I didn't realize he was back there. "They are only found here, on Sabaak, and their organs are valuable for many things. Their glands specifically are used for very fine cosmetics," he says with pride.

My ears heat with anger. It pisses me off that someone would kill these amazing animals for something as trivial as makeup.

I awkwardly lift my leg and try to get my foot in the stirrup that is out of reach.

"Allow me." Hot-Breath grabs my waist and heaves me into the air. I get my foot in the footrest and push myself up the rest of the way. The amount of exertion he had to use to get me up is not good for my ego. I settle into the cushioned seat, my legs spread-fucking-eagle. My bare legs rub uncomfortably against the rough fur.

"Good girl, Daisy. We got this." I lean down and pat her side affectionately, also to double-check that she's still alive. The other h'axom are stomping around and she's hardly moved.

"Daisy?" Tai asks from atop his h'axom. I glare at him, annoyed that he looks so comfortable sitting on his ride, while I struggle to find a workable position.

"I named her Daisy. Isn't she such a pretty girl?" I coo at her, oozing as much sweetness into my tone as I can. I love Tai's dramatic eyeroll every time I put on this syrupy voice. He thinks I don't notice, but I do, and now I make it a point to make sure he's close enough to hear it.

Tai rolls his eyes and shakes his head. I steal a glance at the brethren who are tending to their mounts and flash a middle finger at Tai when I'm sure they aren't watching us. Unfazed by my gesture, he flips me off in return. I must be rubbing off on him, because he's mastering the subtleties of these human mannerisms quite well.

Boss directs his h'axom toward me. His looks fast and athletic, in sharp contrast to mine.

"I picked the calmest one for you," he says.

"Maybe a little too calm," I say.

Ignoring my complaint, he says, "It is my honor to travel ahead of the group and prepare resting places for you today."

I'm grateful. Daisy isn't the most comfortable ride, and it's going to be a very long day.

"Thank you." Hopefully this journey will be much better than stumbling around in circles. All with the added bonus of being away from Boss all day.

"I trust you will tend to the goddess en route," he confirms with Tai. I wince at the condescending tone.

"You really want to talk about how to tend to females?" Tai spits back, not one to be talked down to. This scrappy side of Tai is wildly and inappropriately attractive.

"Don't let anything happen to her," Boss says before galloping back to the head of the group.

Daisy shuffles closer to Tai without my direction. I take the opportunity to ask a few probing questions. "What's going on there?"

"What do you mean?" He sounds defensive.

Another checkmark in the suspicious column.

"Tell me what's going on. I hate being kept in the dark."

"There is nothing going on. I simply want to get off this planet and back home." His body language is tight, and from a few feet away I can see the muscle in his jaw tick. Tai is usually a quiet guy, but right now his silence feels loud.

"Please follow me. I will show you the way," the brethren I've dubbed Baby Face Brethren, for obvious reasons, says while coming up behind us. We all secure the dark goggles. My eyes relax immediately, no longer squinting into the bright sun.

Tai's h'axom lurches forward with a flick of the reins. Daisy remains unbothered by my gentle prodding to get her to move.

"Come on, sweet girl. Time to go," I tell her and tap her sides with my heels. I tug a little at the reins.

Still nothing.

"Daisy, if we are going to be friends, you can't make me look bad in front of him," I whisper sternly.

She finally takes one lumbering step, followed by another slower one, content to move at her own speed. I continue the sweet-talk, hoping it will motivate her to catch up with the group. She is even slower than the team of h'axom dragging a heavy sled. The load is stacked tall and covered with thick fabric. I assume our supplies are under there.

I'm tired and grumpy from hardly getting any sleep last night.

The unwelcomed memory agitated me, and it was impossible to get comfortable in my bed after that. I tossed and turned, and every time I'd get close to falling asleep, Tai would make some noise, a reminder we were sharing a room. All it took was a light breath or rustle of blankets for me to get worked up again. I should have let the brethren drag him back down to the dungeon.

"You okay over there, Sunshine?" I can't tell if he's concerned or being sarcastic. Knowing him, it's sarcasm.

"I'm a little tired. Maybe if you weren't snoring all night, I could have gotten some rest."

He doesn't snore. The soft sounds of him sleeping only heightened the feelings that came up from the memory.

"Maybe if you would have stopped flailing around in your bed last night, I could have fallen asleep and you would hear what snoring actually sounds like."

If he knew what kept me awake, his ego would explode.

"Don't let me hold you back. Don't you have some brethren to spy on?" I need to get him and his knowing eyes away from me.

His ride kicks up sand as he catches up to the rest of the group. I'm equally irritated he was holding back to stay with me and that he took off so quickly when I gave him an excuse.

Which is it, Bri? You want him or not?

It doesn't matter. We might have a temporary shared goal, but I still can't stand him and I don't trust him. Regardless of how hot that one night was—it's not happening again.

The scorching wind blows back my borrowed headscarf as we amble forward. I adjust it, trying to find the right position to keep the sun off my face. Sweat has been dripping down my back since the second we stepped on the surface.

A cloud of sand appears over the rolling dunes. Table Mountain waits for us in the hazy distance.

I hate being in the back of the caravan. I can't talk to any of the brethren from back here. With Boss up in front, this would be the perfect opportunity to feel them out. No one has expressly said they hate Boss, but it's clear they are afraid of him.

I tap Daisy's flanks with my heels and flick the reins up a few times to get her to speed up. She's either completely unaware of my intentions or she is the most stubborn animal on the planet.

The slow pace gives me too much time to think. At some point throughout the day the h'axom formed a single file line, winding our way between the dunes.

It's embarrassing to admit to myself that Tai's secretive nature has me feeling pulled toward him even more. Let's call it curiosity and nothing more. Because if I let myself be drawn to Tai, I'd be in danger of repeating a very toxic pattern I have worked very hard to avoid.

The source of my curiosity is right in front of me, and it's impossible to look away from how he sways and moves in the saddle. His hips rocking back and forth. I twist my neck to the side, desperate to find something else to look at, anything else to think about.

My dad would probably love it here, the barren desert landscape. Endless dunes to climb, craters and dried-out canyons to explore.

From the outside, my parents were happy. With four kids there was always something going on, and when there wasn't, my dad would invent something for us to do.

I always suspected our impromptu backpacking trips were a way for him to temporarily escape. But one day, they weren't enough and he left for good.

My mom adored him, and completely fell apart when he left. We never had answers. One day he was there, the next he was packing up and leaving. I promised myself I'd never do what my dad did. I'd never let myself hurt someone in that way.

He can rot in the desert for all I care.

NINETEEN

Tai

Bri's fake laughter is grating on my nerves. I know what her real laugh sounds like. It's obvious when she's forcing it.

By the look on his face, the brethren she's talking to believes the laughter is sincere. It took her a while to coax her animal to catch up, but over the last hour, she has been subtly dropping hints that Boss is not good for the brethren.

Bri is quite impressive, I'll admit. It's a master class in persistence. At first, she used her sense of humor—but it was wasted on him. She's currently using flattery, but he is so blinded by her beauty and charm, nothing is sticking in that oddly shaped head of his.

"You're a fantastic brethren. I'm one lucky goddess. You know I'd never treat you poorly, or put myself above you, right?"

"But you are above us! We are lowly brethren here to serve you," he says back, more confused than ever.

Bri tosses her hands up in the air, finally giving up on this one. She scans the group of brethren and her eyes narrow on her next target.

Time passes slowly on Sabaak. We haven't even reached our first rest stop and my legs are killing me. My mount comes to a stop right in front of Bri. Her animal bumps into mine, knocking us both sideways.

"Something wrong, Tai?" she asks sweetly—too sweetly and I hate it.

"Nope, everything is great," I say through gritted teeth.

"You are both so lucky to be here this time of year. During the hot season, we wouldn't have been able to make it to Table Mountain!" a brethren says, the one Bri has been fake-laughing with for a while now.

"This isn't the hot season?" Bri asks, fanning herself with the end of her scarf.

"Glorious One, this is our coolest."

She looks over at me eyes wide and makes an odd gesture with her finger drawing across her neck. I'm not sure what it means, but she looks cute doing it.

I have a high tolerance for discomfort, courtesy of my early years. I won't enjoy today, but it's unlikely to be the worst place I've visited. However, Bri is used to a climate-controlled environment. I mentally prepare myself to hear a lot of complaining out of her.

A small bright red tent flaps in the distance. It's about time. I'm ready to get off this thing. I urge my h'axom to a trot and bounce uncomfortably on the saddle the faster he goes. He's equally eager to stop and rest. I'm much bigger than his usual riders. I reach down and pat his neck affectionately in silent gratitude.

I go straight to the trough of murky water. The h'axom's trunk takes long steady pulls of water. Leaving him to hydrate, I heave my half-asleep leg over and slide down his side. I'm already dreading how sore I'll be tomorrow.

A low table and a cushion sits under a canopy. Enough shade for one person. I don't have to guess who it's intended for. The tent is unnecessarily far from the trough, carelessly set up so we all have to walk through the deep and shifting sand.

The brethren are rushing around preparing for their "goddess." I roll my eyes each time they use the word. She's not a goddess. She is a demon. She's shrill and devious and the longer this goes on the thinner my patience wears.

Bri is the last one to arrive. There must be something wrong with her h'axom. It's slow and looks older than the dunes. Five brethren rush to her side to help her down from its back. She gratefully accepts their help and a wince flickers across her face when she hits the ground. There is something about the brief glimpse of pain that tightens my chest.

Bri gently pushes their hands off her once she has her feet on solid ground. She trudges through the sand and grabs a canteen of water from the table as the hot wind blows through the tent flinging sand right in her face. The least they could do was put some walls on this thing. She eases herself onto the cushion. Her movements are stiff and she braces her lower back with her hands. Why aren't they helping her?

These brethren annoy the shit out of me. They are all up her ass but aren't even good at taking care of her most basic needs. They are too busy competing for her favor to pay attention to what is going on around them.

If we are going to keep up the ruse that I'm her servant, I should probably tend to her. It's the only reason I'm going over there to help her out. This is all to keep up the act. And that's it.

I grab a handful of dried fruit from a basket on the table and take it to her.

"No, thank you, I'm okay," she says to a brethren kneeling at her feet. She reaches down and pushes his hands away from her sandals, which he has already untied.

"Supreme Beauty, it would be my honor to massage your feet and legs. You must be tired from today's exertions." This poor deluded idiot doesn't know when to stop.

"I appreciate the offer, really. Give me a minute to cool down." She sounds tired. When she looks up at me, I toss her a long strip of dried yellow fruit. She catches it midair and mouths "thank you."

The brethren at her feet jumps up. "You're hungry, Our Precious Light!" He runs over to the table with food and grabs two of everything with his dirty hands that were previously on her feet. I lean up against the tent pole and watch this unsanitary act of desperation unfold. Who says there's nothing fun to do on Sabaak?

"I'm good, really," she says, her voice heavy with exhaustion. He rushes back to her, kicking up sand everywhere. He dumps his armload of food into her lap. She slowly blinks and takes a deep breath, collecting herself before she loses it on him. I'm hoping she tears into him.

Another brethren steps up behind her and massages her neck and shoulders. From all the way over here, I see her entire body tense up at his touch. She awkwardly laughs and declines his offer.

Her eyes catch mine and she mouths the words "save me." I mouth back "you're on your own." I've already helped her once. She's on her own this time. Actions have consequences, and these are hers.

"Oh no!" Bri yells, laying it on thick. The brethren have no idea that she sounds so insincere it's laughable. "I think your h'axom got loose!" She points dramatically toward the trough, which is out of her line of sight, blocked by the doting brethren surrounding her. There is no way she would know that. A clever way to get some space.

Panicked that he might have to walk all the way home, the brethren behind her takes off at a run, his headscarf flapping behind him as he looks for his ride.

"A little solidarity would be nice," she says to me with narrowed eyes when they are all out of earshot.

"You handled it perfectly fine. You are the goddess after all, aren't you?"

I can tell the sun and heat are affecting her. She doesn't have the same level of fight in her that I've gotten used to.

I grab my canteen and wet the end of my headscarf, soaking it with the cool water. I take her hand and press the damp scarf to her wrists first then behind her neck.

She leans close to my ear. "Thank you," she whispers. "pt'Alquon, did you do something nice for me?"

"Don't get used to it."

Bri lets out an audible sigh and leans back into the wet fabric on her neck.

I look away into the hot wind before she realizes what keeps catching my eye. She doesn't need me drooling after her like all these pathetic brethren. I anchor my arm behind her and nudge her back to let her know she can lean against me. Her skirt shifts and the split falls open all the way up to her hip.

"Any progress on Operation Savior Complex?" I whisper in her ear.

Her sharp elbow lodges itself in my side.

"I'll take that as a *no*."

"It's incremental," she says, full of righteous indignation. "You should know this about me. Once I've made up my mind, there is very little that can stop me."

The brethren Bri sent to go chase down the h'axom is back, out of breath and covered with sweat. If he's unhappy with the false alarm, he doesn't show it.

"What's the deal with Table Mountain?" I ask him, trying to direct my attention away from her smooth, far-too-distracting leg.

I catch one of the other brethren leering at her chest. I loudly clear my throat, breaking his concentration. He knows he got caught and looks guilty as fuck when he finally meets my gaze.

"When we first arrived on this planet, we landed at the top of Table Mountain. We were greeted by a glorious sunrise and we knew we had found the place the clouds had foretold." He conveniently left out the part where they were banished from their home planet because of their violence toward women.

"How long have you been here?" Bri asks.

"Eleven turns of the wind, Divine One," he says with reverence.

"And you've just been waiting around for your goddess to show up?" she asks skeptically.

She is making a giant miscalculation with the brethren. Their extreme religious beliefs make them far more dangerous than she knows.

"It's our highest calling," he states as if it's a matter of fact.

"Sitting around for eleven years? Sounds boring," she says.

I laugh under my breath. Leave it to Bri to state the obvious.

"We have kept the colony prepared for your arrival and we do our patrols."

"Patrols?" This time I have the follow-up question. On this desolate planet what could they be looking for?

"We have been tasked with patrolling the sands around here to ensure the Others can conduct their business without interference."

"Others?"

"Time to leave, Majestic One," Bug-Eyes interjects.

I stay close to Bri so I can be the one to help her up this time. The brethren need to keep their creepy hands to themselves.

Bri settles on the h'axom, and I adjust her flimsy skirt to cover more of her leg. Her skin was not made for this climate.

While Bri is out trying to start a religious revolution, I'll find out who these Others are and how they can help us get the fuck out of here.

From the top of Table Mountain, the sun reflects off Bri's long pinkish hair. The first time I saw her, it was bright pink and piled on top of her head in a messy ponytail with little strands framing her face. Now it's down and blowing behind her from the warm evening winds.

Her skin is golden and shining. Fuck me—she does look like a goddess. The brethren and I all have the same dopey looks on our faces. I shake my head to break the spell she has over me.

TWENTY

Bri

Shocker—there isn't any consensus on the message from the clouds. Our little field trip hasn't solved anything so far. I still have no idea where we are or how to find help. Plus, the brethren are too busy bickering for me to get in there and cast some doubt on Boss. They don't even seem to notice the breathtaking view.

The dull brown sky turns bright with broad pink and purple streaks as the sun hovers over the horizon. For a fleeting moment, the dreariness of Sabaak is gone. Reds and oranges transform the sky into a watercolor painting, the kind painted by a person with a brush, not a computer's poor imitation.

"That one right there! It's the shape of a vessel! See? She alone is the Rain-Bringer of Sabaak! And the rain comes because her prayer *pours* it onto the desert like the water goddess she is," one says, pointing to a flat, shapeless cloud.

I chance a look at Tai, who is mid eye-roll from the ridiculous notion. He's right. This is stupid. But as long as they think I'm their goddess, I can be a positive influence on them. He better not mess this up for me. Also, isn't it rude to make fun of other people's religious beliefs? I shoot him a death stare, and he shrugs back.

How is it that I am more sensitive to the cultural differences between us and the brethren? Wasn't Elowen the one lecturing *me* about this a few months ago?

"No, you fool. It's clearly a flame, representing her works with the power of the sun," another one argues right back. "The power of her fervent prayer *quells* the sun. She's not *only* a water goddess. She works with the sun! She is the Sacred Flame of Sabaak!"

I walk away from the constant bickering and turn back to the stunning view. It's powerful enough to make me forget the overwhelming heat, the gritty sand sticking to every inch of my skin, and the creepy-ass brethren fawning over me. This right here, the view from Table Mountain, is what I craved all those months ago when I was trapped in the muraDome with nothing but work to keep me busy.

One of the brethren and Tai are in deep discussion, and from their body language, it's not going well. Tai's ear twitches when the brethren angrily waves his arms in the air. Tai leans down to meet the brethren's eye and says something through clenched teeth, his hands fisted at his sides. Tai looks over, forces a smile, and pats the brethren on the head in the most patronizing way. The brethren has a similar forced smile that doesn't meet his eyes.

"Majestic Goddess, come this way and take a final look at the barren valley. For the next time you see it, it will be green and flowing with water from your blessings." Another brethren pulls me away and directs me to the valley below.

"Now that you are here, you can restore the planet to paradise."

Now's my opportunity to get some information on what else is out there. "What's over there? Any other holy sites?" I ask, pointing away from the direction we came, curious about a possible escape route in the future.

"No, just more sand. And possibly a Sabaaki village, but we aren't permitted to travel that way," he says.

Perfect. Once I'm done with Boss, that's where we'll go to find help.

The sun dips down below the horizon and the temperature plummets with it. With the brilliant light show over, I notice the brethren staring at me with awe in their eyes. Ugh. I search for Tai. He's back at the h'axom adjusting his saddle, his back to me. Mr. All-Business didn't even take a second to enjoy the view.

Things are still tense between Tai and the brethren. I can't stop feeling there is something I'm missing. Tai is so stingy with details about himself, I can't tell if it's because he's private or because he is hiding something.

At the base of the mountain, a dozen tents are set up in a tight circle. Meat cooks over a small fire. It smells amazing. How am I supposed to go back to boring noodles when this is over? There are a lot of negatives to being here—and the brethren are doing their best to ruin my first experience exploring the vast universe—but the fresh non-modified food might be the best part.

I'm led inside the largest tent. The smell of citrus soap wafts from a clawfoot copper tub set up in the back corner. I feel a twinge of guilt at the thought of the h'axom dragging the heavy sled with a giant tub for me. Since it's here, I might as well put it to use.

An agitating voice reminds me of who I'm sharing my tent with tonight.

"The water will help." In the far corner, Tai reclines on a pile of pillows, looking relaxed and clean.

"A gentleman would have let me use the bath first." I realize how immature I sound.

"Good thing I'm not a gentleman."

I ignore his retort and hobble my way over to the tub. Behind a privacy screen,

I pull off my clothes and step into the lukewarm water.

I groan while I ease my way in.

The water feels nice once I get past the sting of it hitting my raw legs. The bath is perfect, but it's hard to fully relax when I'm sitting across from *him*.

"I have a proposal," Tai says, disturbing my quiet relaxation time.

"Proposing already?" His setup justifies my corny reply.

"Can we call a temporary ceasefire? I'm exhausted. I don't have the energy to spar with you right now," Tai says as he wipes a hand down his tired face.

"So...you're admitting defeat?" I can't help myself.

"I am. I surrender. Please have mercy on me. I'm tired. You are too."

I'd never say it out loud, but I'm relieved. I don't have the energy to go back and forth with him either. Comfortable silence with Tai sounds nice. Having him around isn't all that bad. I prefer it over the creepy fawning from the brethren. One look from the big blue alien usually sends them packing.

"I promise, we can pick up our usual shit-talking later," he says.

"You better not be turning soft on me," I tell him. The words slip out of my mouth before I can snatch them back, an echo of what I said to him the night we hooked up. The taunt that resulted in him pressing his giant cock against me. I scrub my hands roughly over my face, trying unsuccessfully to banish the mental image.

Weightlessness relieves the pressure on my body. My legs, my arms, my back, my face. Everything hurts. Even my hair hurts.

Back above water, I lean against the tub and let the water work its magic. There is a chance he didn't pick up on my comment, but I'm too tired to care any longer. I peek over at him.

He's in a similar position. Head back, eyes closed. I seize the opportunity to get a good look at him. My eyes drift lower, taking in his muscular chest. I don't want him to see me checking him out. He would tease me mercilessly.

Tilaks are objectively good-looking. They are tall, broad, muscular, and chiseled. Blue aliens are hot. Name an attractive trait, and they've got it. So, it's totally normal for my eyes to be constantly drawn to him. The guy is in incredible shape.

Stop thinking about Tai's incredible shape. Especially his thighs. He's got some juicy thighs that could probably... Seriously, stop it.

Nevermind, quiet equals danger. Too much time to let my mind wander. So, I say the first thing that comes to mind.

"Did you name yours?" I ask.

"Name what?" He responds without opening his eyes.

"That giant thing between your legs today. Your h'axom, obviously," I clarify with a grin.

Tai chuckles. "Name it whatever you want, but we're not going to be here long enough for it to matter. You've got a few days to take care of Boss, then we leave and never come back."

"Such a hurry to get home! What's the matter, Tai? Your hand not getting the job done anymore?" The possibility occurs to me that somewhere back on his home planet, a beautiful Tilak female could be waiting for him to return. The thought makes my stomach twist.

Tai's tone turns more serious. "Very funny. Just don't get too comfortable around these guys. They aren't safe."

"I haven't forgotten. But what I want to know is why they are so weird with you."

"I'm a threat. They don't have their goddess to themselves anymore," he says, fluffing up a pillow and placing it behind his head. It rings true, but there is something nagging at me that there is still more to the story.

"Well, being worshiped is a nice change of pace. You should try it," I say. In truth, it's annoying as shit.

"We can't all worship at the altar of Bri," he says, flexing his bionic hand, and the arm drops limply on his stomach.

"How's the...equipment?" Why does my voice sound so husky? *Pull it together, girl.*

"Equipment?" He lifts an eyebrow. Seriously. Everything is a challenge with this guy. And for fuck's sake, I can't back down from a challenge.

"Yeah, it looks..." I gulp. "Unreliable."

He is up and strutting toward me in the time it takes me to blink.

"Oh Sunshine, the equipment is fine, and more than reliable." He looms over me, and all of a sudden, the room is sweltering.

I run my fingers down his bionic arm from shoulder to wrist. A smile cracks my face when I see it twitch from the touch. "It's looking a little...limp these days."

"Just waiting for the right time."

"I think you need to cool down," I say, splashing him playfully. He's not the only one.

With an arrogant laugh, he turns and strides out of the tent, giving me a full view of that ass in his tight cargo pants. The brief glimpse makes my entire body clench. I slide down the edge, submerging myself in the water, and scream.

What gives this alien the right to have such big dick energy?

TWENTY-ONE

Tai

I had to get out of the tent before I did something that couldn't be taken back, so it's back in the sand for me until I'm confident Bri is fully dressed and preferably asleep. The hint of her body under the water was enough to send all the blood in my body straight to my cock. Her casual flirtatiousness made me feel impulsive. Putting some distance between us is the best way to get myself back under control.

It's dark and cold out here. It should be a nice break from the pounding heat of the day, but it's bitterly cold, my breath fogging in the air a testament to how quickly the temperatures change here.

The brethren hardly register my presence when I slide into an empty space around the fire. That's alright with me. I don't want to talk to them either. The flames are hypnotic as they flicker and wave. An open flame is unheard of on j'Tilak. It would be too dangerous in the hydrogen-rich atmosphere. Even a small flame could erupt into a fireball that would consume everything.

Brush shifts in the firepit and embers spiral up to the sky. I watch the sparks until they disappear into the stars. This strange place has these brief slices of beauty.

My peaceful thoughts are rudely interrupted by the frantic hushed tones of the brethren. Boss must be approaching. He really does put everyone on edge.

Bouncing from station to station showed me how differently everyone reacts to power. The vast majority were cruel and punishing. Unchecked power corrupts. I thought that was how the universe worked. Until I learned about my home planet.

On j'Tilak noble houses share responsibility to maintain balance. I wouldn't have believed it if I didn't see it with my own eyes. When someone becomes too powerful or does something to endanger the planet, they lose influence. The planet itself insists on balance.

In an almost mystical way, j'Tilak challenged me. I became attached to the stability it brought me. When the humans came, it threatened the foundation my survival depended on, or so I thought. I worried my world would change too much for me to feel safe and in control. I didn't know it then, but I was ready to change. More than that, I needed to. It was time to learn what I should have known all along: coexistence is only the beginning. The real work is letting someone different from you leave a mark and leaving one yourself.

I watched Aro grow into someone who stopped avoiding responsibility and stepped up. He harnessed the ancient power of battleform to protect his mate. And it opened my eyes to the future possibility of a life that includes humans. Sometimes, I let myself picture life with one specific human.

Just as I had suspected, Boss comes into view, his robes swishing in the sand like a snake.

"I see the goddess let you out of her sight for once," he hisses at me.

"Go bother someone else," I say, dismissing him.

"Tilak scum don't tell the brethren what to do." He spits the word "Tilak" like it's poison on his tongue.

"Fine. If you won't leave, then I will." I get up from my comfortable seat and stomp into the dark and away from the tents. Whatever reason brought him over to me, I don't want any part of it.

Yellow light shines from a tent with its window and door flaps pulled open. At a table in the center, the Oo'rahim that Bri calls Baby Face is cutting up fruit and veg. I step inside, grab a knife, and start chopping next to him.

He's the one who breaks the silence. "You should go attend to the goddess."

"She's alright. I needed something to do with my hands."

"Isn't she magnificent?" He sets down the knife and sighs.

"She's not so bad," I say and keep chopping.

"Don't ever tell Brethren, but I had begun to give up hope she would ever arrive."

I know right away which brethren he is referring to.

"What's he got over you all anyway?" I ask, genuinely curious how this all came about.

"The brethren are all equa—"

"Don't start with all that 'we are all equal' bullshit. You and I both know he's the one in charge, and none of you are doing a damn thing about it."

He looks at me, confusion all over his face. Now I can see why Bri is struggling to make any headway on her mission.

"Whatever. It's not my job to convince you to want better," I say, repeating something I've heard before. The Westgate Orbital station manager said those exact words to me. It took years to understand what he meant. I needed to want it for myself, and I deserved something better.

"We have everything we could ever desire now that the goddess has blessed us with her presence."

"What about the 'Others'? Do they expect her to rule over them as well?" It's not the smoothest transition to where I want the conversation to go, but I need information.

"The Others? Oh no, they are not brethren."

"Who are they?"

Before he can answer me, Boss steps into the tent. Baby Face clams up and goes back to chopping. That's my cue to leave.

"Have a good night, Brethren," I tell Baby Face as I step out of the light and back into the shadows.

I go straight back to Bri's tent and quietly open the flap. It's completely dark inside. Bri softly breathes from her bed in the corner. The attraction I was trying to hide from earlier comes roaring back to life.

What would it be like if she invited me to her bed?

I would never want to leave.

TWENTY-TWO

Bri

"The maiden had been wandering in the desert for days when her glass vessel was nearly empty. She held it up to the sky to see only a splash left, not nearly enough to get through the miles of desert in front of and behind her. She sank down into the sand on her knees. She had given up all hope and was prepared to welcome death when a warrior stepped over the dune and tumbled toward her. He was lost and confused, mumbling about eternal life and cool waters. He fell at her feet on the brink of death."

The Brethren pauses for dramatic effect.

"Although she was frightened, she offered the last of her water to the warrior. First, the water came out in a trickle, barely wetting his lips. Then it poured out faster than he could drink it. It soaked his clothing, then the sand, and filled the valley, making the beautiful Wahadi we will see today."

Another dramatic pause.

"The warrior was no ordinary warrior. He was a demigod who was banished to Sabaak. To reward her act of kindness, he gave her the gift of eternal life as long as she stayed in the Wahadi with him." Hot-Breath brings his story to a close.

"That's a beautiful story. Well, except the part where she's stuck in the Wahadi with someone who, for all we know, could have been a total asshole," I tell him.

The most hostile environments always have the most fascinating mythologies. I notice he doesn't seem bothered by the part of the story where the maiden is essentially held captive for eternity.

"A beautiful story, for a beautiful goddess. When we discovered this Wahadi after our arrival, we knew it was the place of your birth in our holy texts," Friar Tuck says, directing his h'axom to be next to mine. His long, white robe flits in the wind behind him. The brethren have all changed from their usual brown rough robes to lightweight gauzy white ones, tied off in the middle with their signature bell.

"Over the centuries, you must have forgotten your genesis." It feels wrong to not correct him. He's so earnest in his belief in me. It doesn't feel right to let them think I'm their goddess. Maybe once Boss is out of the picture, I'll get them to understand.

Daisy is in her usual form, slowly making her way through the sand. I got lucky today and was able to coax her into formation in front of a few others. She's been forced to keep up with the caravan. Each time she slows down, Tai's h'axom, who I've named Brutus, gives her a little nudge.

From the top of a dune, I look down at the oasis below. Cerulean water surrounded by tall green palms. A wide stone path skirts the edge of the basin. It leads all the way down to a raised platform with steps that overhang the water. I shade my eyes from the sunlight reflecting brightly off the surface. The water looks inviting and cool, but I'll never know for sure. I've been warned it's completely off limits. No one, not even the Goddess Divine, is allowed to touch the sacred pool. The water cannot be disturbed, or it will frighten away the warrior and his maiden.

Daisy takes a slow step forward as we begin our descent. Brutus passes us in a hurry to get to the shade below. I try to prod Daisy along gently, but she ignores me. I love my girl, but I'd appreciate a little more hustle from her.

Tai skids to a stop at the bottom of the hill, hops off with one graceful movement, and ties off Brutus under the shade of an enormous palm tree. A smirk stretches across his face as I slowly make my way over. A silent declaration that he won.

"Not everything has to be a race, you know," I say.

Tai would fit in perfectly with my brothers. The easy confidence bordering on arrogance feels familiar in a way I didn't realize until now.

"If it was, you'd lose," Tai says as he reaches up and helps me down. His strong hands on my waist. I feel the loss of them when he sets me down and pulls away.

We follow the stone path leading to the overlook, letting the brethren go first, as they had planned. I'm grateful to be back on solid ground. Trudging through the soft sand of the dunes has been brutal on my calves.

Throughout the day, we go over every single agonizing detail of the ceremony, and the brethren push through the afternoon and don't stop for any breaks. It's excruciatingly hot. Even my sweat dried up hours ago. I'm ready to say, "fuck it all" and cannonball right into the center of the water.

I want to get this over with as quickly as possible.

"You think they really believe this stuff?" Tai asks, referring to the story of the maiden and the warrior.

"I think they do. And I don't think any of them stop to question how their goddess could be born from an oasis on a planet where they've only been for the last eleven years." I keep my voice low.

They all gather on the landing and move in single-file lines that create a steady stream of brethren in a figure eight quietly praying to the maiden and warrior.

"They are waiting for the maiden to reveal herself," Friar Tuck whispers as we climb the stairs.

"You never know. Today could be our lucky day," Tai says loudly as he passes me on the stairs.

The guy has zero situational awareness. Everyone is quiet and reverent, and he's stomping around and speaking at full volume.

A glass decanter is placed in my hands. I follow the specific instructions and stand at the ledge over the water. My arm shakes as I lift the glass bottle and slowly tip it over, pouring the water into the pool to honor the maiden and the warrior.

I'm vaguely aware of someone taking the glass out of my hands. Everything sounds muted and out of sync. Bodies on every side press closer to me, sucking the air out of my lungs. I push my way forward, with no sense of direction, just the need to get away.

I focus on the one clear thought: water. I need water. Pushing becomes shoving, but the crowd only presses in harder. My head spins, everything around me tilting on its axis. Suddenly, it's hard to breathe.

"You okay?" a far-off voice asks me. I blindly wave in the direction of the question. I need air.

"Bri, look at me." This time I use all my strength to put some distance between me and the person who has invaded my space. A high-pitched scream and a splash wake me up from the haze.

The brethren wail, loudly. My senses return to me one by one. When my vision comes into focus, Tai is treading water below and looking mad enough to commit murder. My stomach drops.

Oh fuck. That's on me.

Bile rises in my throat, and before I can hold it back, I turn to the side and heave into the sand.

I wipe my mouth with the back of my hand and go down to help Tai out of the water. He's stomping his way toward me, seething with rage. His soaked clothes cling to his body, and I have a renewed appreciation for his form. My eyes track down to his chest, the white fabric translucent against his blue skin. Black pebbled nipples poke the wet shirt. I stagger back a little—from the sand, *not* the view of this guy climbing out of the water.

"Tai, I am so sorry. That was an accident," I explain over the loud wailing the brethren have fallen into.

"I don't want to talk to you right now," he says without looking at me.

"I really am sorry. I thought I was going to pass out, and I didn't realize it was you." I'm desperate for him to know how awful I feel.

"Now is not the time."

I silently trail behind him, trying not to laugh as water sloshes out of his wet boots with every step.

Maybe someday in the very distant future we can laugh about this.

I bury my face in Daisy's coarse fur. "We are in big trouble, girl."

Canteen in hand, I sink down on the hard ground in the shade a few trees over from the resting h'axom, giving the brethren and the soggy Tilak some space.

I am mortified that I pushed Tai in the Wahadi. Although, he did get cooled off. Maybe. Possibly at the expense of the brethren's religious ceremony. Hopefully they will get over it. Someday. From the sound of their mournful cries, it's going to be a while.

Sopping wet, Tai sits down next to me. "The wailing is getting old," he says.

I'm too embarrassed to make eye contact with Tai. I keep my gaze fixed on my fingers, drawing swirls in the sand. He nudges me with his damp arm. The gesture eases some of the tension from me.

"I've heard happier funeral dirges," I say. I'm a terrible person for making a joke at their expense.

He looks around. "If there is a holy site on this awful continent, this would be it."

Tai pulls his shirt off over his head and presses the cloth to my forehead, then the back of my neck, and wrists. My temperature drops immediately.

"And you desecrated it," I say to see if we have already gotten to a place where we can laugh about this. I sneak a glance at him from the corner of my eye.

"I would throw your ass right in if I didn't think Boss would return me to the gods, as he likes to say." Tai laughs and looks at me. "Be careful. The Wahadi has made me into a demigod. All shall fear me," he says in a joking voice.

"I could never fear you," I say. It appears I was wrong. It didn't take very long to get to a place where we could laugh about it.

"My life would be so much easier if you did."

TWENTY-THREE

Tai

Bri chews on the inside of her lip, punishing herself for the accident. The normally confrontational attitude has been replaced with avoidance. She will hardly even look at me, and I find myself wanting to cheer her up even though I was the one shoved into the oasis.

I don't need to lecture her. She's clearly scolding herself enough for the both of us. When I dragged myself out of the water, I was prepared for her to be unapologetic and blame me. I was wrong. And the way she is gulping down water makes me think she might genuinely have heatstroke.

"You look like a drowned rat," she says, finally looking me up and down. I can tell she's masking her vulnerability with jokes.

"I've heard rats are very intelligent and incredibly attractive."

She smiles at me out of the corner of her eye. It feels good when I make her smile. That thought sets off a deadly chain reaction. If it feels this good to make her smile, there are a few other emotions I'd like to wring out of her. Every once in a while, I let myself remember *that* night.

I replay the scene in my mind, every perfect detail. I reached for her when I woke up, but she was gone. Bri never mentioned it again. So, I did what I'm best at and buried the memory as deep as possible.

A dried piece of grass from Daisy's lunch sticks to Bri's shoulder. Without thinking, I brush it off. The feel of her skin sends a vibration up my bionic arm.

She leans into my touch, and the back of my hand skims her neck. The entire world melts away, and it's only me and Bri. Everything fades away except her eyes locked with mine, until they flicker away to focus on something over my shoulder.

"Don't look now, but Boss is watching," she says and lays a hand on my chest.

I don't need to look back to know his beady eyes are on us.

The rational part of my brain says to pull away, to not aggravate the situation. The other part of me wants to kiss her, to send the message that she is mine, not his. She draws me in closer. I'm power-less to the way she looks at me. Like I'm hers as well.

I'm so focused on her and the sound of my heart hammering in my chest that I don't hear the commotion around the h'axom at first. Yelling and pounding hooves break the spell and jerk me back to real-ity. Three h'axom stampede straight for us, their leather reins hanging loosely. I pull Bri up and spin us around, putting a palm tree between us and the charging animals.

We stand there slack-jawed and watch the h'axom throw them-selves into the holy water of the Wahadi.

"Oh...that's bad," Bri says.

In shock, the brethren all stand suspended in silence as the h'axom spout water in the air from their trunks. Bri holds a hand over her mouth, desperately trying to hide the horrified smile on her face.

"Don't you dare laugh," I tell her, biting my cheek to hold in my own laughter.

The brethren drop to their knees. They plant their faces on the ground and wail even louder. Next to the remaining tied-up animals, Boss is not on the ground like everyone else. He stands there staring at me.

Somehow, I don't think the h'axom got loose on their own.

With a handful of dried grass and a deadly calm gait, Boss approaches the h'axom. His demeanor is at odds with that of the distraught brethren, who resume making those awful sounds. It doesn't take long for the h'axom to catch the scent of their next meal, and they follow Boss out of the Wahadi and back into the shade.

"What's his fucking problem?" Bri mutters, watching Boss as closely as I am.

"I don't know. Whatever it is, I don't like it."

TWENTY-FOUR

Bri

Daisy finally decided to speed up, which has put me next to Tai. Every time he slows down or veers away, she stays right by his side. It's not horrible being next to him. I expected him to lay into me after I pushed him into the water. He was shockingly kind and compassionate. Which I needed. I needed a friend today. I didn't want to be worshiped. I wanted someone to simply be with me for a minute, and it was nice.

His presence distracts me from replaying what happened today over and over again, and blaming myself for everything. I'm also paranoid the brethren are looking at me differently. I've let them down in some massive way. Being put up on a pedestal feels awful, because at any time I could fail them and come crashing down. Tai's never put me up there. He might annoy the shit out of me, but at least I can be myself.

"Your arm okay?" He's been wiggling his fingers and fiddling with a tiny embedded panel on his forearm for a while now.

"It's okay, I think. It doesn't agree with the sand," he says and stops messing with the arm.

"Oh good. I mean…not good. I worried it was the water."

"A bionic arm that can't get wet wouldn't be very useful," he says and smiles over at me. A real smile, one of the rare ones.

"True."

My mind is completely blank. It's rare that I struggle to find something to say. I'm usually trying to stop talking. Maybe it was his kindness earlier today, or the heatstroke, but I want to keep talking, and I can't think of anything to say.

"You know, you can ask," Tai says, interrupting my thoughts.

"Ask what?" I'm confused. What should I be asking?

"You want to know what happened to my arm. How I got this," he says and waves at me with his bionic arm.

"Oh, no. It's none of my business."

"Since when has that stopped you?" he asks rhetorically.

I look down. He must have interpreted my silence as me waiting for him to talk about his arm now that we're, dare I say it, cool. In reality, I was trying to think of something to talk about other than the weather.

I don't want him to feel obligated to tell me. But if he wants to tell me, I'll listen.

"It happened right before I joined the military. I had gotten myself into some trouble. Then it all sort of blew up, literally, and I lost my arm. I was given the options of prison planet or military. They told me they would give me a bionic arm if I enlisted. 'Prisoners don't need two good arms, but soldiers do,' they said."

Who is this Tai stringing together sentences and telling me stuff about his past, like he almost wants me to know more about him?

"There's not much of a choice there," I tell him. I know it takes a lot for him to talk about his past. The Tai I know doesn't easily admit his mistakes or weaknesses. This insight is a big deal.

It appears I'm not the only one who's been thinking about the past since we crashed here. Being away from j'Tilak and the military has disrupted his life more than I realized.

"Part of me wanted to go to the prison planet out of spite. I was angry and stupid back then."

I can relate to that. "I didn't take you for a bad boy," I tell him, returning to our normal teasing.

"Got it all trained out of me. I don't think about it much anymore." He looks down at his arm deep in thought.

"I bet it's hard not to think about it, when a reminder is right there every day."

He looks off in the distance, and I take it as a sign he doesn't want to go any further. I probably wouldn't either if I lost an arm, and from what it sounds like, he's not proud of the circumstances.

"Doesn't everyone on your planet have to do mandatory military service?" I ask.

"I could start three years early or be shipped off," he says quietly. "I didn't even know about the mandatory military service on j'Tilak. Even though I imagined the worst, it was still better than a prison planet." His voice trails off.

Daisy and Brutus slow down to let the brethren pass, glaring at Tai the entire time. The guilt hasn't gone away. Somehow, in all the commotion, the fact that it was my fault slipped right by them.

The two h'axom walk side by side, close enough for my leg to brush against Tai's. My bare skin against his khaki-covered leg. Tai looks down at where our legs graze.

"Is the military all that bad?" I ask. The words come out as a whisper, sounding more seductive than they should.

"Absolutely not. It was the best thing that happened to me."

"You're lucky. On Earth, most people in your situation are forced into the military because they don't have any other option and they are tossed to the front lines of some dumb war over who knows what." My mind plays a sequence of faces of all the boys I grew up with who left right after high school and were never seen again.

"That is troubling, your people would sacrifice human lives for something trivial," he says. "Service on j'Tilak is different. Even calling it the military felt silly until recently. We are a peaceful people but have seen battles where we come to the aid of those who are under threat."

"I wish it was like that everywhere."

We ride quietly for a while. I mentally process how fucked up it is that putting one's life at risk is the only way out of poverty for so many. It's clothes on your back and food in your belly, but I wish there were another way. One that didn't involve bloodshed.

It feels like I'm being watched. I am relieved to see it's Tai and not one of the brethren. They have been on my last nerve. All of my attempts at getting them to doubt Boss have completely fallen flat.

"How much do you hate me for making you stay here to help them?" I ask and nod toward the group of brethren in front of us.

"I should say 'a lot,' but the truth is, I agree with you. These weirdos deserve better than Boss, and it's admirable that you want to help them."

I could fall off my h'axom in shock. I was half joking when I asked him the question and he answered it with sincerity. Admirable? I didn't know Tai was capable of that emotion, especially toward me.

It's quite possible I have judged Tai unfairly. Well, not totally unfairly. Because he has been a total ass more than once. But for the first time since I met the grumpy bastard, I'm understanding him a little.

"You're getting a sunburn," he says, nodding towards my leg. He's right. My scantily clad legs have been exposed to the sun all day, and my skin feels hot and stretched tight.

"Yeah, it's gonna be a bad one," I say, spreading the small piece of fabric over my leg. The wind blows it away immediately.

"Here, I can help." He brings Brutus to a stop and jumps down. He steps to me and puts his hands out. Instead of grabbing my hands to help me down, he clutches my waist and pulls me down to the ground softly. Being this close to him, I can smell the clean water on his skin even though he dried off hours ago. I don't know where to put my hands, so I rest them on his broad shoulders. The corded muscles bunch under my fingers on one side, and the cool metal shifts on the other. Up close, my eyes are met with the concern in his. I feel cared for. He doesn't seem so overbearing anymore.

Tai holds me to him longer than necessary. I wait for what comes next, hoping he leans a little closer. But he doesn't. I stand there frozen and awkwardly wait for something to happen. My eyes drop to his lips.

"What are we doing?" I whisper, unable to stand the tension for another second.

Tai reaches for his belt and, in one swift motion, has it undone.

Fuck me. That was really hot.

Like an idiot, I stare open-mouthed.

Tai undoes his pants and drops them to the sand. He carefully steps out, shakes the sand off, and holds them out for me.

"Here. Put these on."

"I can't take your pants!" I push them back toward him. A warm wind blows against my sweaty body and I shiver a little. It was totally from the wind and not the sight of Tai with his pants off. Underneath his pants are tight black shorts clinging to muscular thighs.

I close my eyes and keep pushing his pants back toward him. It's too much effort to not look down.

"I'll be okay. My skin can tolerate the sun better than yours," he says and pushes the pants into my hands. "Here. Let me help."

He does an unspeakable thing and gets down on his knees in front of me.

"May I?" he asks, pointing to my leg.

Speechless, I nod. *Bri, get it together. Words! Use words.*

He picks up my foot and pulls one pant leg over it up to my knees and does the same to the other. His rough hands on me sends another shiver. I focus on everything else as Tai tugs the pants up my legs and secures them at the waist. He unchains my skirt's waist and wads up the flimsy material in his hand. Suddenly my throat dries up, and I resist the urge to lick my dry lips.

The pants are way too big. He folds up the cuffs and rolls the waist a few times to get them to stay up. When he stands back up to look me over, I see a similar want in his eyes that matches mine.

"Are you sure?" I croak out. My voice betrays me, sounding far too eager.

"Totally sure." The look is gone, replaced by his serious business-like tone.

He grabs a canteen off his saddle, takes a long drink, and hands it to me. I take a slow sip, not wanting to choke on the water.

I take a beat to get myself together. It's fine. He's just being nice. I'm being weird because it's been a long time since...

"We should, um, get going," I tell him. Before I can struggle up Daisy's side to get back on, he grabs one of my legs and hefts me up into the air. I easily swing my leg over and settle into the saddle again. It feels weird to be wearing pants that Tai was in seconds ago. I purge from my mind the thoughts of what parts of him were touching the same fabric I am wearing now.

<hr>

The path down into the canyon almost does me in. I contemplate if it would be less painful to toss myself over the ledge instead of the slow zigzagging path down. What's a few broken bones compared to a slow descent? It's the final stretch, but there's not a single muscle left in my body to hold me up. I cling to the saddle for dear life, hoping I don't slip off and get trampled under Daisy's huge, flat feet.

The small shack covering the staircase down to the colony reminds me of the countless stairs standing between me and my bath.

"Fuck me," I mutter.

"What?" Tai asks.

"Stairs. So. Many. Stairs."

"You can do it, Sunshine. You're a goddess, remember?" he says. "First one down gets the bed!"

I channel my brother's competitive spirit for this final push.

There isn't anything a sense of humor and healthy competition can't fix.

"You're on!" I swing my leg over and try to dismount, matching his movement. My body doesn't cooperate, and I land with a face full of sand. Before I can peel myself up off the ground, Tai has me up and back on my feet.

He brushes the sand off my arms.

I step away, suddenly needing to put space between us. These feelings that I am struggling to suppress are not a good idea. I need to remind my libido. I clear my throat and hike up the oversized pants.

"Ready. Set. Go!" I shout and sprint toward the door, taking him off guard. It's a dirty move, but I need the advantage of a head start. I get through the door before him and step into the narrow stairway leading down. The lower half of my body is numb, but by some force of will, I find the energy to run down the stairs. There isn't enough room for him to pass, so I set the pace. With every step down, my legs regain feeling. Sharp pain shoots up from my feet with every stride.

Tai's heavy footsteps close behind fuel me to go even faster. There are a few widened landings where he could pass me. There is no way I'm going to lose my bed, so I speed up and somehow manage to keep him behind me.

We're almost to the bottom. By my count, there is only one landing left and I'm still in the lead. It comes into view and I give it my all. Tai's pants are slipping down my hips, and my foot catches on the hem. I'm pitched through the air and land with a hard belly flop on the stone floor with a wheeze.

I look up to see Tai's face next to mine. He's crouched down watching me, his face a blank slate.

"You okay?" he asks.

I roll over onto my back and look straight up at him. A small smile creeps across his mouth.

"Don't you dare laugh," I say, holding back a sour smile myself. My pride hurts more than anything else.

"You're a clumsy little thing, aren't you, Sunshine?" he says as the smile spreads across his whole face. "That bed is going to feel so good tonight!" he says over his shoulder as he continues down the stairs, leaving me on the floor.

I don't move from my spot on the ground, staring up at the blank ceiling until a bell warns me of an approaching brethren. Footsteps quicken and the last face I would ever want to see comes into my field of vision. Boss.

"Blessed Resplendence! Why are you on the ground? Are you alright?" he asks and pulls me up to a sitting position.

"I'm okay. Just missed a step." I stand up and straighten the oversized pants.

Boss's eyes narrow on the borrowed clothing. I can almost feel his thoughts, and he is not happy.

"Those rags are not fit for the goddess," he says with a sneer. "Allow me to find you something more...suitable."

I return the look. "Don't bother yourself with such a menial task. Surely you can find *someone else* to do it." I jab at the way he treats his fellow brethren.

"Sweet Divinity, I am your humble servant and equal to all the brethren in your servitude."

I'm not buying it for a second. His over-the-top choice of words are less and less genuine every day.

"Cut the bullshit," I say, getting straight to the point. "We both know that isn't true."

He recoils. A flicker of shock before he recovers quickly and returns to the phony subservient tone he uses with me.

"I will admit to taking leadership when the brethren require it. When we landed here on Sabaak, there was pandemonium. If I hadn't stepped in, we would have perished. I would think our goddess would be appreciative of my efforts." Vitriol sneaks back. Apparently, he can only maintain the facade for so long.

This motherfucker. If he thinks he can intimidate me, he's got another thing coming.

"Listen here, *Brethren*," I say, emphasizing the title to help get my point across, "You need to chill the fuck out."

"Chill? I am not overheated. Perhaps you need to cool down from the trip on the surface." If he is trying to rile me up, it has the opposite effect. My irritation manifests as ice in my veins.

"It means you need to back off." I poke his broad forehead with my index finger, adding fuel to the argument. I'm ready to fight.

His eyes blaze with anger and then he bows, "If it pleases you, consider it done."

He slithers away into the colony without another word. I was not expecting that. I was ready to finally have it out with him and lay it all on the table!

The abrupt end to the conversation leaves me unsettled. As I walk the tunnels back to my room, I try to put the disturbing interaction behind me and instead focus on the giant warm tub waiting for me.

TWENTY-FIVE

Tai

I sink down into the tub and resolve to never ride another h'axom as long as I live.

Before long, Bri steps into the bathroom and our eyes meet. Fuck. I still want to kiss her. I want to do more than just kiss.

"I'll close my eyes," I tell her and squeeze my eyes shut. The sound of her clothes hitting the floor goes straight to my cock. I blindly swipe my arms across the water, gathering bubbles around me, hiding evidence of my reaction to her. Anyone in my situation would have a similar response to a beautiful woman getting naked.

"You can open them now," she says. I peek through one eye and she's across from me, the water lapping at her collarbones. She has a serious look on her face, and I can sense something is wrong right away.

"Everything okay?" I ask.

"Yeah, everything is fine. I've had it with Boss's shit," she says while she unties her long braid. The way she gently pulls apart the three sections is fascinating. How does she not let it all get tangled up? She turns, and her pink hair cascades down her back, concealing her soft golden skin from view. My fingers itch to reach out and touch her.

"What did he do now?" I ask, suddenly concerned he did something between the time I left her face down on the ground and now. I feel terrible for leaving her down, just so I could win the stupid bet.

"His normal bullshit."

"What happened?" I press for answers. Whatever it is she doesn't want to say I really want to know.

She squints and quirks her mouth to the side in the most adorable way.

"I don't want to tell you," she says and turns away, pretending to inspect the line of glass bottles along the edge.

"Now you really need to tell me." I wade toward her.

"I'm not getting anywhere with the brethren. They refuse to believe that Boss is taking advantage of them. They all think that's how things are supposed to be around here."

"You're doing the best you can. You've made some excellent points. That guy is a massive asshole and should be banished."

"You don't count. I'm too tired to talk about it anymore," she says and sinks under the water, ending the conversation.

She comes back up for air, and waterdrops stream down her face and neck. A smudge runs across her cheek.

"Here, you've got..." I step toward her and rub my thumb across the mark, wiping her face clean. Her soft skin feels like I could damage it with one touch of my rough hand.

"Oh." She touches where my fingers were and looks up at me with those eyes. "Thanks." And this time, there isn't anger or frustration in them, but there is a different heat.

I move before rational thought has a chance to stop me and my lips crash into hers. Every time I've resisted has built up to this kiss, and it's hot in my veins. More and more fuel to the fire. It was inevitable.

She holds tight to the back of my neck as my hands wander over her curves, memorizing every inch of her. They go to her gorgeous ass, and I pull her up and closer to me. Her long legs wrap around my waist, locking me against her. My cock is hard, throbbing between us.

"Tai." I silence her with another searing kiss. I skim my fingertips down her long neck and across her collarbones.

"No more talking." My voice is low and rough.

I lift her up and place her on the edge of the bath and push her legs apart. She opens for me so beautifully and throws her head back. I stroke my cock at the sight. She's absolutely perfect.

I get down on my knees in front of her and kiss my way from her knee and all the way up the inside of her perfect thigh. She shivers from my touch. Her pleasure turns me on more than anything else in the universe. I'm greedy for more—and I know that I'll never get enough.

I drag a finger over her slit and follow it with my tongue. She arches against my face wanting more, searching for more friction. I push a finger inside her, then another. My bionic arm is programmed for maximum sensitivity, and I feel every inch of her. Her pleasure races up my arm like a bolt of lightning.

She groans in complaint when I pull my fingers back. Her eyes light up when I lick my fingers. I'm desperate for more and descend on her pussy, covering my face with her. This time when she arches her hips, I give her what she wants and slide my fingers inside. I lap at her clit with the flat of my tongue and relish her grinding against my face.

She grips my hair while I go to work. My fingers pump in and out in time with my tongue, drawing out moans and gasps from her. There's no stopping until she screams my name.

Her legs shake beside my head and her panting gets louder. I double my efforts to make her come. Her face contorts with pleasure bordering on pain. She spasms around my fingers and tongue.

I stroke my cock slowly, spreading my precum over the sensitive head, and watch her regain her breath. She hooks her ankles at my lower back and draws me closer.

"Inside. Now." It's my turn to moan from her ordering me around. With my dick in my hand, I push slowly inside her. She pulls me in, and every inch is paradise.

I move my hips slow and measured. *Fuck.* She takes me so well. I can't decide which is better: watching where we are connected or the pleasure etched on her face. I'm so wrapped up in watching her that my hips move on their own, faster and harder, taking me well past the point of no return.

Water splashes out of the tub and floods the tiled floor. The sounds of our bodies colliding together are accompanied by heavy breathing. I grab her hips and anchor myself there. With every thrust, I am one step closer to madness.

Bri grabs my shoulders and pulls herself against me—and that's all it takes. My vision goes spotty and all the pent-up pressure bursts out of me in ground-shaking pulses.

She doesn't shout my name but whispers it against my lips. Somehow, it's so much better than I could have ever imagined.

TWENTY-SIX

Bri

Well, that happened, Again. I wish I could say it was a mistake and I regretted it. The truth is far more complicated. Does it have to be? People fuck on vacation all the time. Away from the realities of life, they indulge in some harmless fun and then go back to their lives. No harm, no foul.

Tai climbs out of the tub, water dripping down between defined muscles. His beautiful thick cock hangs between his legs. It's a good hang.

"Excuse me, my eyes are up here," he says, catching me staring.

"I can't count how many times I have caught you staring at my chest instead of looking me in the eye." I splash water at him, which he dodges with ease.

"Who could blame me?" he asks and extends his hand out to help me up.

My legs are still wobbly from the multiple orgasms he deftly wrung out of me, but Tai doesn't let me stumble. He holds me steady and wraps a towel tightly around my shoulders.

"What does the Divine Goddess of Orgasms and Perfect Tits desire?" he asks and sucks a sensitive nipple into his mouth.

"Oh no, don't ruin the afterglow." I smack his chest. The gesture serves as a reminder of how hard his body is.

"You *are* glowing," he says between kisses up my neck to my earlobe, sending shivers over every inch of my skin. Dammit—he is good at this.

It's impossible to think straight when we are naked and pressed together. My resolve to stay emotionally detached fights a losing battle with the desire pulling me toward him. Of their own volition, my hands wander up his muscular back, and my fingers rake through his damp hair.

"I can't believe I'm about to suggest this, but I think we should get dressed and find some food," Tai says. He must feel conflicted, because he doesn't put any distance between us or stop the all-consuming kisses.

"Food sounds good," I say and haul myself away. Clarity returns along with the reminder of who is beyond these doors. The tiresome brethren who wouldn't know a critical thought if it smacked them in the head are always lurking around. Every attempt at liberating them from Boss has been met with blank stares. It is proving to be more difficult than I had originally thought, but I'm not ready to admit defeat.

"Come on. Let's go find some of those red berries you like," he says, leading me out of the bathroom.

We are both dressed in seconds, suddenly ravenous. Tai pauses at the bedroom door and turns back to face me. He guides an errant strand of hair back behind my shoulder and kisses the tip of my nose. The sweet gesture is not something a fling would do. He throws open the door and pulls me along with him. I decide to enjoy the moment. *Carpe diem* and all that shit. We can figure everything else out later. For now, in this strange world with these weird aliens, I'm right where I want to be.

TWENTY-SEVEN

Tai

Bri and I grab the same piece of flatbread and neither one of us lets go. She scrunches up one side of her face and tries to tug it out of my hand. I hold even tighter and refuse to give an inch. We're both enjoying this battle of wills when Boss slinks into the dining hall. Bri looks over at him and drops her grasp on the flatbread. I let go as well, no longer hungry. With one look, he managed to ruin my appetite.

"The goddess is needed in the prayer room," Boss says and yanks Bri up from her seat.

"I suggest you let go of her right now, or I'd be happy to relieve you of that hand." I'm on my feet and towering over Boss with Bri standing between us.

"The rain hasn't returned. You must summon more. Or you no longer serve a purpose to us."

Bri looks up at me with rage in her eyes. "Sure, I'd be happy to pray," she says awkwardly and overly sweet. He doesn't know it yet, but that saccharine voice is dangerous. I follow them down the tunnels to the prayer room, not wanting to let Bri out of my sight.

I was ready to go to blows when he grabbed her arm. But the look in her eye told me I didn't need to fight this battle for her. She'd get him back in her own way.

The prayer room is empty and dark. Boss shoves Bri down to her knees in the center of the room. His rough treatment of her sends a wave of fury through me, one that threatens to completely take over. The only thing calming me is the hatred in her eyes, and I know that his days are numbered.

"Now pray. And you, Tilak," he spits, "Leave her in peace so she can fulfill her destiny."

I plant my feet to the ground and dare any one of these fuckers to try and make me leave. But Bri catches my eye and gives me a quick nod, silent permission to leave. My ear twitches at the dismissal. Every instinct tells me to stay right here.

"Really, I'm okay," she says.

Reluctantly, I back out of the prayer room and into the hall. I'm about to sit in the alcove facing the door when Boss calls out.

"Follow me," he says over his shoulder as he walks down a tunnel I've yet to see, one I haven't mapped out yet.

I can't help myself, and against better judgment I follow. If he's with me, he isn't harassing Bri, and he's the only one I think is a possible threat. We go down another narrow tunnel I'm not familiar with. This one is older than the rest. The walls are crumbling, like they could collapse at the slightest touch. He stops abruptly and turns back to me with malice in his eyes.

"I warned you, Tilak, and now you have crossed the line."

"What the fuck are you talking about?" I roll my eyes. What does he want now?

"I'm talking about you seducing the goddess. I saw how you looked at her at the Wahadi. The scriptures clearly say her pleasure must come from the brethren, not some Tilak scum. Your time has run out."

I saw this coming.

"Yeah, okay. You got me. I'll leave."

I've already got a plan. I'll leave peacefully then sneak back in. I'm confident I can grab Bri and get out without being detected.

"No. You misunderstand, Tilak. It's time for you to return to the gods." A swarm of brethren fill the tunnel, blocking me from every side. I might be three feet taller than them, but they outnumber me twenty to one.

I would kill for my blaster right now.

Before they have a chance to organize around me, I shove Boss hard enough to take three brethren down with him. I easily shove my way through to get back to Bri. I should never have left her alone.

Baby Face stands in my way and raises his fists. As if his tiny hands could stop me. I lift him off the ground by the throat. In a futile attempt, he bangs against my bionic arm, begging for freedom. My tight metal grip makes his eyes bulge before I toss him onto the pile of fallen brethren.

Another one swings a wooden broom handle, smacks his brethren in the face with his backswing and brings it hard across my abs. I yank the stick out of his hands and snap it across my knee, breaking it in two. He panics and runs in the opposite direction. The remaining brethren scatter and clear a path for me.

I'm nearly to the end of the tunnel when two brethren jump on my back at the same time. I reach behind and grab one by the hood of his robe and toss him aside. The other wrestles my bionic arm down and slaps a cuff on my wrist. A shock knocks me to my knees. My vision narrows when my other arm is wrenched back and cuffed.

My yell echoes off the stone walls when another shock radiates through me. I grind my teeth together to get through the pain, counting every shallow breath while I wait for it to stop. I deepen my inhales and the current comes to a stop.

"You arrogant Tilak, thinking you can come in here and take what is ours," Boss says, brushing dust off his robes. He stalks toward me. From this position, he is taller than me. I look up and spit right in his face. He pulls out a blaster and points it right at me.

TWENTY-EIGHT

Bri

I wait a few minutes in the prayer room and listen for Boss. Hopefully he's convinced I prayed long enough and I can get back to my room. This is such bullshit. It's past time to plan a little retaliation for Boss being such a prick.

On tiptoes, I creep through the tunnels toward my room and wonder if Tai is there. Maybe I'm still in the sex haze, but I'm excited to get back to him. I smile despite myself.

That little voice in the back of my head whispers warnings.

You'll only hurt him.

You weren't made to settle down with anyone.

By the time I reach our room, I'm completely conflicted. Part of me wants him. In some weird way, we work. The other part wants a life free of guilt, and that means no one gets close enough to get hurt.

I take a deep breath and open the bedroom door. No more of the hottest sex to ever exist. We'll keep it friendly and plan our revenge on Boss.

The room is dark and empty. I don't have to see anything to know

Tai isn't in there. Something is off. There aren't any brethren hovering around, Boss isn't anywhere to be found, and Tai is missing.

I turn on my heel and begin my search.

"You arrogant Tilak, thinking you can come in here and take what is ours."

I hear Boss's condescending tone down the hallway. *Excuse the fuck outta me? Theirs?*

Oh, hell no.

I step around the corner and into absolute chaos. Tai is on the ground, wrists cuffed behind his back. Boss looms over Tai, pointing a blaster down at his chest. Brethren are scattered all over, rubbing jaws and inspecting injuries.

"What is going on here?" I ask innocently. Boss and Tai look at me in unison. Tai looks concerned, but that concern is not for himself, It's for me. Boss has his familiar arrogant air about him.

This bastard loves it when he can reign over anyone.

"Glorious Light-Bringer, the Tilak has broken the sacred laws. He has defiled the Wahadi and deceived you. It is time he paid for his transgressions," Boss says keeping the blaster firmly pointed at Tai.

"How has he deceived me, loyal Brethren?" I slip into character. I'm going to need to be convincing to get Tai out of this.

"He has not told you the truth about his past. He was here, on Sabaak, when he was caught for his crimes," Boss says. "I knew he looked familiar. I checked our records and confirmed it was him."

"Tai?" His name slips from my lips.

He looks ashamed, caught in a lie. His reaction tells me everything I need to know. Boss is telling the truth.

Betrayal hits me right in my chest, and it knocks the air out of my lungs. Why didn't he tell me this before? That feeling disappears, quickly replaced by anger. I feel manipulated, and I didn't expect that from Tai.

"Bri..."

Tai struggles on the ground, and the cuffs shock him so hard, he is knocked unconscious.

"Lower the blaster. He can't do anything now," I tell Boss, sadness and disappointment soaking my every word.

"We will return him to the gods."

"No! Wait." I stop them from picking up his limp body. "I give him mercy. No returning him to the gods. Take him to the dungeon. And take those cuffs off—it's inhumane."

"But—" Hot-Breath steps in.

"No. As your goddess, I decide what happens to him. Take him to the dungeon or you can join him there." I stare him down, daring him to defy me. I'm not fucking around. I'm tired of this shit and want to go home.

It takes a dozen of them to drag Tai down the stairs to the dungeon. The plan has officially changed. No more trying to get through to these guys. It's not worth risking Tai. He has become far too important, and I want answers. He owes me the full truth.

What I need is a distraction. I need something so big, so monumental that the brethren won't even remember Tai exists.

There is one thing that could take their minds off the giant blue prisoner in the dungeon: the mere thought of their goddess performing one very specific ceremony I refused to participate in previously.

I grab my pack from the bottom drawer and check the contents. No hydropacks, no nutrigels, but everything else is still there. I look down at my clothes and wish I had my nasty coveralls. This goddess costume they have dressed me in is not ideal for a daring escape, but I don't have any other options.

I bolt to the bathroom and grab a handful of the bottles of soap from the edge. I spin around, looking for anything else that could be useful. Seeing nothing, I stash the pack under my bed.

I crack open the door. Bug-Eyes sits on a wooden chair facing me. Just sitting there. Staring. Waiting for me to open the door.

Creepy fuck.

"There you are! I was hoping to find you." I should have been an actress with how convincing I sound.

"What can I do for you?" He yawns. Someone isn't excited about being on guard duty.

"I need to speak with Boss. Can you go find him for me?" I ask sweetly, hoping a little charm will help get me what I want.

"Boss?" he asks.

Dammit, why do they only go by *Brethren*? It's so fucking confusing. I suspect he knows exactly who I'm referring to. He's just being difficult.

"Brethren, *the* Brethren. Long eyebrows that connect with the long gray beard? Ever heard of him?"

"Wait here. Don't leave your room."

The illusion that I had the upper hand fades fast. I might not be locked up in a dungeon, but I am a prisoner just the same. I wait impatiently in the doorway, watching for a possible break in the steady stream of brethren walking past. Why are they all in this part of the colony today? Don't they have better things to do with their time?

Boss finally shows up, his thin lips pressed tightly together.

"Yes?" he says impatiently. I notice he didn't address me with any of the over-the-top titles I have come to expect.

"The brethren have proved their loyalty to me. You have found the traitor in our midst. I would like to reward you all. Tonight."

He raises one skeptical bushy eyebrow at me.

"The ceremony, the one we didn't finish," I clarify, hoping I can get away with saying less. I refuse to say the words "pleasure" and "completion" around these guys.

"Goddess, the ceremony requires purification of the brethren before we can begin, and we still have the Tilak to deal with."

"Don't worry about him. He's locked up, right? He can't go anywhere. I want to do the ceremony tonight. I'll do my own little purification thingy as well, and I am not to be disturbed. I'll come out when I'm ready."

His eyes light up at the tenacity in my voice. He's fucking crazy if he thinks I am getting anywhere near any of their cocks.

"I am happy to see you have come around. I will notify the brethren to begin preparations." He bows low and backs away.

"Tell them to prepare the rooms on the third level," I call after him before closing the door. They will be out of the way up there so I can get down to the dungeon while they are doing whatever they do to prepare for this.

Back in my room, I strap on my pack and wait with my ear to the door until I am completely satisfied that the brethren are busy "purifying." Gross. I shudder at the thought.

Outside the safety of my room, the coast is clear, but I don't have long. The tunnels are quiet, not a bell or robe in sight. I dart from alcove to alcove carefully. My eyes scan my surroundings for stray brethren around every turn.

Tai better be conscious by now. There is no way I can drag him up on my own.

Moans come from a darkened room, and I scurry past as quickly as possible. As I suspected, these idiots are jerking off to prepare for the ceremony.

Down the hall, a curtain is pulled back. I slip in the doorway to my left and ease it shut, closing myself in. Scratchy robes push against my back in the tiny pitch-black closet. A lucky move on my part. I slip into one of the robes and leave the bell behind—they don't need to hear me coming.

A brethren shuffles by and takes the staircase up, heading to the third level.

I dash to the stairs on the other end of the tunnel and take a dark, narrow staircase down, praying to the Goddess of the Radiant Sunburn that this is where the dungeon is.

TWENTY-NINE

Tai

"Wakey, wakey." Bri's blurry face comes into focus inches from mine. Her eyebrows are pinched together. I can't hear what she's saying over the ringing in my ears. My arms shake as I push myself up off the dirty floor. Bri steadies me when I sit up and sway a little, struggling to find my center of gravity. She checks my pulse at my throat and smiles up at me when she confirms a regular heartbeat.

Bri's voice cuts through and her image sharpens. "You have some explaining to do." She grabs both sides of my face and watches my eyes, checking for any sign of brain damage.

"I know, I'm so sorry—"

She stops me. "We can talk about this later. Are you able to get up? We should get going."

"How did you get in here?" I ask.

"It's not hard to sneak past a sleeping guard," she says and helps me to my feet. The room spins and I stagger back. Bri catches me before I fall and crack open my head.

"He's still sleeping? Shit. These guys are so useless."

Bri laughs. "The rest of the brethren are busy. As long as we avoid the third level, we should be good," she says.

I lean heavily on her, still trying to find my balance. "My pack and blaster should be right out here." I step through the wide-open door on wobbly legs.

My belongings are right where I last saw them. I sift through the pack, making sure nothing is missing. It's all there: a handful of hydropacks and nutrigels, tent, translator, and best of all, my blaster. I tuck it into my belt and breathe a sigh of relief. It feels good to have it back.

"We're going to need provisions." I hold open the pack, showing her how little we have left.

"Let's make it quick. I don't think we have much time left," Bri says.

"How did you get away from them?" I ask. A multitude of possibilities run through my head: poisoning, barricading them in some room, setting off explosives. I rule the last one out. If she had access to explosives, she would have used them on me by now.

"Let's just say I flexed my goddess powers," she says with a sly smile.

"Bri, what did you do?" I ask again. This time more forcefully.

"I told them I wanted to reward them for uncovering the traitor in the colony." She bites her bottom lip to hold back a smile.

"And that reward would be...?" I cross my arms over my chest.

"I told them I'd do the ceremony."

"*The* ceremony? Like, the pleasure one?" I ask.

"What other ceremony is there? It's the perfect distraction. Plus, they needed to 'purify' themselves to prepare. I don't want to think too hard about what that means." Bri looks extremely proud of herself. Truth be told, I am too.

"Those poor idiots are going to be so disappointed when they whip their dicks out and you are nowhere to be found," I say with a grin.

"I stopped feeling sorry for them when you were on the ground unconscious," she says. "Are you okay?" Her eyes pass over my face and chest, checking again for injury.

"I'm fine. Let's get out of here. This place sucks." I grab her hand and pull her behind me. The point of contact between us feels right. Even in the middle of this insanity, her presence has this strange effect on me.

By some miracle, we find a walk-in pantry filled with dry goods and a faucet down the hall from the sleeping guard. We quietly look for food we can easily carry, trying not to shift around too abruptly. I grab a bag of some weird grain mixed with dried fruit, as many flat-breads as I can hold, and all the dried jerky meat I can stuff into both our packs.

Bri fills up our canteens at the faucet and tosses me one. The two of us working together feels like everything is clicking into place. Nothing can stand in our way, not a colony full of murderous cultists, not a planet that's actively trying to kill us. Nothing.

THIRTY

Bri

Tai is up and around like nothing happened. However, I am not so convinced he's completely okay. I watch him out of the corner of my eye while he moves around the pantry grabbing supplies. It was really scary finding him unconscious on the ground. He catches me staring at him and flashes me a brilliant smile.

"I'm okay, really," he says reassuringly.

"I know. I'm just trying to figure out if you got an upgrade from the shock. You don't happen to have X-ray vision, do you? Lightning hands?" I keep my tone light to hide how worried I was.

"Come to think of it." He points a finger toward the hallway, but nothing happens. "Damn. Maybe next time?"

"Should I go find a pair of those cuffs?" I ask. "We could try again."

"And what exactly would you want to do with them?" he asks and pauses, clearly waiting for a response.

"You sure you want to talk about this now?" I say, impressed with myself that I can stay on task. We still need to escape, and Tai is over here talking handcuffs.

"You're right," Tai says. "If my mental math is correct, they should be finishing their 'purification' any time now."

The annoyingly familiar cockiness is back. It usually gets under my skin, except now it's a relief because he sounds like himself again.

"So, what do you propose?" I ask, hoping he's got some grand plan in place. I certainly don't.

"I don't have superpowers, but I've got this." He pulls out the blaster.

"We aren't blasting our way out of this. They are weird, but we aren't killing anyone." I don't need murder on my conscience the rest of my life.

"Who said anything about killing? All I need to do is wave it around and everyone will back off." He models the movement, waving the blaster over his head, he looks silly, not menacing.

"It was implied. Plus, you seem a little too eager to whip it out," I say.

He shrugs and tucks the blaster back into his belt.

"You're already dressed like them. I'll grab a robe and we can pass ourselves off and make a run for it," Tai suggests.

"There is no way you'll pass for a brethren. You're eighteen feet tall."

"Seven," he says, correcting me.

An idea pops into my head.

The robe should work for me. I'm only slightly taller than the brethren. But there is no point in trying to make Tai look like anything other than a Tilak.

"I've got it. I'll be the brethren and transport the prisoner. We get to the top and get the fuck out of Dodge. And don't you dare ask me what Dodge is. It's just...Dodge."

The look on his face tells me he likes the plan. All the worry and concern from before is gone. Now he's ready to start a war.

"Fine." He says something under his breath about always having to do things the hard way. The crooked smile gives him away even though he's pretending to be annoyed.

He shoves a final handful of dried meat into the pack and cinches it closed.

"Once we get to the surface, I think we should find 'the Others.' They can't possibly be worse than the homicidal sex cult down here," I suggest.

"Exactly," he says. "We get out and go south."

"Do you think they'll help us?" I ask, optimistically, hoping for some good news.

"Not really. But I remember you saying that nothing can stop you when you really want something."

There he goes, using my own words against me. Tai steps up to me, blocking out everything else but him.

"I should have told you I've been here before. I was so close to telling you the whole story when we came back from the oasis. I don't know what stopped me. No. Wait. That's not true. It was shame. I'm ashamed of who I was back then."

I'm surprised by the sudden confession. I don't fault him for not wanting to admit his past mistakes. I should be mad. I should be livid, but somehow, I feel closer to him than ever.

Maybe I'm letting him off the hook too easily, but I stand up on tiptoes and brush my lips across his. It's my way of telling him we are okay. It's not an apology or victory. It's a truce. I smooth his hair back, and when he leans into my hand, I know he understands.

"Let's get out of here before I change my mind and leave you here to deal with the brethren on your own," he says, laughter lighting up his eyes.

"Oh, he's got jokes! Someone must be feeling better." I lift up my hood. "Ready to go, prisoner?" I say with a low voice, trying to imitate the brethren's accent and tenor.

"Bri, play this by the book. None of your bullshit," he warns.

"I resent that." We fall back into our normal banter easily. It's second nature at this point.

I yank his arms behind his back and push him forward and out of the pantry with a smile.

There must be something wrong with me. A normal person wouldn't have this much fun running for their life.

We manage to get down the first hallway without rousing the guard or running into anyone. Tai whispers directions through the tunnels, leading us to the main level of the colony and closer to the surface.

A brethren scurries toward us. Putting on a show, I push Tai forward off balance. "Come on, prisoner," I say with a comically low voice.

The brethren knocks into my shoulder in his rush to get past.

"Watch it!" he yells over his shoulder.

"What the fuck?" I whisper to Tai.

"Don't blame the guy. He's in a hurry. He needs to purify himself for the goddess." He looks back at me with a crooked smile.

"You're never going to let me live this down, are you?" I ask, pretending I am not enjoying every second of this.

Get it together, Bri. Your life is in literal danger! Now is not the time to flirt with Tai!

"Definitely not," Tai whispers over his shoulder.

"Keep it moving, Tilak." I continue the charade.

"Bri." The low rumble of his warning hits me right between the legs.

Down, girl.

Tai crouches down to fit into a low stairwell I've never been in before. His broad shoulders nearly touch both walls, blocking out everything. I follow him up a steep incline, the air getting warmer with every step.

"Where to next?" I whisper.

"Now we blast our way out." He laughs. "Just kidding. We're almost there."

I give him a little shove forward, thoroughly enjoying the roles we are playing. "No blasting," I say, throwing cold water on his suggestion.

We keep moving forward. I hope our luck holds out a little bit longer.

THIRTY-ONE

Tai

The cold metal of the blaster against my waist provides some comfort as we work our way through the colony. We are so close, I don't want anything to stop us now. Even though it's unlikely I'll need to use the weapon, it's a relief to have it back.

"Follow my lead when we get up there. I'll take us to the nearest exit," I tell Bri, taking the opportunity to remind her I'm the one calling the shots.

"You're the prisoner. Follow *my* lead."

"Bri." It comes out as a growl.

"Relax, I'm joking. You're the big bad alien in charge. I fully acknowledge you know the best way out. I'm not that stubborn."

"I think you are exactly that stubborn." I resume walking.

It's only a matter of time before they realize we left. We need to be as far as possible by the time they come looking for us.

The main level of the colony shows signs of activity. Feet scuffing on the stone floor and bells warn us that we aren't alone.

A brethren approaches us and I slow my steps, feigning defiance to the "brethren" at my back.

"Come on, prisoner. Pick up the pace," Bri says with a deep voice and nudges me forward.

She has some sharp elbows for a little human.

Her pathetic attempt to imitate the brethren is comical. If they fall for it, they are dumber than I thought. I shield Bri from the approaching brethren. The two of them are deep in conversation when they pass by, completely oblivious to us.

We approach the main hub in the colony's center and tension from Bri emits behind me. We carefully avoid the dining hall. My heart rate picks up and a cold sweat clings to my skin. Bri steps closer to me, her body pressed close as we wind our way through the crowded space. Brethren are hustling through, all of them distracted and in a hurry. Bri's plan to distract them with the promise of the ceremony was brilliant.

She keeps us moving through the maze of tunnels as I subtly tilt my head to signal her as to where to go next. I keep my head down, doing my best to convey "dead man walking." The human reference I learned fits the situation perfectly. Bri would be so mad that I knew this one without her having to explain it to me. I can tell she enjoys correcting me whenever possible.

"Stop! Or I'll shoot!" a brethren yells from across the space. Our luck has officially run out.

Bri stiffens behind me. She grunts an acknowledgement and murmurs something low. My stomach drops. She pushes me forward slowly, pretending like she didn't hear the warning.

"Stop! I'm serious!" he calls out, and I hear footsteps and bells approaching.

Shit. Fuck. Shit.

I shuffle my feet forward. We've got to get out of the main area. I can take him on, but I don't want to risk the entire colony coming down on us at once.

"Hey! You! Did you hear me? Where are you...? Wait, where is your bell?" The voice is louder and sounds alarmed. From over my shoulder I recognize the sleeping guard, who inconveniently chose this moment to wake up.

"Fuck. Let's go." Bri and I break into a sprint. Those fucking bells. The tunnel winds around, giving us a few seconds of cover from the brethren at our heels. I skid to a stop after a sharp turn and Bri collides into my back with an "oomph."

I push her behind me and stand ready to meet him head-on. A wide-eyed brethren comes around the corner. Before he can say a word or call out a warning, I slam his head against the wall, just hard enough to knock him out. He crumbles to the ground with hardly any noise.

Shock freezes Bri's face, her eyes darting between me and the unconscious brethren. I walk toward her and she steps back away from me.

I grab her shoulders, holding her still, and step closer. Eyes locked on mine. Briefly, I forget where we are and why we're here. All I can see is her beautiful blue eyes boring into me.

My lips graze the outer edge of her ear and her eyes close.

I whisper, "I'm sorry." It takes every ounce of strength to pull back.

Her eyes flutter open and a tiny little line appears between her eyebrows. I want to smooth it away.

"For what?"

I'm pulled back into reality.

"For this."

I push her shoulders until she's off balance and falling straight back into the nearby garbage chute.

I look back at the brethren one last time and jump in after her.

THIRTY-TWO

Bri

I never want to think about that trash heap ever again. Unfortunately, the smell makes it impossible to forget. Daisy snorts at me when I step into the stable. Even my loyal h'axom is bothered by my smell. My hair, my robes. Everything stinks. I could kill Tai. He could have warned me or found another way out!

"Yeah, Daisy. I know. I smell terrible."

"It was that or wave the blaster around, and I was just honoring your wishes," Tai says as he grabs the giant saddle for the h'axom.

"I didn't know those were my only two options!" I suspect this was his way of getting back at me for the Wahadi.

"Neither did I, but I made an executive decision," he grins at me, a failing attempt at innocence.

"I should have left you in the dungeon." It's an empty threat, and we both know it.

Brutus snorts and stamps his feet when Tai approaches, also offended by our smell. I slide my hand up Daisy's snout and over her furry ears. With lazy eyes, she looks over at me and slowly chews through the pile of small grass at her feet.

"You take that one," Tai says and nods toward another h'axom farther down. One I don't recognize. I know Daisy has her faults, but at least I'm sure she won't toss me on my ass in the middle of the desert.

"I'll take Daisy."

"No way. It's too slow," he whispers, shooting me his most stern look. A look I have gotten used to and no longer has an effect on me. Well, at least not the one he intends.

"*It* is a she. And she's mine." I couldn't leave her behind. Plus, she comes with the added benefit of getting under Tai's skin.

"Fine," Tai says through pursed lips. He moves quietly around the stable releasing the rest of the h'axom. I'm impressed. It's a good call. One I didn't even think about. Now it will be near impossible for the brethren to catch us.

"Oh, come on girl. I know you're happy to see me."

I grab the saddle horn with one hand and brace myself when two strong hands circle my waist and lift me up. His eyes sweep over the saddle and h'axom, checking to make sure everything is in its place. Once satisfied, he returns to Brutus and easily pulls himself up and onto the giant animal.

With a snap of his reins, Brutus lurches forward. I tug on Daisy's, urging her along. She nibbles at the grass before slowly dragging her feet and stepping into the bright morning light.

"Keep up. The brethren will not be happy when they realize we got away." Brutus breaks into a gallop. Tai moves gracefully, like he's been doing this his whole life.

Miraculously, Daisy follows at a much quicker pace than I thought she was capable of. I smugly lean forward and give her a grateful pat on the neck. I knew she wouldn't fail me.

We climbed through deep piles of garbage for hours, the smell curdling my stomach the entire time. If I could have taken a full breath, I would have screamed at Tai the entire way out. When pushing garbage out of my way, I got a tiny bit of pleasure from pushing it right into his path. Right now, microaggressions are the only thing keeping me going. And we take it wherever we can get it.

Tai leads us through the winding channel that was once a thriving river. The feeling of the unknown gives me a rush of adrenaline crackling under my skin. I know we're still in danger, but against all logic, I haven't lost my taste for adventure.

"I can't believe we made it out," I say.

Tai looks over his shoulder behind us, checking if we are being followed.

"We aren't in the clear yet."

"Tai, you need to learn how to celebrate the small stuff." He's right, of course, but I'm still impressed we broke out of the colony.

The canyon narrows and widens over the course of the morning. I'm grateful for the high walls surrounding us, which keep the direct sunlight off. It's not as cool as down in the colony, but it's a break from the oppressive heat above. We travel in complete silence for a while, listening for any hint of the brethren.

"We need to get to higher ground," Tai says reluctantly.

"But the shade!" I whine. I know it is inevitable that we would end up in the blazing sun but doing it willingly when there is perfectly good shade feels wrong.

"We are vulnerable down here. Someone or something could sneak up on us."

Dammit. He's right. Begrudgingly, I pull on Daisy's reins to follow Tai up the slope. I slide forward on the saddle when Daisy lurches up the hill. My core clenches, and my legs tense from the incline. I'm still painfully sore from the last ride. If only the brethren could've waited on their plan to murder Tai for another few days. I would have appreciated the chance to let my muscles recover.

The sun heats up my dirty robe, sending off a fresh wave of hot garbage straight to my nose.

"I can't wait to get out of this robe. It smells almost as bad as you do," I say and pluck at the robe, putting a little space between the disgusting garment and my body.

"Soon," he says, returning to his monosyllabic ways.

"Good girl, Daisy. You're the best h'axom in the world." I turn my attention to Daisy. She doesn't respond to my attempts at conversation either, but Brutus grunts and tosses his trunk in the air.

"I couldn't agree more, Brutus," I say. Fine—if I can't talk to Tai or Daisy, Brutus will be my friend. "I prefer the shade as well."

"I prefer not being ambushed," Tai grumbles.

The farther we get from the colony and the brethren, the better I feel. It might be every woman's fantasy to be worshiped as a goddess but not mine. I much prefer it out here with Tai, braving the hostile environment and being proactive about our escape. I file that under "Things I'll never admit to Tai." This particular file seems to be growing by the day.

"What?" Tai asks, head cocked to the side.

Oh shit—did I say that out loud?

"Huh?" I ask innocently.

"I thought I heard you say something. You were mumbling," he says, scrunching his eyebrows together.

"Oh, nothing. Just having a little discussion here with my friend Daisy. Aren't we, sweetie pie?" I scratch the tuft of long fur on the top of her head. She grunts and shakes her head side to side.

"I want to get to higher ground to see if anyone is following us," Tai says, spurring Brutus on with a simple flick of the reins.

"You're worse than Jamie." My thoughts verbalize.

"Is that your boyfriend on Earth?"

His question makes me smile.

"No, he's my oldest and most serious brother. He thinks it's his job to keep everyone in line."

"He's a good male."

"He is overbearing and bossy. But he's the best. He would probably love it here. All my brothers would. They'd love the chance to prove how tough they are." The words spill out. It feels good to talk about my family. I avoid bringing them up because I'm afraid it would open the floodgates of emotion I've tried so hard to keep closed. Missing them has threatened to take over since I left Earth.

"How many brothers do you have?" Tai asks.

"Three. I'm the baby of the family, and the only girl."

"Ah, the princess. That tracks," he says with a tiny little smile pulling up one side of his mouth. I'm never going to live this down.

"Not at all! I had to keep up or get left behind," I clarify. For some reason, it's important that Tai doesn't view me as some weak spoiled human.

"Really? I assumed they would all favor their little sister."

"They did. I mean...they do. In their own weird Mitchell family way."

"How's that?" he asks.

I'm surprised by the follow-up questions. We might even be approaching something resembling a conversation at this point. I proudly sit a little taller on Daisy's back. I managed to draw Tai out of his one-word answers!

"Well, we believe you've got to be strong and think fast to survive. No one is going to take it easy on you. When I grew up and started doing well in school, things changed a bit, I guess."

A memory flashes in my mind of my family sitting around the dinner table passing around the yuriOS with my latest grades. The look of pride on their faces brings a tear to my eye.

Wow. I'm damn near crying. All of this repressed homesickness must be finally catching up with me.

I pull up the hood, choosing the smell over the sweltering sun and the vulnerability written all over my face.

"That explains why you're so tough," Tai says, slowing Brutus down and coming up next to me.

"You think I'm tough? Tai, that was verging on a compliment." I smile over at him behind my hood. Sarcasm shrinks the lump in my throat a tiny bit.

"I didn't mean to verge," he says.

"Oh okay, fine," I reply swiftly with a playful tease.

"What I meant to say, if you would let me finish, it wasn't a verge. I meant it as an actual compliment."

The lump is back. Bigger than ever. I gulp at air to try and diffuse it. It doesn't work.

"You haven't complained once, not about the unbearable heat, or the endless sand, or the weird brethren. You have every right to whine endlessly, but you haven't once. You have proved me wrong time and time again."

Oh shit. The lump is still growing and moving north to my mouth. I bite my lip to try and keep back the tears welling up in my eyes. I didn't realize how much a few kind words would affect me.

"Never let it be said I didn't rise to the occasion." I try to lighten the mood. His sincerity is making me uncomfortable. Tai has so many facets. He is more observant than I ever realized.

"Do me a favor and tell that to my brothers when you meet them," I say absentmindedly. Come to think of it, I don't know when he would ever meet them face-to-face.

"Where are your brothers now?" Tai asks, watching me intently.

"Let's see. They are all still on Earth. Nate and Jamison work for a mineral extraction company. Hollis is probably charming some rich old widow at the luxury hotel he works at. And my mom, Talia, is a housekeeper at the same hotel."

What I don't mention is that all four of them are working extra shifts to fund my trip. I wonder if they've heard the news about j'Tilak and the station I was evacuated from. I hope they haven't. Who knows what lengths they would go to if they thought I needed to be saved?

"And your dad?"

"Your guess is as good as mine. He took off when I was little." From time to time, I've wondered what happened, where he went. Anytime I would raise the topic, my family would shut it down immediately. My brothers especially didn't like discussing it.

Tai lets out a noncommittal hum.

We're back to grunting. Conversation must be over. But I'm not done talking. "How about you? Where's your family?"

I'm prying into his past, something I know he struggles to be open about, but I do it anyway. What's he going to do? Take off on Brutus and leave me and Daisy here in the desert? He's stuck with me for the time being.

"I grew up in the system," is all he says. For how messy my family is, my heart sinks at the thought of not having them. I know what 'the system' means. It's one of those phrases that crosses boundaries and planets. It's what happens to kids who don't have anyone, ones who are left to survive on their own.

"Oh, I'm sorr—"

"Don't be. It's fine. Everything worked out." Tai fiddles with his bionic wrist and grimaces.

I pick up that he doesn't want to relive all the sad details of his past. I can relate. I've always hated being looked at with pity.

"Where did you grow up on j'Tilak?" It's a safe question—his home planet is paradise, and his face always softens when he talks about it.

"I grew up on a few space stations. The first time I saw my home planet was when I enlisted."

Way to go, Bri.

Stations are no place for a kid. Even I know that. The fueling station we stopped at on our way to j'Tilak was an absolute nightmare. I imagine a younger Tai growing up there. The thought makes me sad.

I audibly clear my throat to try and force down the uncomfortable feelings rising up. This small insight is a reminder that I know so little about him. I always associated him with Aro, so I assumed they had a similar background. An ideal life on a perfect planet.

We ride for a while. Even though we have been joking around, I still need to talk about why he wasn't honest with me. The silence hanging over us feels heavy and uncomfortable. My mind keeps circling back to why he lied to me about being here before. Initially, I was hurt and mad. Hurt because he should have trusted me enough to tell me, and mad because he is such a stubborn ass sometimes. Maybe once I know why, then I can stop obsessing about it.

"So..." I start slowly. "Why didn't you tell me you'd been here before?" I hold my breath, waiting. I need an answer from him. For some reason, it feels important.

"I didn't tell you, because I was an idiot."

"Was?" I interrupt, half joking.

"Well, even more back then. I got mixed up with the wrong crowd and ended up here, hiding out. I got caught and you pretty much know the rest." He looks out toward the horizon, avoiding me.

"Tai, you could have told me. I would have understood. Do you think I'm so awful that I would judge you for something that happened years ago?" I hope he says no. He's got to know me better than that. The weight on my shoulders could be lifted if I knew it wasn't me. I'm self-aware enough to know Tai thinks I'm a hard-ass, but I'd never want him to think I was unforgiving.

"It's not you. It's me. I thought I dealt with it over the years, but it turns out I buried it instead. Being back here brought it all back up." He finally looks over at me with sad eyes.

"I get that. But no more secrets. We're in this together now." I don't like being lied to, and I especially hate being kept in the dark. Tai doesn't owe me his entire life story, but this was information that could have been helpful.

Learning it from Boss made it so much worse. Being here brought up some painful memories for Tai, but his deception brought up some painful memories for me as well.

I'll never forget the day my dad left. There was no explanation. He was just gone. Mom fell apart and cried for days. She hardly got out of bed. My brothers filled in the gap, making sure I was fed and got to school. It took years for her to recover, or maybe she never did. From the day he left, I promised myself I would never hurt someone the way he hurt us.

This situation with Tai brings up a familiar feeling, a tightness in my throat. The ache of holding back tears. These are two very different situations, but the similarity of a truth unsaid ties them together in my mind. You think you know somebody, and then one day they show you who they really are. Sure, Tai isn't my dad, and part of me understands why he did it. The scariest part is how much it hurt that he kept the truth from me. It's a warning I have let him get too close. Hopefully he'll go back to the "one-word answer Tai." I don't feel as exposed with that guy.

THIRTY-THREE

Tai

Over the last six years, I have never told anyone about my upbringing. As far as Aro and my unit are concerned, I came into existence the day we enlisted. I showed up with my bionic arm, ready for a new start. That Tai, the one who survived on scraps and stealing from travelers, was gone.

My eyes stay fixed on the horizon. A narrow strip appears, separating the hot air from the burning sand. Slowly, bit by bit, a mountain range appears. There is one lingering thing I need to tell Bri, and it's going to bother me until she knows the full truth. Maybe if she knows the context of what led me to Sabaak, then she'll understand.

"Spending my life jumping from station to station was not a good life for a kid," I tell her.

She doesn't say anything, and with half her face covered by her hood, it's impossible to tell what she's thinking.

"Six years ago, I was on the run. I finally got off the station, which is a whole other story. I ended up here in some village. When I was hungry and thirsty, they brought me in and saved my life. I was there only a few days when the Authority found me. I set up an explosive on the outskirts of the village to cause a distraction, so I could get away. I didn't know what I was doing, and the explosion was a lot bigger than I thought it would be. It was chaos. Sabaaki and the Authority were all running around trying to put out the fire. I got hit with some of the explosion. It's how I lost my arm."

I pause and take a deep breath. My heart is racing out of my chest while I tell Bri the whole story.

"A good person, a good Tilak, would have helped the Sabaaki. Would have made sure everyone was okay. I didn't. I ran like a selfish coward. I tried to save myself instead of helping others. In the end it didn't matter because I got caught, and I'll never forgive myself for what I did here."

The heavy quiet between us stretches on. Her expression is unreadable, but it's not the anger I was prepared for. The neutrality on her face is just as terrifying. I wait and wonder if I made a mistake. I thought telling her was the right thing to do. The thought that scares me the most is that I doubt she will ever look at me again like she did yesterday.

"Thank you for telling me," she says, flooring me with one sentence. "I know it's not who you are anymore. People make mistakes when they are desperate. It was a shitty thing to do, but I know you'd never do that again."

"You can't possibly know that," I say, doubtfully.

"I do. I know you were looking for people on the station when we were evacuated. You didn't even have to tell me. I just knew it. You put yourself in danger for strangers. That's who you are now."

A sad smile spreads across my face. "You forgive me? So easily for something so awful?"

"Don't worry about me. It sounds more like you need to forgive yourself."

We ride next to each other in silence, both of us deep in thought.

"I'm sorry if I made you feel like trying to save the brethren was wrong. I don't blame you for delaying our escape from the brethren. You were trying to do the right thing and what matters is we got away without anyone being returned to the gods."

Bri cracks a smile but narrows her eyes at me. "I think it's time for what humans call a 'do over'. If that is what we are doing, you're gonna have to go back farther than that," she tells me with zero anger in her tone.

"Hi, Bri. I am happy to see you unharmed here at the space station. Would you care to return to j'Tilak with me?" I say, making my voice sound overdone and sarcastic.

"Farther," she says, laughing.

I pause, just now realizing I really messed shit up before that. I swallow hard, and take a deep breath.

"Do I need to apologize for the night of the party?" I ask. Time stands still while I wait for her answer and for what it might mean for our future.

"No. Not that. I liked that. But what I didn't like is how you totally brushed me off afterwards!" she says. Damn, her vulnerability is a superpower.

"I liked it too. I thought you regretted it, so I avoided talking about it."

"We both fucked up there, didn't we? But don't let me stop you from your continued apology." She says with a laugh that sounds like music.

"Hi, I'm Tai. I'm in a foul fucking mood because Aro kicked my ass in training and is dragging me to the rec room to be his wingman so he can flirt with his mate and you are here and getting the brunt of it." I put my hand out awkwardly imitating the uniquely human gesture.

"Almost there," she says and looks forward again, leaving my hand hanging there.

I clear my throat.

"Welcome to j'Tilak. I'm Tai, and I'll be taking you to the mura-Dome. Please dispose of your vomit here in this receptacle."

"Hi, I'm Bri." She looks back at me with a smile. She takes my hand roughly and shakes it up and down.

"See? That wasn't so hard," she says and faces forward again.

"Now, your turn."

"I don't have anything to apologize for," she says.

"You have got to be fucking kidding me," I practically shriek in frustration.

Her shoulders shake and the laugh she was holding bursts out. "Hi, I'm Bri. I'm feeling a bit cooped up here in the muraDome, and out of boredom I'm going to pester you because it's the best entertainment I've had in months," she says.

That's a very accurate description of the first time we really got to know each other.

"We've been terrible to each other, haven't we?" I ask.

"A little bit," Bri says. "It's okay. I kinda liked it."

We both go quiet. Inside I feel a sense of relief.

"What's that?" Bri points forward, finally seeing the cliff ahead.

"*That* is where we are going. The Veilfall." I shift uncomfortably on my h'axom. My legs went numb hours ago. "Let's take a quick break.'"

I slide off Brutus's back in one swift motion. I hurry to Bri's side before she can attempt the dismount on her own.

Her face has smudges of dirt across her cheeks, and she's glistening with sweat. She has never looked more beautiful.

She rests her hands on my shoulders as I grab her waist and lower her to the ground. A loud sigh pours out of her when she touches the ground and rolls her neck back and forth. Her face contorts when a fresh wave of smell wafts off her robe. This close up, I can smell her, and it's awful. The stench coming off me is equally bad. I pull off my shirt and wad it up.

"Here, let me," I say quietly and pull the dirty robe from over her head, exposing her goddess costume. Her hair hangs loose, framing her face. Even though she's tired, her eyes are bright and full of excitement. She looks wild and ready to take on the entire universe.

The wind blows a thick strand of hair across her face and before I can stop my fingers, they tuck it behind her ear. The touch reverberates all the way down to the soles of my feet. Her eyes drop to my exposed chest before she pulls away.

"What sorts of snacks did we pack?" she asks awkwardly, ducking away and rifling through the saddlebag behind me.

I clear my throat and focus my thoughts on our survival. Between the conversation and being close to her, I'm struggling to keep my mind straight. Her dodge makes me insecure about where we stand. Are we those people who just occasionally fuck? Or is there something happening between us?

"Flatbread, dried meat and that grainy sticky stuff they try to pass off as food," I say, doing my best to sound normal. Although I'm far from it.

She digs around in my bag and pulls out long strips of the meat. "I'd rather eat sand," she says and swallows with a grimace.

"Hopefully, it won't come to that." There is one absolute certainty: I will do anything to protect her and get her home safely.

We aren't going to make it to the Veilfall before dark after all. It's slow going through the hot sand. I can't even blame Bri's h'axom. We are all struggling. The adrenaline from the escape has worn off and bone-deep exhaustion has settled in.

Bri is drained too. Her eyes are tired, and she hasn't talked shit to me in hours. I'm going to call it off. We need to rest. We have a lot more journey ahead of us, and it's extremely doubtful the brethren would be able to catch us without any h'axom.

I slide down Brutus's side and hit the ground. My feet have been asleep for hours, so the sudden rush of blood hurts like stabbing needles.

"Let's stop for the night," I tell Bri. She nods and swings her leg over the saddle. I grab her before she can drop to the ground, catching her mid fall.

"You rest. I'll set up camp while you have some water." I place her on the ground and shove a canteen into her hands before she can argue.

"Thanks. It caught up with me all of a sudden," she says and takes a long drink from the canteen.

I've been drinking as little as possible, conserving water for Bri. I worry I pushed her too hard today. She looks like she could pass out right here in the burning sand.

My tent pops up without a problem. I pull out my BioDent. I bite down on the disc and it goes to work cleaning my teeth. The foam is minty and fresh—and I've never been more grateful for the tech. I'm covered in sweat and sand, which I can deal with, but there is no way I can make it without a clean mouth at the end of the day.

I step around Bri, who hasn't budged from the spot where I deposited her. I pull off her pack and dig around for her tent. I'd rather she sleep in my tent, but she's tired and probably wants her own space. I take my time setting up her tent, giving her the opportunity to tell me she doesn't need it.

She doesn't say a word, so I reluctantly stake it to the sand next to mine. Close enough to keep an ear out for trouble through the night.

I am about to toss my BioDent in my pack when she asks, "What's that?"

"A BioDent. You've got one in your pack. It cleans your teeth." I dig through her bag and toss it to her.

"This is the best thing I have ever seen." She opens the disc and puts the mouthpiece in place.

"Bite down, not too hard, and it'll turn on," I instruct.

Her eyes roll back in her head when it hums to life.

I distract myself by dealing with the h'axom. My fingers twitch and my wrist clicks when I tether Brutus and Daisy to my tent stake. If they try to wander away in the middle of the night, the jolt will wake me up. The last thing I want is to wake up without our rides.

She spits out the foam and carefully puts the BioDent away. "That was so good, I think I came."

I try to laugh at the joke, but I'm too concerned about my arm.

"You okay?" she asks, looking at my bionic hand. Her keen eyes never miss anything.

"Yeah, it's acting up again." I flex my hand to try to make it act normal.

"Here, let me see." She calls me over and pats the sand next to her.

I drop down, close enough for our arms and legs to touch. She grabs my hand and turns it, inspecting it from the outside.

"Here. This is where you open it." I show her the seam in the metal and pop it open with my fingernail.

In the fading light, she brings it up to her face for a closer look.

"Hm...let's see." She gently runs her finger along the neural wires.

"That tickles!" My arm jerks involuntarily.

"Hold still!" She brings my wrist even closer. Her soft breath is warm on the highly sensitive metal cover. "Oh, lookie here."

A thin layer of sand clings to the components. Bri gently parts the synthetic muscle fibers and blows away the grains of sand that had worked their way in. My hand goes numb when she removes the alloy synovial joint. She cradles the limp hand and rotates it back and forth, studying the movement.

"Aha!" She smiles and replaces the joint exactly how she found it but crosses muscle fibers and reconnects them in the wrong place.

"Those don't go that way—"

"Hush, I know what I'm doing." She levels me with a look that means business.

"That should do it." She closes me back up. Moving my hand feels...smooth. No more clicking in the wrist.

"How did you do that?" I'm honestly impressed. It took me years to figure out how to repair my arm, and she does it within seconds the first time she looks at it.

"I dunno, I'm good with tech."

I sit there awkwardly waiting for an invitation into her tent as she stands and brushes sand off her clothes.

"Good night, Tai," she says as she climbs into her tent and closes the flap behind her.

By tomorrow, we should be at the Veilfall, and I'm nervous about the reception I'll get from the Sabaaki. Will anyone there recognize me? I hope not. Even if they don't know what I did, I'll still know.

I wish we only had one tent. Then we'd be forced to sleep next to each other. I could rest easy knowing she's safe with me. I could *accidentally* rip a giant hole in my tent when I pack it up in the morning. She would be so mad. A price I'm willing to pay.

How is it possible that only one night ago Bri and I were together in her bed? I hate the brethren for a lot of reasons, but especially because they spoiled my good mood with their pathetic attempt to kill me.

A perfect moment ruined by a homicidal cult. Not something I ever thought would happen to me.

My lips still buzz from her kiss. It's unclear if this was all an inevitability or impulse. I don't know how to describe what happened. All I know is I got swept up by her. I saw a side of her and it felt like it was just for me. The vulnerable Bri that hides behind her sharp words and strength. She trusted me enough to let her guard down.

I wish I had done the same. Trusted her enough to let my guard down and tell her the full truth about my past from the start. If I'd done that, she could have decided a while ago if there was a place for me in her life.

I always felt safer being by myself. For the first time in my life, being alone feels like loneliness.

THIRTY-FOUR

Bri

Something is out there. From the heavy fall of feet and the loud sniffing—it's got to be big. I hold my body still as can be, hoping that whatever it is moves on. Where is Tai with his blaster when I need him?

After a few laps around the tent, it stomps away and I release my breath. In the distance, I hear snorting. Lots of snorting.

Correction, some *things* are out there. Curiosity gets the better of me. Throwing caution to the wind, I unzip the tent flap and peer out into the early morning light.

Not far off is a herd of h'axom sniffing and snorting away at the ground, searching for their next meal. Daisy pulls at her tether, trying to join them. Brutus has already gotten free and is in the center of the group. I laugh to myself. Tai's plan to keep the h'axom tied to his tent failed miserably.

I scramble out and shake Tai's tent. "Wake up! We've got company!"

He jumps out of the tent half dressed and half asleep, his hair sticking out in every direction. I could have admired that sight all morning if it wasn't for the herd of h'axom ambling away.

A sharp whistle comes from the other side of a dune. The herd shifts directions and slows to a stop.

"Bri, do you still have your translator?" Tai asks without taking his eyes off the herd.

"I think so."

"You might want to grab it. You're going to need it. We found the Sabaaki. Rather, they found us."

My hands shake as I fish the tiny square patch out of my bag and stick it behind my ear. I'm excited and nervous about meeting the Sabaaki.

They can't possibly be as bad as the brethren.

Did I just jinx us? Shit.

Tai packs up our tents with short jerky movements. The downcast expression on his face combined with the rounded shoulders is not what I expected to see. This is good news! We found the Sabaaki before we were baked alive by the desert sun.

A tall, slender alien guiding the h'axom steps out from around the dune and crouches down in a defensive stance when they see us. Its long legs bend at the knees, ready to run at the first sign of danger. Thin arms spread out ready to deflect an attack. The color of its hairless body shifts to match the sand. The only clothing is a small pair of tight shorts.

The large egg-shaped head with round unblinking eyes resembles an old caricature—from a time long ago when aliens were figments of human imaginations.

"Hello! We are trying to find our way home. Can you bring us to whoever rules here?" Tai says in universal language. The translator works with a slight delay, passing along the message in Sabaaki.

I laugh despite the tension. Did he really just say "take me to your leader"?

The irony is completely lost on Tai, and he shoots me a death stare that says, "Pull it together."

The Sabaaki replies in a language made mostly of vowels. "Who are you?" They slowly rise to their full height. The translator echoes in my ear with a slight delay.

"I'm Tai. This is Bri. We crashed here and have been trying to get home to j'Tilak," Tai answers for both of us.

"That one is not a Tilak," the stranger says, pointing their long, thin finger at me.

"She's human, but she lives on j'Tilak now," Tai clarifies.

I tuck away the little spark of happiness that flares up when Tai refers to j'Tilak as my home.

"My name is Eio'sh," he says, placing his hand over his chest.

I'm flooded with relief. A name. Finally. Not some weird collective identity that hinges around worshiping me.

"Can you help us get home?" I ask.

"I might know someone who can," he says. "It appears your h'axom cares for you greatly."

Over the course of the short conversation, Daisy wrapped her trunk protectively around my waist. I give her a pat to reassure her that I'm safe.

"Thank you so much. We'll take any help we can get." I peel Daisy off me and shoo her toward the herd. She happily joins the group and prances around with an agility I didn't know h'axom were capable of.

"Come with me. Perhaps my elder, Maia'el, can help," Eio'sh says. He whistles one long note, and the herd follows obediently, including Daisy who miraculously keeps up.

The Sabaaki's steps are deceptively fast. Tai and I have to hurry to catch up. Our translators make up for the language difference, but I can tell there is a lot unsaid between us and our new friend.

Still not fully recovered from the traumatic events of the brethren and desperate to avoid conflict with another alien species, I decide to make Eio'sh my new best friend whether he likes it or not.

I spend the next few hours telling him what happened after we crashed on Sabaak. Tai interjects here and there to correct me when I exaggerate for dramatic effect, totally ruining the entertainment value of the story. Other than that, he's completely silent. Eio'sh is appropriately shocked by the presence and behavior of the brethren. Another reassuring sign that we aren't walking into another shitshow.

We take breaks throughout the morning to let the h'axom graze. Eio'sh slowly warms up and eventually tells us about himself.

"I am the head shepherd in our town," he says proudly. At least I think he's proud. His face is expressionless and the tone of his voice never changes inflection.

"You have an impressive herd," Tai says.

"This is nothing. It used to be three times this size." Eio'sh looks over the herd.

I follow his gaze and try to imagine what a larger herd would look like. Daisy waves her tail happily and willingly keeps pace with the group. "Where did the rest go?"

"They have been disappearing, slowly, little by little."

"Do you think it's sand hunters?" Tai asks. Clearly, a creature he's intimately acquainted with.

I remember the brutal slash through his shirt when he first arrived at the colony. Whatever it is, it must be nasty.

"They would never approach a herd of h'axom. Maybe one by itself, but never when they are all together," Eio'sh explains.

"I hope you figure out what it is," I say.

The looming mountain turns out to be two. As we get closer, a giant crack down the center comes into focus and more mountains appear closely behind. In so many ways, things up close are never what they seem from afar.

"And here we are. Welcome to Veilfall." In the shadow of the mountains, a round pen made out of wood and brush waits for Eio'sh and his herd. He drags a wobbly gate open, and the h'axom file in and head straight to the pile of dried grass in the center.

"What's going on with you? Why are you so tense?" I ask Tai when we are alone. Finding Eio'sh has brought me alive, but Tai has been guarded. No, more than guarded. He keeps positioning himself away from us and staring off into the distance, more than usual. Something is obviously bothering him.

"Nothing, I'm fine."

"Liar." My epic eye roll is completely wasted on him. He refuses to look at me.

THIRTY-FIVE

Bri

A path threads through a narrow gap between the sheer faces of the neighboring mountains. Reds and browns swirl together, resembling wood grain texture in the stone. The dry wind whistles through the passageway like an eerie song welcoming us to Veilfall.

"If you would just tell me what's wrong, we can fix it and you might be able to enjoy this amazing place." I drop my backpack on the ground and spin around, taking it all in.

"This is me, enjoying it," he says with zero expression in his voice.

"You forget, sir, I have seen what you look like when you are enjoying something."

We've been through too much to go back to this nonsense. We have survived Sabaak and the psychotic brethren. He even opened up about his past.

The truth hits me all at once.

That's it.

He's worried about what it will mean to face the Sabaaki after all these years.

Eio'sh meets a group of identical Sabaaki where the path begins. They stand completely still, communicating in absolute silence. The only indication they are communicating is the change in expression and shape of their eyes. Eio'sh gestures to us and they all turn to look. Tai and I shift uneasily on our feet from the scrutiny.

I grab his hand and hold it tightly, a show of support. A reminder that he isn't facing this alone.

At last, Eio'sh rejoins us near the pen. "Let us begin the final part of our journey."

The other Sabaaki spread out and position themselves around the h'axom.

"Lead the way!" I say with renewed enthusiasm, hoping it will be contagious and cheer up Tai.

"I got this." Tai swings his backpack over his shoulders and grabs mine before I can.

We follow Eio'sh through the twisting path, excited to see what is around each turn. Sure, I feel lighter without my pack, but the real buzz comes from my mind teeming with the possibilities of what could be at the end of this road.

As we walk, I drag my fingertips along the stone to feel the texture of the walls. Sand drops away from the gentle touch. The stone is a paradox, soft and hard at the same time. Strong enough to withstand centuries of wind and water, yet it gives way to the softest touch.

Tai puts his hand on my lower back, guiding me around a boulder blocking half the trail. His touch triggers the memory of his hand in other places.

Bri, don't get too close.

I spent all night thinking of ways to keep a healthy distance from the massively appealing blue alien who is systematically breaking down all the walls I've worked so hard to put up over the years.

Distance. Boundaries. Going our separate ways after this. I repeat the words a few times in my head.

I can't help but laugh a little at myself. One look from Tai and all my resolve crumbles like sandstone.

"What's that smile for?" he asks.

"I'm always smiling."

"Sunshine, you could burn someone with the looks you give me."

"Okay, fine. It was an inside joke with myself. You wouldn't get it." I skip past him and take the lead the rest of the way through the narrow winding path.

When the tunnel finally widens, a city carved into the face of the cliff looms overhead. Rows and rows of homes and shops stack neatly on top of each other. Doors and windows are framed with either braided molding or columns. Others are ornate with sunbeams and flowers.

I'm fascinated by the way everything is cut straight from the mountain. Sunlight peeks over the mountain, giving the city a golden glow and landing at our backs.

The Sabaaki all freeze and crouch down in the same stance Eio'sh had when he saw us as we step into the empty space between the mountain and the city. The males are dressed similarly to Eio'sh, and the females wear beautiful flowing kaftans, each of a different color.

Eio'sh faces the crowd silent and still, wordlessly communicating something to his fellow Sabaaki. Every few seconds, their eyes flutter toward us in staggered succession.

"Tai, are we good here?" I ask quietly, disguising my question with a nervous smile. I made the mistake of underestimating the brethren. I'm not doing that again.

"I think so. They seem more scared of us than we are of them," he whispers.

If Mr. Head-on-a-Swivel thinks we are safe, then I do too. His radar for danger is better tuned than mine. He knew from day one that the brethren were not to be messed with, and I didn't believe him. I push down the guilt rising up from putting us in danger.

Eio'sh motions for us to follow and guides us along the city. Sabaaki wander in and out of the bottom-level shops and stop to stare when we pass by. The bright reds and greens of the fabric overhangs draw a sharp contrast to the dull brown of the desert.

We follow Eio'sh through an open-air market where stalls and kiosks are packed tightly together under canopies. I'm mesmerized by the patchwork of the shade overhead.

Eio'sh steps through an unmarked door, simply a notch in the mountain. A group of chubby Sabaaki children bracket the door on both sides and giggle as we follow Eio'sh in. We must look so strange to them.

The cool darkness of the room is a welcome relief. In the far corner, I hear a vowel-heavy language being exchanged. It's quiet. My translator can't pick up the words.

"Alright. Let's see how this goes," Tai whispers as he sets our bags down near the entrance.

"Come in, come in. You must be weary from the great desert." My translator comes to life now that the Sabaaki in the room are speaking to us. Tai and I tentatively step closer, my eyes still not fully adjusted to the darkness. An older Sabaaki sits comfortably on a rug, legs crossed in front of her. She is lit by a single lamp with an open flame in the corner.

Eio'sh motions for us to sit on the rug. "This is Maia'el. She can answer your questions."

"Thank you for your hospitality," Tai says nervously.

"Were you separated from the Boraei?" she asks. My translator doesn't have a comparable word.

"We crashed here alone. We aren't familiar with the...*Boraei*," I answer, struggling with the pronunciation.

"You don't look like them, and we are all still living, so that tells us that you are different. These days we are uneasy with visitors."

"Where did they come from?" Tai asks.

"We don't know. Boraei is an ancient word we use, which means 'Dangerous One.' Anyone who gets close enough to ask gets shot down and buried in the sand."

Dread pools in my belly. When will this planet stop trying to kill us? I'm over it. I just want to go home.

"Do you have transportation off the planet?" Tai asks, his thoughts in sync with mine.

"No. We have no need to leave Sabaak. We cannot survive anywhere else. The only way off the planet is the ship the Boraei arrived on." Maia'el watches us with interest. Her expressions are impossible to read, but her calm demeanor has an effect on Tai and I both. His shoulders relax down from his ears, and his breath deepens and evens out.

Great. Fucking great.

Not ready to fully give up hope, I ask, "Maybe a comms system? Could we get a message out to our people?"

"They destroyed our interplanetary communications when they arrived," Maia'el says.

Eio'sh returns with a tray of food and a clay jug of water with two matching cups. "The Boraei showed up one day, without warning. They attacked everything around them. Entire villages were destroyed in a single day. For a while we watched them, hoping to learn of their purpose. They would set up a camp, search the area for a few days and move on. Over and over again. We began to worry for our scouts' safety and called them home before they could be caught," Eio'sh says.

This news delivers the defeating blow to my last shred of hope. I thought we were finally going to leave Sabaak when we escaped the brethren. Now we have to confront an even more dangerous group. Fuck this.

I look over at Tai, expecting to see the same resignation. Instead, he looks more resolute than ever. His shoulders are back up and he's clear-eyed.

"I'm getting you home. Nothing is going to change that," Tai says, looking into my eyes.

Dammit if those words didn't do something to my insides. A tiny bit of my feminist credibility leaves my body when I realize how good it feels knowing he's looking out for us.

"Your bravery is admirable. Please stay and rest. You will need your strength for what is ahead of you," Maia'el kindly offers.

Eio'sh leads us up a spiral staircase lined with tapestries. The stone staircase is worn down in the center from years of use. He welcomes us into a bedroom with a single bed in the center and a wide cabinet tucked into the corner. On top is a basin and a stack of towels. Eio'sh pulls away a privacy screen from the window, letting in the light.

"Take as long as you need. The room is yours."

We circle the room, checking out all its charming features. Soft linen blankets make up the bed. A mural of a sun on the wall. The view from the window is my favorite part. We are just above the multicolored canopies shading the market.

"When you are ready, come find me at the Oahe." His offer hangs in the air until my translator clarifies with "communal kitchen."

"Thanks!" I answer for both of us. Eio'sh gives me a kind nod and leaves, giving me the opportunity I've been waiting for.

"It's got to feel weird being here with the Sabaaki after everything that happened last time."

His guilt and agony are written all over his face. "I think I need to tell them. If they know up front, then they won't take it out on you."

"Tai, we're in this together. Whatever you decide to do about the Sabaaki, I'll face it with you. But maybe we could get cleaned up a little before you go clear your conscience."

"You go first." He waves to the basin and towels. "I have some-thing I need to take care of."

"Wait!" He's out the door before I have a chance to argue.

My clothes are tattered from escaping the brethren. The tears in my skirt show even more of my ass and thighs than before. The straps around my neck hang on for dear life. I remove them carefully. I need these clothes to hold on a little while longer. At least until I can wash the robe.

The soap and shampoo I appropriated from the brethren are waiting for me at the bottom of my pack. I pour a generous amount of soap into the water and wet the small towel and scrub my entire body. Between the rough material of the towel and the sand, my skin is glowing and soft by the time I'm finished.

Tai loudly clears his throat from outside the door. I scoop up a thin blanket from the bed and wrap it around my chest, suddenly feeling self-conscious. I don't exactly know where we stand.

My resolution to stay away is getting harder to stick to. We are somewhere between casual hookup and the person who scares the living shit out of me because they are getting too close.

"I, uh..." Tai steps into the room, eyes fixed on the ground. "I found you some clothes," he says nervously as he places a flowing dress at the foot of the bed.

"Thank you!"

"I'll give you some privacy," he says and turns toward the door.

"Tai, wait. It's okay. I'm all done." I snatch the clothes off the bed and hold up a floor-length orange kaftan with golden stitching down the front. I drop it over my head and it flows gracefully to the floor, only a few inches too long.

A heavy sigh escapes my lips. Finally, something clean and comfortable.

"Where did you find this?" I ask and twirl a little, letting the soft fabric spin around me.

"One of the shops below. I did a little bartering."

"What did you trade?" I ask, genuinely curious. I silently hope it wasn't the BioDent. It's not technically a necessity, but needed nonetheless.

"Don't worry about it," he says while pulling his dirty white shirt over his head. I didn't notice anything new for him to wear. It means a lot that he got clothes for me first, and I'd like to return the favor.

"I can go grab something for you too," I offer and look around for my pack. There has got to be something in there I can trade to get him some clean clothes.

"Nah, I'm good. I don't think they'd have anything that would fit me anyway," he says as he smiles and gives me an infuriatingly handsome wink. He's right. The Sabaaki are all very thin, the opposite of Tai. It would be hilarious to see him squeeze into those tiny shorts they are all wearing though.

He moves for his belt buckle and my knees go weak.

"Don't tell me you're going soft on me now," he says with laughter in his voice.

There he goes, using my own words against me—again.

I am an absolute disaster of conflicting emotions. One minute I'm promising him I'll face his greatest shame with him, the next I'm thinking of every reason why we can't be together.

Words start pouring out of my mouth and I'm helpless to stop them.

"Here's the thing. We have a good time, you know, in bed. And that's great, and I'm open to continuing. But I just. I don't really know what I want as far as a relationship goes. Or even if I'm capable of one. Or even if that is something you are thinking about. You don't want to get all tangled up in my mess."

Tai stands there with an amused look on his face until I run out of air.

"Feel better now that you got that out?" he asks with a glint in his eye.

"As a matter of fact, I do," I say and throw a pillow at him.

"Good. Let's take this one step at a time. We can figure all that out later." His pants hit the floor, and I can make out his hard cock against his thigh under his tight shorts.

THIRTY-SIX

Tai

The way Bri hovers around the room while I clean up tells me everything I need to know. Regardless of her little rant, she wants me. The air crackles with anticipation. I wash up quickly and wrap a towel low on my waist before sliding the privacy screen closed over the window.

"That's a bit presumptuous of you," she says with a quirked eyebrow.

"Oh, really? I guess I could move it back." I slowly reach for the shade. She darts over and grabs my arm to stop me.

"I didn't say that."

My thumb traces slowly and deliberately across her chin to her jaw and down the column of her throat, savoring every inch. Her eyes flutter closed and a ghost of a breath leaves her lips. All restraint and intention to go slow snaps.

I don't know what is happening between us either, but I am too far gone to think about it. Right now, all I want is her.

Her mouth gently closes around my bottom lip, pulling me closer and deepening our connection. My towel drops to the ground and I leave it there. The only thing between us is the soft fabric of her dress. The one I painstakingly selected, thinking it would look nice with her pink hair.

She steps backwards toward the bed and pulls me by the shoulders with her, not breaking the contact between us. I love it when she leads. She could lead me off a fucking cliff and I would follow. Willingly. Enthusiastically. Smiling the whole damn way down.

She stumbles on the long hem of the dress and lands on the bed with a laugh. I gently pull the fabric over her head and drape it next to the water basin on the table.

I run my hands up her body. Her hard nipples graze my palms. My mouth joins my hands, and I tease her nipple with my teeth.

She writhes against me. With her hands on my dick, she positions me at her entrance and thrusts her hips up to mine. In one movement, I am inside her and moving.

"Are you going to scream my name this time, Sunshine?" I ask, thrusting deeper into her. She gasps and digs her nails into my shoulder. I nip at her forearm, driving into her.

"You don't know when to shut up," Bri says, pulling my head toward her and silencing me with an unrestrained kiss.

I'm building toward an orgasm and need her to get there as well. My plans to make this last have failed spectacularly. I grab her arm from my shoulder and push her hand to where we are connected. I can't take my eyes off her fingers pressing on her clit. It happens before I can stop it. I let go, or maybe I just finally stop pretending I was ever in control.

Bri and I reluctantly get up from the sex haze and go down to the ground level. In no hurry to find Eio'sh, we wander through the market and take it all in. Every sense is on overload. The sounds of the Sabaaki language being translated in my ear. The smells of dried herbs and spices shoved under our noses with offers of the best price. Dates and figs generously pressed into our hands.

We follow the smell of roasting meat to a spit-roasting stand that's big enough to feed half the city. A group of Sabaaki stand around the meat and offer opinions about how to cook the communal meal. For such willowy people, they look ready to dig in. We watch them bicker and critique the cook's methods.

Bri and I stand back, mindful of their suspicion. It's not every day a Tilak and a human walk into their small city. As soon as they notice us, we are beckoned into their circle. A warm bowl of rice is pushed into our hands.

One of them inspects Bri's kaftan and clicks their tongue approvingly at her attire. I can't help but puff up with pride.

"Your wife looks lovely," they say and pat me on the back.

Bri's head snaps to me at the misconception. Part of me is tempted to let them think we are married. It feels fun to pretend. If I had my visor, it could calculate the odds of Bri and I being together. The chances would be less than 1%.

I decide to go with it before she can correct them. "Yes, she does."

Bri laughs and shakes her head. Maybe after everything we have been through the odds have ticked up slightly.

"We heard you are seeking out the Boraei so you can return home. Are you sure that is a wise decision?" they ask.

"It's our only way," Bri says with a mouthful of rice. One of the Sabaaki places a thick slice of meat in her bowl and she tears into it.

"Then may the winds guide your path," one says and piles my bowl high with the sizzling meat. The flavor hits my tongue, and I take three more big bites before I swallow.

It's the best thing I've ever eaten.

"Do you know where we can find the Boraei?" I ask while trying to swallow the piping hot food.

"They were across the plains the last time we encountered them."

"Past the deep sand, the ground hardens and levels out. Then you will pass the canyon with water. Follow the river and pray they don't find you first," another adds solemnly.

"Sounds fun," Bri says. Her sarcasm goes straight past them.

"Yes, thank you so much. You've been so generous. It's a nice change of pace from our last encounter," I say.

"Who else have you met on Sabaak?" they ask.

"There's a group that call themselves brethren.

"A cult," I interject.

"Whatever. They thought I was their goddess. When they decided this one," she says, angling her thumb at me, "needed to return to the gods, we got the hell out."

"Goddess? An easy mistake," says the one who thinks we are married.

"It wasn't as great as it sounds," Bri says. "Trust me."

They lead us to a group sitting around a fire. We lower ourselves to the ground and sit shoulder to shoulder as we finish our food. The sun dips below the mountains around us and the circle widens to accommodate the Sabaaki who have trickled up to the fire. Drums show up. They play a simple beat together that branches out into a polyrhythm.

A waterskin gets passed around. When it gets to me, I take a small sip, not sure what to expect. A sweet and spicy liquid burns my tongue and all the way down my throat. I gasp for air and cough from the sting. The Sabaaki all have a good hearty laugh at my expense.

I hold it out to Bri. "This one has a kick."

She grabs it roughly from my hands and takes a long drink. She wipes her lips with the back of her hand and gives a satisfied "ah." She passes it along to the next person in the circle, earning nods of approval from our hosts.

"Your mate is stronger, yes?" Eio'sh says coming up behind me.

It must be my lucky day because Bri didn't hear the comment. I don't think her confidence needs another boost, even though they are right.

More wood is added to the fire and the waterskin comes around again. I'm prepared this time and take a long pull before handing it off to Bri.

This reminds me of the night back at the muraDome when Bri dragged me into her room. All those months ago, I would never have guessed I would find myself here on Sabaak with her.

When everyone clears out for the night, Bri and I stumble up the stairs to our room and pass out face-first on the bed.

THIRTY-SEVEN

Bri

Our gracious hosts, the kind and helpful locals that I *knew* were here somewhere, insist on a visit to the underground gardens before we leave to track down the Boraei. My palms get clammy every time someone says the ominous word. Boraei, Dangerous One. Why couldn't they be called the Friendly Ones or Helpful Ones? I would even be satisfied with the Chaotically Neutral.

Just beyond the cliffside city, they lead us down a sloping ramp into the ground.

"Not this again," I groan as we descend. I remind myself these are different circumstances. This is not the brethren. No weird sex ceremonies, no controlling Boss—just a few kind aliens wanting to send us on our way with some food.

"Took the words right out of my mouth," Tai says, nudging my arm with his. We both have a little unresolved religious trauma.

The ramp doesn't go very far. Unlike the brethren's dark and creepy colony, it's bright here. It's obvious they went to great lengths to let as much light in as possible. Stone archways are colorfully painted in bright golds and reds. It's as cheerful as the other colony was dreary. Tucked into the walls are small plants with vines climbing up to the sunlight. Small purple berries cluster along the way. A Sabaaki gently pulls fruit off the tree and tucks it into the bag strapped around his narrow waist.

I mirror their careful movements, gently picking the fruit, not wanting to damage the delicate berries and vines.

"Come this way." Another Sabaaki motions for me to follow.

Through the pathways, intricate murals of flowers, sunsets, and Sabaaki embracing cover the walls. The artwork is impressive, but it's the sentiment behind the paintings that brings a tear to my eye. These lovely, peaceful people don't deserve to be harassed by the Boraei, and the brethren don't deserve to even share the same air as the Sabaaki.

My thoughts are interrupted when I step into an open courtyard. In the middle is a tree that looks hundreds of years old. Its green canopy covers the expanse above, protecting us from the harsh sun like a mother bird taking us under its wing. Bright yellow fruits hang down out of my reach, but my guide has no trouble collecting them one by one, storing them in his pouch.

I spin in circles. Speechless from the beauty in every direction.

"Our ancestors built this garden. It has fed us for generations."

"Thank you for bringing me here. I'll never forget your kindness and generosity," I tell them. I'm feeling extra emotional today. Being here with the Sabaaki is a dream come true. A place and people so different from Earth. I do my best to lock each detail securely in my mind. Sometimes I need to be reminded that it's not all brethren and Boraei out there. Goodness and beauty has a place in this universe as well.

"I believe we have enough for your journey," they say, patting the satchel.

I look back at the group of Sabaaki behind me. My eyes are drawn to the big blue guy picking berries along the wall. I stand next to him and pluck a few berries and pop them into my mouth. Tai opens his mouth expectantly and I toss one in.

"Oh hey, I've got something for you." Tai reaches into his bag of berries. He's making me nervous. I'm not ready to be in a gift-giving arms race.

He pulls out a small white blossom and hands it to me. The smell of citrus and honey fills the air while I braid the flower into my hair. "It's beautiful," I tell him.

I've learned to identify the differences in Tai's facial expressions. Some are feisty, some suggestive. This one is warm.

I like him. And it's terrifying.

I clear my throat. "Oh shoot. I got some dust in my eye." I pull at my eyelid, faking the injury. "I'll catch up with you later."

I run for the exit, like a coward, but I can't outrun the scent of the flower tucked into my hair.

THIRTY-EIGHT

Tai

The city is quiet. All the merchants close their stalls during the hottest part of the day. Everyone is inside the mountain, taking shelter from the heat. The occasional Sabaaki hurries from one shadow to another. One smiles kindly when he walks by and gestures for me to follow him into a dark doorway.

Laughter and the dull murmur of conversation greet us when we step into a large room with a high ceiling painted with vibrant colors.

The room is crammed tight, and in the center of all of it, Bri and Cubes. Of course. Three Sabaaki hunch over the table in tense discussion while Bri sits there comfortably like she doesn't have a care in the world. She casually drapes an arm over the chair next to her. The entire room is on the edge of their seats, except Bri.

She must feel my eyes on her because she looks up and smiles broadly. My entire body vibrates from that one look. It's all fire, confidence, and challenge. I know that smile. It's the same one I saw all those months ago the first time we played.

Between us, everyone whispers back and forth. I hear a word here and there about the various strategies of the game. Bri waits patiently for her turn, relishing the utter chaos around her.

I lift an eyebrow at her as a silent question. *How did this happen? Where did she find a set of Cubes on this planet?* I would never guess the Sabaaki were the type to enjoy a game built on bluffing, but they are completely engrossed.

Bri shrugs back, giving me a non-answer. She returns her attention to the game. These Cubes are different from the holographic ones we played with on j'Tilak. These are roughly carved from sandstone. The glyphs on each side barely resemble the high-tech version I'm used to.

These poor guys. They don't stand a chance against Bri.

This game was my first introduction to her. I'll never forget that night. She was ferocious, and it was one of the hottest things I've ever seen. She played the game with swagger. It came naturally to her, while I fumbled repeatedly and couldn't remember the rules.

So much has changed about us, but not that. She still owns every room she walks into.

The two Sabaaki counseling the player go quiet and lean back. The nervous opponent extends a trembling hand, ready to make his next move. He rethinks and pulls his hand back. The crowd groans and goes back to whispering feverishly about what he should do next.

My empty stomach pulls me to the table pushed up against the wall that's piled high with food. I load up my plate and drift back to the game, sure not to miss any of the action.

My eyes are zeroed in on Bri, and I miss what the Sabaaki does with his turn. I don't need to see what he did, I can read it all over her face. A sly smile spreads across her features. Whatever he did was the wrong move. She's got him in her clutches now. No one else realizes it yet, but the game is over.

With a quick move, Bri takes her turn and slams down her set of Cubes, declaring victory. The room erupts with everyone talking at once. Some are still trying to understand what just happened, while others congratulate Bri on her win. The defeated player holds his head in his hands, softly chiding himself for losing the game.

She pushes her chair back and stands with a stretch. Graciously, she goes to her opponent and shakes his hand, congratulating him on a game well played.

The Sabaaki continue debating. Who should have done what and when. Why her challenger made the wrong move at the wrong time. It doesn't matter, none of them ever stood a chance against her. None of us do.

"You missed most of the action," she says, stepping up next to me. She grabs a plump berry off my plate and pops it in her mouth.

"I think I get the gist," I tell her and hold my plate as far from her as possible.

"You want a rematch?" she asks.

"Oh, no. I learned my lesson."

"Scaredy-cat," she says.

I don't need to know the definition of the word to catch her meaning.

"They are ready to play another round, though." I nod over to the table. The next challenger sits at the table and waits for her to return.

"Okay, fine." She passes in front of me on her way back to the table and snatches up the rest of the berries. She eats them in one giant bite and smiles back at me, unfazed by my territorial growl.

The room goes quiet when the game starts up again. I step back and watch Bri work her magic over the room. Everyone here is completely under her spell.

She has managed to win over the Sabaaki. Bri has this divine ability to connect with people, to draw them in immediately. She's familiar and mysterious at the same time. And I'm lucky enough to be a bystander and watch it all happen.

Maia'el comes to stand next to me. My anxiety spikes from the awkward silence between us in the loud raucous room.

"Would you like to talk about what is weighing you down, Tai?" she asks kindly. I'm not surprised that out of everyone here, she would pick up on what's happening in my head. It feels like the right time to confess and deal with the consequences from before. I can only hope that whatever punishment follows will be enough to silence the guilt.

I take a deep breath and follow her through a dark hallway that leads farther into the mountain.

She brings us to a small, cozy room away from the noise. Sitting cross-legged on a thick rug. Maia'el motions for me to join her and hands me a clay mug. I politely take a sip before setting it down. The herbal sweetness has a slight medicinal flavor in the back of my mouth. I can't drink much. My stomach is in knots from the impending dread I've had since we arrived.

"You've been here before, yes?" Maia'el asks. An opening rather than an accusation.

"I have."

"I know the story of a Tilak who came here once," Maia'el says softly.

I brace myself for what comes next. Whatever it is, I deserve it. If the tea was poisoned, I hope it acts quickly, and that they will take mercy on Bri. They must know she had nothing to do with me back then.

"Maia'el, when I landed here six years ago, I was desperate and angry. I'll never forgive myself for what I did." I'm not trying to defend my actions, but she must know how truly remorseful I am.

She rests her long, thin-fingered hand on mine. "It was a tragedy, but not a tragic ending."

"What do you mean? Sabaaki were hurt, probably killed, because of my selfishness." Why doesn't she understand how abhorrent I was?

"It was not the end, for the Sabaaki nor you. No one was killed. A village was destroyed, yes, but no lives were lost," she says with a kindness I don't deserve.

"I still shouldn't have run."

"Tsk." She clicks her tongue at me. "Do not worry yourself with 'shoulds'. Embrace the path that Sabaak sent you on. After all, it led you to *her*." Maia'el doesn't say Bri's name, but there is no one else she could have meant.

I let her words sink in. What would it mean to truly embrace the path my life is taking?

THIRTY-NINE

Tai

"Thank you for everything," I say to the group of Sabaaki who gathered to see us off this morning. They're quiet, but I detect smiles now in place of blank expressions.

"May the Goddess bless your journey," Eio'sh says.

Bri's eyes widen, and she belts out a laugh.

I'm completely lost. No clue why she's laughing so hard.

"I knew I should never have told you that story. Get over here!" She steps towards Eio'sh and wraps him in a tight hug. His long gangly arms hang loosely, unsure of what to do. She holds on long enough for him to catch on and return the hug. My jaw drops at the affectionate exchange. Only Bri could manage to pull this off in less than two days.

"Do you remember which way to go?" Maia'el asks.

"That way." I point straight ahead. "Until the ground hardens, past the river, and keeping close to the shadows so they don't find us first."

"Good. You remembered every word. I trust you will find your way home." Maia'el pushes a woven bag into my hands. Inside are berries wrapped in soft material and a tall stack of flatbread.

"You can always return and find your place here with us," Eio'sh says.

"That's a kind offer, but the blue guy doesn't like sand," Bri says, saving me from having to respond.

I lift her up easily, and she settles onto Daisy's back. I double-check the straps and harnesses and tap her on the leg.

"Scooch over."

"Wait, what? Where's Brutus?" she asks and looks around for my missing h'axom.

"I traded him," I say, hoisting myself up behind her. Her back stiffens and she twists around to look me in the eye.

"Why would you do that?" She doesn't sound happy.

"How else was I going to get you new clothes? Plus, half of their herd has gone missing. They need him more than we do." My eyes wander down to the pretty dress perfectly catching the wind. The orange fabric swirls around her feet. I'm glad it's long enough, so she won't get a sunburn on her legs while we ride.

She narrows her eyes and turns forward without a word. Her body relaxes. Daisy throws her head back, forcing Bri to lean even closer.

Her back finds my chest, and she melts into me. I get more comfortable in the saddle as well. My warm metal arm lands gently on her hip.

FORTY

Bri

Maybe he doesn't realize his hand is on my hip. I can't think about anything else. It's a lightning bolt down to my toes. I am keenly aware of every point of contact between us.

I look down at his bionic arm resting on my hip and smile a little half smile. I'm curious as to what it feels like for him compared to his other arm. I'm very aware of more places than my hip.

Stop it. Stop it right now, Bri. Shut. It. Down.

I remember that conversation I had with Elowen back on j'Tilak. Me trying to get through to her, convincing her to open herself up to the possibility of a happy life with someone she loves. Man, it's so much easier said than done. The thought of Elowen reminds me of the looming possibility of fate. I never had a chance to find out what Tai thought of all the mate stuff.

"Do you think you have a mate out there?" I ask before I can think twice and keep my thoughts to my damn self.

"A mate?" Tai nearly chokes on the word.

"Like Elowen and Aro. Someone out there in the vast universe you can hulk out for." I keep my eyes trained forward, too embarrassed to look back at him.

"No, I doubt it. I think mates are reserved for certain Tilaks. Aro's ancestors could do it, and I don't think that's in my bloodline."

"What does that mean?" I'm defensive on his behalf and ready to list all his good qualities, even if he doesn't want to admit them to himself.

He's one of the best males I know. Some sweet little thing would make him perfectly happy back on his home planet. The image of Tai with a pretty Tilak woman makes me slightly ill.

Now is not the time to catch feelings.

"I'm station trash that got lucky," he says matter-of-factly. I bristle at his comment. If everyone's life was limited by their origins, where the fuck would I be right now?

"It doesn't mean you don't deserve a mate. I'm sure some pretty Tilak woman would love for you to smash some shit for her."

Damn. I hadn't planned on saying that out loud! I really need to work on the filter between my brain and my mouth.

"Battleforms are more than just smashing shit," Tai says with a laugh. "The biological response to protect what's most important is a big deal. Anyway, that's not what I'm into."

The slightly ill feeling in my belly turns into fluttering. I can't resist the follow-up question.

"What are you into?" I hold my breath waiting for his answer.

He takes his time. "Loud and opinionated. Someone with zero survival instincts who constantly underestimates danger."

A smile creeps across my face, but I look straight ahead, not wanting him to see my reaction. I know it's only teasing, but I can't stop the tingly feeling in my chest at his admission. We are dangerously close to crossing the line from casually sleeping together to forming a real attachment.

"Good luck finding that." I diffuse the situation with my normal amount of sarcasm.

"What about you? What's your type?" he asks.

"Hm. Let me think. I'm looking for someone short, small teeth, big gums, only slightly homicidal."

His laugh echoes through the valley. Irritating Tai is fun, but nothing compares to the feeling of making him laugh.

"I think I might know someone."

I catch myself thinking that a mate like Tai wouldn't be the worst thing in the world, and then I question my own sanity for letting the thought finish. Elowen struggled with the idea of free will when she realized that Aro had recognized her as his mate.

Maybe because of my background in genetics, the idea of a mate doesn't feel as abstract to me as it might to others. DNA is a blueprint, but it also carries history, personality, and predisposition. With DNA, much of our lives are written long before we are born. I don't find it so strange to think that somewhere out there, in all that vast and indifferent universe, there's someone whose biology would recognize mine.

"Where did you go?" Tai's voice interrupts my thoughts.

"Nowhere. What makes you think I went somewhere?"

"Come on, Sunshine. Give me a little credit." He lifts an eyebrow at me. "I want to know, what were you thinking about just now?" he asks again.

"I was thinking about DNA."

He laughs. "That is not what I was expecting you to say."

"I remember the first time I saw a DNA strand, the double helix that all of life is built from. I realized that no matter how much I knew, there would always be more to learn. It sparked something inside me, and I never considered anything after that."

"I've always wondered about my own DNA, where I came from," Tai says.

"You never met your parents?"

"No memory of it. Can't miss what you never had."

Daisy's steps slow, and she comes to a stop. Tai flicks the reins and nudges her flanks with his feet.

"What is it, girl?" I ask and pat her neck.

In the distance, a low rumble shakes the ground under us. The sand vibrates from the sound. Behind us, a tall brown wall approaches. The sky darkens from the sand being kicked up.

"What the fuck?" Before I can finish that thought, Daisy starts digging. The forward shift flings Tai and I off over her head. I land hard on my side, gasping for air.

The rumble grows into a roar, and sand violently swirls around us.

FORTY-ONE

Tai

"Sandstorm!" I shout over the howling wind.

I crawl on hands and knees towards Bri. She's on all fours, her hair whipping around her face when she looks up. The sand below me gives out, and I scramble to not sink down with it.

In the blink of an eye, she's gone.

I frantically spin around, but I can't see more than a few inches in front of me.

"Bri!" I bellow into the wind.

After a dozen or so steps, I stop and yell for her again. I can't lose her. Not after all this.

"Bri!"

Somehow through the wind I hear her call my name. I blindly sprint in that direction, barely able to keep my eyes open.

"Bri!" I get a mouthful of sand. I spit it out and call for her again.

For a split second, the wind clears and I see her huddled on the ground, sand coating her body and piling up around her.

I pick her up and pull her into my pounding chest. Her eyes are plastered shut, her hands clinging to me.

I put her hand on my waist and wrap her fingers around a belt loop. "Don't let go!" I have no idea if she heard me. Her hair has pulled free from the long braid and is whipping her face, getting caught in her mouth and around her neck.

I pull off my backpack and fumble around for the tent pouch. Hopefully, it's strong enough to withstand the storm.

I let go of her hand to pull the tent out of the pouch. It breaks free from the bag and pops into shape in front of us. I hold down one corner of the tent with my foot. Sand is pelting the fabric and piling up on the sides. I grab Bri's kaftan at the chest and push her into the tent ahead of me.

Using sand as an anchor, I half bury the tent in the ground and hope it's enough to keep us from blowing away. I get in the tent with Bri and collapse against the ground.

It's still loud, but at least we have a barrier between us and the pounding sand. Bri is on her hands and knees sputtering, trying to get sand and hair out of her mouth. I reach over and pull her hair away from her face and wipe away the sand from her cheeks.

"Are you hurt?" I ask, examining her for injury.

"I'm okay. You?"

"Never better." I laugh. I'm not having much luck brushing the sand off my shirt, so I pull it off over my head and toss it in the corner of the tent. Bri's eyes widen when they land on my chest. The boots come off next and end up next to the dirty shirt.

Bri brushes the sand off her arms and legs then goes to work on taming her knotted hair. Fascinated, I watch as she combs her fingers patiently through, working section by section.

"Have you seen my hair tie? Are you sitting on it?" she asks.

I shift forward and look under me and don't see anything. I pat my hands all over the floor of the tent looking for her hair tie. I look under my shirt and boots while she searches her side of the tent.

"I don't see it," I say reluctantly.

"Fuck."

Defeated, she hunches and sinks farther down to the ground. Her face crumples and she bites her lower lip, keeping it between her teeth. It takes me a minute to realize what's happening: she's crying.

She sniffs and rubs her wrist across her face.

"Bri."

"It's nothing. I really needed that hair tie," she says and more tears pour from her. "It's just a hair tie. It's not a big deal. I don't even know why I'm crying." She hiccups and hides her face from me with her hands.

I scoot up next to her and pull her hands away. "It's okay. I'll go find it."

"No. It's gone. I'll be fine," she says and I see a wall come up over her face. The one that is stronger than I thought possible, and I hate it. I prefer when she lets her guard down. She let me in for a brief second, then put the wall back up.

"Whatever you need, it's yours."

"Knock it off. You sound like the brethren." She laughs between sniffles and pushes playfully at my chest.

"You've been through a lot. If you need a hair tie, then I'll find it." I search for the softness I got such a short glimpse of. I know it's in there somewhere.

"I have been through a lot." The tears start falling again. This time I pull her to my chest and hold her against me. Her body goes rigid for a second before relaxing into me, letting me support her.

I rub my hands up and down her back, comforting her and letting her cry it out. After seeing Bri stay strong this whole time, watching her in awe as she's handled every single thing that has come her way, I'm glad I get to be the one she lets in. The one she trusts enough to fall apart around.

"Does the hair tie have important human significance?" I ask.

She laughs through her tears. "No, not at all. It was my only one. It was the straw that broke the camel's back."

"You're going to need to explain that one to me." I keep rubbing her back, worried that if I stop, she'll pull away. "I know what a camel is. How could a straw break its back?"

"It means someone can cope with a lot of tiny things, but after a while they pile up and get heavy, and eventually the last straw becomes too much, and it breaks the camel's back."

It crushes my heart that she feels this way. She has been carrying a lot. All on her own, never once asking for help. Something inside me comes to life at the thought of being the one to help carry her burdens.

"You're stronger than any Tilak I've ever met, but you aren't alone. I'm here. Let me help you." I was hoping to make her smile, but instead, she sobs into my chest again.

"Thank you, Tai."

She pulls away from me far too soon. She straightens her dress and uses the hem to dry her tears.

I grab my shirt, rip off a strip of fabric, and twist it up. It's a poor substitute for the hair tie that means so much to her.

"Here, try this." I hand it over.

She pats down the tangles, pulls her hair back and ties it off.

With nothing left to do, and now feeling incredibly awkward about staring at her, I lie down and stare at the ceiling, watching it billow from the sand and wind above.

Bri lies next to me and inches her way closer until our bodies are touching shoulder to shoulder, hip to hip, all the way down our legs.

"You give good hugs," she says without looking at me.

"Not too bad for a first-timer?" I ask.

"That was your first hug?" Surprised, she jerks her head toward me.

"Yeah." I don't dare look over at her. There was never a person to hug. And now, I can't imagine sharing a hug with anyone else.

FORTY-TWO

Bri

Last night was a harsh dose of reality. We aren't out of the woods yet. I'm getting really tired of this place trying to kill me.

I awkwardly climb out of the half-buried tent and take in the aftermath of the storm. The sky is hazy yet calm. Fine particles float in the air looking for a place to settle. I can't be sure, but the dunes seem steeper this morning. While we slept, the desert rearranged itself around us.

Daisy is gone. I hope she made it out of here before the storm got bad. It's a miracle the tent didn't blow away with us in it. The only thing that kept me from totally losing it was Tai. I stayed tucked into his side the entire night. Occasionally, he ran fingers up and down my arms to comfort me.

"So, what do you think?" I ask Tai, who's sitting on the sand, facing the sunrise.

"You want the good news or the bad news?" he asks.

"You pick."

"If we can't find the Boraei, we are going to be here for a long, long, long, long time," he says.

We are both tired and beaten down. Hopefully the good news will perk us up.

"And what's the good news?" I say and tug on the tent, pulling it out of the sand.

"That *was* the good news."

If that was the good news, I do not want to know the bad news.

Tai stands and helps me break down the tent while I process our dire situation. There has to be something we aren't thinking of. Some obvious thing staring us in the face.

"Aren't you one of those guys?" I ask.

"What guys?"

"Yeah, you know. A handy guy."

"Handy?" his voice goes up in pitch, and he quirks his head at me.

"Not like that! Handy, as in survival skills. You go into the desert with a roll of tape and a multi-tool and you build a spaceship."

"I don't have any tape," he says, totally missing the point.

"Never mind." I kick at a rock poking out of the sand, and it moves. That's no rock. It's Daisy's hoof! I jump back, giving her space as she pushes her way up. Daisy emerges grunting and shaking off the extra sand.

"Daisy! You made it! I was so worried, girl!" I wrap my arms around her thick neck and pepper her with kisses, getting a mouthful of sand and fur. I can't believe she buried herself next to us and didn't run off.

"You are the best h'axom in the whole universe!" I coo at her in full baby-talk mode.

She gives one last massive shake, flinging sand everywhere. It makes me realize her saddle is gone, along with my pack. It was strapped to her last night when we fell off. All we have left is Tai's backpack and the dwindling supplies we took from the brethren.

Tai must know what I'm thinking because he comes up behind

me and wraps his arms around my shoulders. "We're going to be okay. We're both too stubborn to quit."

I soak in his confident words. He's right. We got this.

"I'm going to walk." We both say at the same time and let out a nervous laugh. I guess we are both feeling a little awkward about last night. Or maybe it was the position of our bodies when we woke up this morning. All tangled together.

"Are you sure?" he asks.

"My thighs are raw, and my hips are killing me. I need to walk it off."

"Want me to go grab a brethren? I'm sure they'd love the opportunity to give you a massage," he says, stifling a laugh.

"Ha, ha. Very funny. Don't tell me you aren't sore from riding the last few days."

"I'm in absolute agony, but I couldn't very well complain when you were handling it like a champion," he says, rubbing his neck.

"As long as I don't lose another hair tie, I should be fine."

"I've got plenty of shirt left if you do."

My ovaries do a double backflip.

Daisy affectionately rests her trunk on Tai's shoulder and walks right alongside us. Dammit, why does that have to look so cute?

My legs have been getting used to walking in the sand. Even though it's hot and the terrain is uneven, it feels better than riding.

"Never thought I'd say this, but I think I'm getting used to it here," I say.

"I wish I could say the same thing," Tai says and flexes his elbow. The joint in his bionic arm creaks. There is no keeping the sand out of the tiny cracks. I hope no permanent damage is done.

"Is it acting up again?" I ask.

"Yeah, but not as bad as before." He wiggles his fingers at me and sighs. "This thing cost me a fortune."

"They didn't give it to you when you enlisted?" I ask, trying to piece together the small bits of information I know about him from his past.

"I got a smaller version when I enlisted. I sized up a few times as I bulked up. This one should have been a permanent replacement, but I don't know how much longer it will last now."

I really didn't think about the impact of this place on him when I demanded we stay, so I could force my savior complex on a bunch of dudes who were not interested.

"Tai, I'm sorry..." I say, wanting to acknowledge my part in this.

"Nope. Don't do that. We started over. Remember?" he says.

"Well, at least let me cover part of the cost when we get home," I offer. I wish I could buy him a brand-new arm as a thank you for everything he's done for me.

"You have credits like that laying around somewhere?"

"Eventually. I'll get back to my research and discover some DNA sequence to reverse the appearance of wrinkles or whatever and sell it to rich people."

"Is that why you chose genetics?" he asks, squinting into the sun when he looks over at me.

"No, it's not." I kick some sand his way at the implication that my motivations are that shallow. "But it can pay the bills until I can do what I really want."

"And what's that?"

"Genetics was an interesting subject in school. I thought there might be some good career opportunities there. Which, for the record, I was right about. But once I have enough credits, and pay back my family, I'm going to start a foundation."

"A foundation?"

"It's basically a program with money used to support a cause." j'Tilak, the paradise planet, wouldn't need something like this, but the rest of the universe could really benefit from it.

"It's a great idea. There were a lot of kids where I grew up who needed something like that." His expression softens. "Me included."

I take a risk and ask, "What was it like? I can tell you've tried to downplay it, but it must have been really hard."

"I'll tell you, only if you promise to not feel sorry for me," he says.

"Deal."

"It was rough. I learned to survive by any means necessary. All of us kids formed a little gang. We came up with all sorts of ways to steal from travelers. We learned pretty quickly not to steal from other residents. So, we went after anyone passing through."

I don't say a word, hoping he'll continue and tell me more.

"A crooked mechanic taught me how to fake an engine failure. We used to find the nicest ship docked on the station. The other kids would follow around the captain and crew while I'd sneak onboard. When they would return to their ship, it would look like a massive engine failure. They would go to the mechanic, the only one on the station, to fix it. Once the payment was received, I'd return and put the part back."

I promised him I wouldn't pity him, so I do my best to keep a neutral face and not think too hard about why he had to resort to scams to survive.

"I eventually got caught, and somehow managed to undock a ship and fly it. I'd never flown anything before. It's how I crashed on Sabaak the first time."

And there it is: the full story about how he ended up here. It all makes sense. I can tell he hardly wants to admit the truth to himself, let alone say it out loud to someone else.

"A lot of people on Earth are stuck in shitty jobs, being exploited and treated worse than a bot. It could have been my future if my family hadn't stepped in. I want to help people in the same way, give them opportunities. Help them reach their goals, even if it's to have an adventure on a distant planet where everything possible goes wrong."

Tai stops walking and stares at me, his eyes searching my face. It's impossible to tell what he's thinking. He probably thinks I'm ridiculous for thinking I could make a difference in this vast universe that is tipped in the favor of the wealthy and powerful.

"What?" I ask, feeling self-conscious from his stare.

"I had you completely wrong," he says. "You seem so sure of

yourself, like nothing ever scared you. I assumed life had been easy for you."

I give a small shrug. "Not even close. We didn't have much growing up. It was hard. But it pushed me. Everything I've done came from that."

Tai turns back and starts walking again, both of us quietly lost in our thoughts.

FORTY-THREE

Tai

The water is hardly more than a mud puddle. My boots squelch through the wet dirt as I circle around. My feet slide a bit with each step. I turn to warn Bri but before I can say a word, she has lost her footing and is sliding, each foot going in a different direction. She hits the ground and bursts out laughing.

"You are the clumsiest person I have ever met," I say and put my hand out to help her up. She flings the mud off her hands and reaches for me. Instead of pulling herself up, she yanks down on my hand, pulling me down into the mud next to her.

"Serves you right," she says and flicks mud on my face.

"Oh, you think you're pretty funny, huh?" I grab a handful of mud and swipe it across her face.

"Oh, no you didn't!" A handful of mud hits my forehead. I swipe it off my face and narrow my eyes at her.

"Mercy! Mercy! We're even!" she says gasping for breath between her laughter.

"Hardly."

She has more mud on her than I do from the fall that had nothing to do with me. Bri gets up carefully squelches her way through the soft mud around the corner.

I look around trying to figure out how we are going to get some drinkable water from the murky muddy mess in front of us. The idea to filter it out using the clothes we have on pops in my head—a skill we learned in military training—but I soon get grossed out at the thought. I'm about to lean down and scoop up some water with my hand when I hear Bri from around a bend in the canyon.

"Fuck yes!" she yells followed by a loud splash.

I trudge my way through the mud and follow the sounds of splashing. How did I miss the crystal-clear pool of water in the middle of the desert the last time I was here?

Well, I was preoccupied with other things.

It's wide and looks deep, deep enough that Bri is completely submerged and swimming somewhere under the surface. Across the sparkling pool, water cascades down in a transparent sheet from a ledge above.

This looks much safer to drink than the mud water.

I take off my boots and set them down. My shirt and pants come off next. I leave on the briefs and wade into the cool crisp water. I stop when I'm about waist deep and lean down to splash some water on my face and hair, cleaning off the mud, sand, and sweat.

"Come on, Tai, it's even cooler down here," Bri says, treading water in the center of the pool. Her eyes are bright and shining. If I knew how to swim, I'd be over there in an instant.

"I'm good."

"No, really. Come on, it's better over here."

"I can't swim," I admit.

She moves closer. Her dress is wet and see-through, the top clinging to her chest and her hard nipples peeking through the fabric. I'm glad my lower half is underwater because I'm immediately hard.

"You can't swim?" she asks, looking skeptical.

"Never learned. Not many bodies of water on fueling stations," I tell her. Water is a precious commodity in space. I would go months between baths. And when I did, it was pretty much a bucket of dirty water poured over my head.

"That's a terrible excuse. I happen to know there was a pool at the muraDome. You could have learned anytime you wanted."

I wade a little closer to her. I'm extremely turned on right now. Her body is incredible, and I want to remember how it feels against me.

I'm about to snatch her wrist and pull her toward me when she screams and jumps into my arms.

"I felt something! Something touched my ankle!" she shrieks as she shakes and looks back frantically.

"Are you sure?" I ask, searching the clear water along with her.

"Yes, I'm sure!" She smacks my chest and grabs my arms to keep herself perfectly still.

Our eyes meet, hers terrified and wide. "Tai. I think it's on me," she whispers.

"Okay, okay. Where?"

"Here in the front," she says, motioning down at her lower half.

My eyes follow hers down her chest, belly, and between her legs. "Please get it off me." I watch her face go pale and notice she's hardly breathing or moving at all.

"Okay. Don't move."

I reach down and my fingers graze the soft skin of her belly. My dick is throbbing. The sheer dress is the only thing between our skin. I gather up her skirt and bunch it in my hand, clearing the way to her bare thigh.

"Don't get any ideas," Bri says. She's scared but hasn't lost her easy humor.

My finger brushes down her leg. On her inner thigh, a sticky bump is stuck tight to her skin. I grab it gently and pull, not sure how it's attached itself to her. I peel it off slowly and reluctantly pull my hand away.

The little thing is an orange and black spotted amphibian of some sort. It's cute. It fits in the palm of my hand and clings to me with four padded feet.

"I think you made a friend," I tell her and hold it up.

"What is that?" Bri squirms and shakes off the feeling.

"I don't know, but it looks harmless." I peer into its big buggy eyes. Its tongue pops out and it licks its own eyeball. Its pupils focus on me, and right when I'm about to stroke its back, it unhinges its jaw and bites down on my thumb.

"Ouch!" I scream and drop it, but it stays stuck to my finger while I try to shake it off. I fling it off back into the water, and Bri and I run for the shore.

Wide-eyed and panicked, I can't help but laugh at the ridiculous sound I made when it bit me. Bri clutches at her middle, laughing so hard she can't even get a sound out.

I collapse to the ground and watch her laugh.

Bri is so beautiful, it hurts. She plops down next to me and leans against my arm.

"I guess the swimming lessons will have to wait," she says and nudges me.

"Yeah, I'm definitely not going back in there." I grin at the sight of her, wet from head to toe, water dripping down her smooth skin.

"Here, let me see that." She grabs my wrist and brings my thumb up to her face. She intently studies the small bite marks left behind.

"It's okay, it didn't hurt that bad." I gulp down nothing, my mouth dry again.

"Do you have anything in your pack to mend it? I don't want it to get infected. Who knows what sorts of microbials are here? I'd hate for you to lose your last good hand."

"I'm pretty good with both hands."

I curl my bionic arm around her and bring her close. With one slow finger, I trace down her throat, around to the back of her neck, following her spine all the way down until my hand comes to rest at the small of her back. All I see is Bri and her gorgeous eyes and lips. Lips that are being licked, preparing for a kiss.

I'm on her in an instant. Her hands comb through my hair when I kiss her. She tastes like salt and smells like rain.

The brethren are right. She's a goddess, and I want it all.

She rips her lips away from mine and scoots away. The distance between us now feels worse than anything I've ever felt.

"Um, I'm gonna go check the pack." She stands up and tries to cover up her exposed body. I watch her over my shoulder. She puts her fingers to her lips absently, touching the place I had my lips on as she walks away, taking my sanity with her.

FORTY-FOUR

Bri

I had been worried the line between hookup and something more was approaching. The combination of the conversation on our way here and the feeling of his hand moving up my thigh officially pushed us into perilous territory. I'm confident that I can move us back into the safe zone where we fuck like rabbits at night, tell a joke or two during the day, and keep feelings out of it.

How ironic. Not that long ago I was telling Elowen to let her guard down with Aro. That she was worthy of love. It's a lot easier to give advice than to take it. If Elowen was here right now, she'd be calling me out.

Especially now, Tai has been giving me these tiny little glimpses into where he came from, who he is under all the gruff exterior. He's got hang-ups about his past. He thinks he's being vague and subtle about it. But he wears it like a neon vest.

And that's the problem. I want to know more.

I shake my head to focus on the task at hand and dig through the pack. There has got to be some first aid here somewhere. My fingers snag on the liquid sutures at the bottom of the bag. I swing around and collide right into his hard, dripping wet chest. This up-close and personal view is exactly what I was attempting to avoid. A smattering of indigo freckles span across his chest and shoulders, begging to be touched.

"I'm trying to figure something out," he says.

I clinch my hands at my sides, squeezing the tube of sutures almost until it bursts. All to keep myself from reaching out and touching the dark blue specks.

"Oh?" *For fuck's sake, Bri. Use your words.*

"I'm trying to figure out if you are running away from me. Or towards something else."

Old habits kick in. The tightness in my throat tells me it's time to make a joke, to shut this conversation down before it goes too deep. My hands don't want to cooperate when I tell them to relax.

"At the moment, I'm running toward a bandage for your finger." I know he didn't mean it literally. But I don't have time to think of anything better.

"Don't do that. I really want to know. Are you pulling away because this isn't what you want? Or you do, and that's what scares you?"

The bottom of my stomach drops away. I do want him. Is that enough to overcome the fear?

"You don't have to tell me. But at least be honest with yourself."

Shaken to the core, my mind races to find the right words. It's too hard to explain something when I'm still trying to figure it out for myself.

He grabs the tube of sutures from my hand. "I'll take that."

His hand is steady and unwavering as he traces a thin line of the adhesive around the bite. I look down at my own hands, which are shaking like leaves in the wind. I clasp them together to hold them still.

"Okay. Now we can go back to talking shit," he says with a smile and tosses me the sutures.

FORTY-FIVE

Tai

"I would kill for a bowl of noodles right now," Bri says. I hear her stomach grumble over the crunch of the sand under our feet.

We've been walking for a few hours. The water hole was nice, but I didn't want to stay any longer than necessary. I didn't want to risk another encounter with a Sand Hunter, or any other predator that might be going for their midday drink.

"You're over there starving, and you're thinking about noodles? If I could have anything right now, it would be a giant Tilaki honey-cake." I toss her a few strips of jerky. Definitely not as good as honey-cake, but it will keep us from starving.

"What's that?"

Now I have her attention.

"It's a j'Tilak specialty. It's the go-to celebration dessert. Birth-days, weddings, returning home from being stuck on a miserable planet. That sort of thing. It has more than thirty-seven ingredients and takes hours to make. It's fluffy and sweet, and melts on your tongue. The first time I had it, I thought I'd died."

"It sounds amazing. Would I have to wait for my birthday, or could we have it when we get back?" she asks.

"The second we land I'll find one for you."

"I'm going to hold you to it. Honeycake first, noodles second, quickly followed by a shower," Bri says with a faraway look on her face. I hope she's picturing the shower and not boring noodles.

"Maybe you should get that shower first." I can't resist the urge to tease her. I used to be scared of feisty Bri, but now, that one is my favorite.

"How dare you? It's not my fault I've been sweating my tits off this whole time." She narrows her eyes at me. Her spark has returned, the one that sometimes scorches and other times warms.

"I suppose you blame me for this." I know she was joking. I'm relieved we can laugh about our circumstances. For a while there, I wasn't sure she would ever forgive me.

"Well, if the shoe fits."

"If the shoe fits? What are you saying?"

"Never mind, don't worry about it."

"So, what's the first thing you're going to do when we get back? After a shower, that is," Bri asks.

Throughout the conversation, our footsteps have slowed. It feels more like a leisurely walk than a fight for survival.

"First, shower. Second, re-enlist. Mandatory service is almost over, and I'm staying on," I say without looking at her. Why does it feel wrong to tell her my plans? It feels like guilt for not including her in the decision-making process and that makes zero sense.

"Oh, come on, G.I. Joe, there's got to be something else you'd want to do."

"What's a G.I. Joe?" I ask.

"It's a who. Not a what. It's this mythical man who has embodied hero worship for centuries. Every new generation has their own G.I. Joe who fights the enemy of the time. I think it began as a toy."

"Hm... I don't think the analogy fits. I'm not re-enlisting to fight. I like the structure, the comradery. I'm doing something that matters."

Out of the corner of my eye, I check her reaction, looking for her approval.

"I get it. I want to feel like that too."

That's all I've ever wanted. To know what I'm doing matters to other people. That I can make a difference and make life better for others.

I hand Bri the canteen and a nutrigel but don't take one for myself.

"Mission accomplished then. Your research saved an entire planet." I can't refer to Earth as *her* planet anymore. She belongs on j'Tilak. With me.

"Oh, I haven't forgotten. I almost regretted it when Earth backed out of the treaty the second it became inconvenient. Regardless of how shitty the politicians are, the people stuck on Earth don't deserve to slowly starve to death."

I scan the horizon, looking for any sign of the Boraei. We've passed the landmarks from the vague directions Maia'el gave us. The ground is flat and hard, and there's nothing for miles.

"Let's stop for the night," I suggest. The sun is low in the sky. There is no point in pushing ourselves to go any farther today.

Bri looks around, assessing our location as well.

"You won't hear any arguing from me!" she says brightly.

"Liar."

FORTY-SIX

Bri

I like this Tai. He listens and watches like he's studying me for an exam later. Each time I open up to him, he shifts his eyes like all of these little conversations are being filed away in his head so he can fully understand me. It's a heady feeling, and more than a little intimidating.

He's already in the tent when I climb in. He smiles nervously as I make myself comfortable in the small space. We are down to one tent. Watching him set it up, I knew we wouldn't be able to keep our hands off each other. Before the "fuck like rabbits" portion of the evening commences, I need to get something off my chest.

"Today you asked me if I was running away from you or towards something else."

He lets out a heavy breath and a heavy swallow at nothing.

"The truth is more complicated than that."

"How so?"

"For a lot of reasons, which I don't want to get into right now." I crawl up his body and straddle his hips. "However, I have a solution." I tug at his hair, pulling him to me.

"You are a problem-solver," Tai rasps against my skin.

"We can do this, guilt-free. And then when we get home, everything goes back to normal."

His grip on me lessens. "Guilt?"

Oh, shit. I said the wrong thing.

"Wrong word," I move his hands back to their previous position. "No strings attach—shit, you won't know what that means. Unconditional, yeah. Let's go with that."

"Do we need to figure all this out right now?" he asks, breathing heavily.

"Not at all."

Our lips crash together violently. It's all need and heat and desperation.

His hands are on my back, pressing into my skin, holding me tight like I could fly away at any second. He arches beneath me, adding to the building friction between us. I circle my hips, indulging in the sensation of us pressed together.

The movement elicits a snarl, and I have never felt sexier in my life. His lips and teeth are at my jawline and throat. Nipping, claiming, teasing me.

My hands are on his shirt pulling up. Before I get it over his head, I'm flipped onto my back and Tai hovers over me, his hips between my legs. He kisses down my chest and pauses above my belly button. He spits and sputters out some sand he licked up along the way.

I can't help but laugh at his expression. My skin is all sand and sweat. The thought banishes the confident sexy feeling that had possessed me seconds ago. I push on his chest and squirm beneath him, trying to put some space between us.

He growls and goes back to kissing and nuzzling deep into my neck.

"I'm so gross—you don't want to do this," I tell him. My voice is breathless and doesn't even sound believable to my own ears.

"You're the best thing I have ever tasted," he says. His breath rushes over my sensitive neck.

"I'm sweaty and dirty." I squirm again.

"You're perfect," he says again, his lips brushing against me with every word. It's my turn to groan against him. My poor attempts at getting distance between us turned into me grinding up against his rock-hard cock that is determined to punch through his pants.

"Tai..." I don't even know what I was going to say.

"Tell me to stop," he says, each word punctuated with a kiss across my shoulder. "Tell me you don't want this. Say you don't want me." The kisses have stopped, and he stares, waiting for an answer, his light blue skin flushed and his pupils blasted out.

I should tell him to stop. I should say I don't want this. But I'm beyond rationality right now. All I am is desire, and I'm sure there are reasons why this is a bad idea, but I can't remember any of them right now. Plus, I can't bring myself to lie to him.

I reach up and grab his neck and bring him down on me for another harsh, demanding kiss. He matches my intensity, and I could come apart from that alone. I drag my lips across his blue chest, tasting his salty skin. It's heavenly. I want more.

Now I'm rubbing the sand off my tongue. It's everywhere. I've never hated the sand more than I do right now.

The tiny strips of fabric between us are too much. My breasts are sensitive and need to be freed from the gauzy dress. I gather it up and pull it over my head. Tai grabs one breast and kneads it roughly. Rocking against me, the seam of his pants hits the right spot and gives me too much and still not enough pleasure with every pass.

I move with him, matching his punishing pace that has me careening toward release in a shockingly fast amount of time. He pushes my hand away when I reach for his zipper.

"I'm going to make you come like this, and when we are out of the sand, then I'll give you what you want."

Oh fuck. That tone of voice makes my entire body shiver. His deft fingers rub up and down.

His erection pushes against my inner thigh while he tortures me with his touch, his hips rolling in sync with his fingers. He slows and has me begging for more. I arch against him and whine, "Don't stop."

"Bri," he murmurs against my neck.

"Mmmm?" I ask, unable to form a full sentence.

"The things I would do to you if I wasn't covered in sand."

I whimper when his finger flicks across my clit. "What would you do?"

He smiles. A predator toying with prey. "After I got you out of these clothes, I would lick every single inch of your delicious skin." Tai nips at my jaw and drags his face over to my ear and tugs on my earlobe with his teeth.

I gulp hard at his words. He moves his hand from between my legs and traces down my neck with one finger.

Goosebumps. Everywhere.

"Then I'd make you come on my mouth." He sounds so cocky, and without his hand between my thighs, I can finally think straight.

"You could try." I taunt him a little. "Many have tried, and none have succeeded at that maneuver." I clap my hand over my mouth. I shouldn't have said that, for many reasons.

His laugh is low and erotic.

"Sunshine, I'm going to make you come in ways you haven't even dreamed of." He runs his fingers down my ribs. His touch is almost a tickle. I gasp and lean toward him, seeking more friction.

"I bet I could make you come before you even pull your dick out." Another challenge. Another chuckle from Tai. Christ on a fucking cracker. He is going to make me come without even touching me. I palm his cock as he pushes it toward me. A small dot of moisture shows up on his pants.

I am pure need. Nothing else matters. Nothing else exists.

"Oh no, you first," he says moving back between my legs, going back to the excruciating pleasure.

"Prove it."

Tai snarls and drags his fingers down my slit. I grab his arm with both hands and buckle from the sensation. The pressure builds in my core. My legs are soaked, and Tai relentlessly flicks his fingers across my clit, playing me like a goddamn instrument.

My stomach drops out from under me and I come apart, clinging to him for dear life. He captures every single gasp and moan with his mouth drinking in my pleasure for himself.

"I think we got a little carried away there." I sound nervous. Why am I nervous? I just came all over the guy. As the haze lifts and the world comes back into focus, a familiar little voice is there waiting for me.

You missed your chance. You should have insisted on conditions before jumping the guy.

"You can carry me away anytime you want."

"Oh, you have all the right words tonight," I say and roll onto my back putting a few inches between us. Tai promptly drags me to him and settles me against him in the nook.

Without disturbing our comfortable position, he reaches over, grabs the canteen, and puts it in my hands.

"Thank you."

I drift to sleep with the sound of Tai's heart beating against my ear.

FORTY-SEVEN

Bri

Last night was transcendent. It was Earth-shattering. It was the weirdest combination of trash-talking and orgasms. All I can think about is when we are going to do it again.

So, I don't know why I shrugged him off this morning.

In the light of day, the old habit came back so easily. The walls went up before I could stop them. Before I even understood what I was doing. Even though it's the last thing I wanted.

I prefer it when he's on the inside of the walls I put up, not the outside. It's all so confusing and contradictory.

The awkward tension in the air between us is only amplified by our desolate location. The scenery hasn't changed in the hours we've been walking today. Just endless, flat, barren land. We don't have a direction or destination in mind, now having passed the landmarks the Sabaaki told us would lead us to the Boraei, and we are on our own.

I shiver at the memory of his hands on me, even though the air is hot and still. Not a hint of breeze today as we trudge through the dirt.

I opted to ride Daisy today, another decision to put distance between me and Tai.

Something tells me now's not a good time to ask him where we are going. I can practically see the tension radiating off his shoulders as he walks ahead.

We should talk this through. We are both grown adults and should be able to discuss this. Except, I have no idea what to say.

Look, Tai. You're hot as fuck, and I'm totally down. My mind draws a blank after that.

Maybe I shouldn't lead with how hot he is and how I want to get in his pants.

My skin gets clammy from the thought of the giant monster cock he's hiding in those pants.

Shit, I'm supposed to be figuring out a solution to this problem, not slobbering all over myself, imagining his dick.

It's not you, it's me. Fuck. Could I be any more cliché?

I think I really like you. But I am terrified I'll make you fall in love with me, and then I'll bolt. And I hate the idea of breaking your heart. I could never live with myself if I did that to you.

Daisy grunts and pulls against Tai's lead, trying to go in a different direction. He digs his heels in the ground and pulls her back in his direction.

"What is it, girl? You know something we don't?" I ask the h'axom.

"She's being stubborn. We need to go that way," Tai says, pointing ninety degrees from where Daisy is trying to go. He pulls on the reins again, unsuccessfully.

"Maybe she knows where to go. We certainly don't," I tell him. I'm taking Daisy's side in this.

"We need to go over there," he says with a grunt, trying to pull Daisy back on track.

"How do you know? They could be literally anywhere!" I hate how shrill my voice sounds.

"The village has got to be over there." He pulls on the reins, and

Daisy comes to a complete stop. Somehow, I've managed to be stuck between the two most stubborn beings in the entire universe.

"Tai, I think we should let her take the lead."

"I'm not letting some dumb animal lead us around the desert. We're going this way."

Tai's words don't hit their mark. They hit me instead. He is a grumpy bastard most of the time, but this is the first time it feels like he's being mean. And Daisy doesn't deserve that.

"She's not dumb. Between the three of us, she's the only one who is from here. She probably has some survival senses that lead her to safety or water or help!" It feels weird to be arguing with Tai from up on her back, so I swing my leg over and slide down to the ground with a thud.

Tai huffs and turns away from me. He sinks down to the ground and throws a handful of sand in frustration. The tension in his back that I've been watching all day slowly lifts from his shoulders. It's replaced with drooping shoulders of defeat.

I sit down next to him. He doesn't even look over at me. I know that I hurt him this morning.

What is wrong with us? We keep saying and doing the wrong things. It's so messy.

This is definitely a sign we don't belong together.

"I don't have it in me to fight both of you right now."

"I guess we did gang up on you," I admit with a bitter laugh.

"I am hanging on by a thread. Have mercy on me and go with me on this, please."

It's the *please* that does me in. I lean over and rest my head on his shoulder. He relaxes against me and drops his head down lightly onto mine. We sit there for a while silently watching the shadows shift across the sand.

Minutes or hours go by. The only indication of time passing is the stretching shadows from the grooves in the dirt. A flash of light catches my eye in the direction Daisy was pulling us.

"What the?" I block my eyes with my hand, trying to make out what caused the reflection.

"A village!" Tai says triumphantly and jumps up from the ground. I stiffly climb up to my feet. He looks so happy that I swallow the inclination to point out Daisy was right.

"Thank you, sweet baby Jesus!" I yell to the sky. Finally, something other than the bare desert around us.

Tai scoops me up and spins me around. He lets out a deep sigh of relief. The hopelessness from moments ago is gone. We are chest to chest smiling broadly. I'm suddenly aware of his proximity and the way he's looking down at me, not quite at my eyes, a tiny bit lower. He bites his lower lip, and I realize where he is looking.

"I'm so tired, I cannot possibly take one more step. If we stop for the day, could we make it by tomorrow?" I ask and take a step back, breaking the spell.

Tai pushes his hair back with his bionic arm. "Easily."

FORTY-EIGHT

Tai

"Thank you for coming to save me," Bri says, breaking the silence.

We've been lying here facing each other in the tent for a while, so there isn't anywhere for me to go to hide the surprise on my face.

"You're welcome. It's the least I could do."

"You didn't have to come. Aro could have sent some redshirt to get me. They probably would have seen my crashed escape pod and left me here to rot."

"What's a redshirt?"

"A redshirt is a person who has no name. They are a plot device in old classic sci-fi movies. They would be the first to get killed, raising the stakes, but there's not enough danger by that point to affect a main character," she explains. "Expendable."

"I'm glad I'm not a redshirt."

"You have no idea how close you were to being one."

"Would a redshirt be the hero, get the girl, and ride off into the horizon on a ship at warp speed?"

"No, probably not."

"Then I was never going to be a redshirt."

I drag a fingertip up her bare arm. Tiny bumps erupt over her skin.

"There are about a million reasons why I shouldn't do this right now, but I'm so sick of trying to remind myself of why this is a bad idea," Bri says and pulls me to her. Her lips crush mine and my hands are on her in an instant.

Simultaneously, we scoot closer to each other. Before I can settle in and get comfortable by her side, Bri pushes my shoulder until I'm flat on my back. She swings her leg over my hips and positions herself on top of me.

My cock nestles against her as she slowly circles her hips on me. She pulls away from the kiss and sits straight up on me. One hand is on my chest. and the other reaches behind her to stroke my dick and cup my balls against her.

"Fuck, Bri. Are you trying to follow through on that threat from last night?" What she said about making me cum in my pants has been playing in my mind all day.

She doesn't say anything but quietly laughs at my comment. I'm panting and can hardly draw in a full breath. Her hand rubs up and down my dick over my pants. I imagine the warm, wet sensation of being inside of her.

I reach behind her neck and untie the strap of the tiny top the brethren gave her to wear, exposing her tight, hard nipples. I need to get my mouth around them. I push up to a sitting position, bringing our chests together and creating a new angle for our bodies to move against each other. I suck her nipple into my mouth and take a hard pull.

She gasps and scratches her hard nails down my back. A growl of approval rumbles in my chest, and I dig the pads of my fingertips into her back, clinging to her for dear life. Every point of contact between us feels like the growing pressure of a static charge. An electrical storm you feel long before you see it.

She lifts off my lap just enough for her to grab my dick and tilt it to her pussy. Using me, she rubs her clit up and down with the head of my cock. My underwear gets wetter with every pass. I am losing my goddamn mind.

"All of this for me?" I ask, my voice sounding raspy and low. Both of her hands are on my chest and push me back to the ground. I willingly let her direct me to where she wants me. If Bri wants me crawling through hot sand, I'd do it in a heartbeat.

Bri rewards me with a long hum and another drag up my dick.

Her movements quicken, and her breath becomes ragged, matching mine. When her hips start to shake and her circular movements become erratic, I explode into my underwear. I should be ashamed, but all I've got is awe from watching her ride me. She collapses onto my chest, and her heart beats wildly against mine.

Slowly, she pulls herself up and drops down next to me, her head going right back to my shoulder.

"I warned you," she says dreamily.

"Yes, you did." There goes my only pair of underwear.

Bri traces lazy circles over my chest and snuggles deeper into me.

"Hungry? Thirsty?" I ask.

"Thirsty," she says. I hand her the canteen, and she takes a small drink. Even though we are running out of water, I don't want her to suffer. I can hold out longer without it than she can, so I push it back up to her mouth, urging her to take another drink.

"We're almost out!"

"Don't worry. We'll get to the village tomorrow, and we can find water there."

She eyes me suspiciously but finally takes another drink from the canteen.

Bri settles back against me, and I tug her even closer. "Good night, Sunshine."

"I'm going to bite you the next time you call me that," she says and nips at my chest.

"Don't threaten me with a good time."

FORTY-NINE

Tai

I recognize that arch. This is the village. *The* village.

"This place is in bad shape," Bri says, observing the ruins.

I wasn't sure at first. I thought maybe my mind was playing tricks on me. But the closer we got, the more obvious it became that this is where it all went down six years ago.

I might as well tell her. Now that she's seen the destruction I caused firsthand.

Bri catches my grimace. "Are you okay?"

"I'm fine. Let's see what we can find." I don't feel fine. I feel very far from fine.

"You don't seem fine," she says under her breath.

I push through the mental block that has kept my past secured away. I am going to tell her.

"This is the village I destroyed before I got caught." I look away, afraid to meet her eye. "I did this. It's my fault."

It's one thing for her to hear about what happened. Seeing it is a totally different story. It's so much more real when you can see the destruction with your own eyes. I never saw the aftermath. I was on my way to j'Tilak before the fire was even out.

"Oh shit."

"Yeah." My words hang in the air. I don't know what else to say.

"If I were in your position right now, you know what I would want to hear?" she asks.

"What?"

Please don't let it be some toxic positivity diminishing the fucked-up thing I did back then. Or some pompous statement about how "everything happens for a reason."

Bri steps up next to me and slips her hand into mine, "The only thing I'd want to hear," she says softly, "is, 'I'm here. You're not alone.'"

The sunbaked clay walls surrounding the village have crumbled in up-and-down zigzagging formations. Roofs are caved in. Doors and windows hang from broken hinges. Sand has blown in, piling up against the remaining structures. We let Daisy loose instead of locking her up in the small sty. It doesn't feel right to stick her in there without anything for her to eat or drink.

Every detail is a stark reminder of that day.

"Hello?" Bri's voice is absorbed by the thick brown adobe as she wanders through the space between the small homes.

It's empty here and has been for a while.

We wind our way through the abandoned buildings, peeking into broken windows or doors left open in a hurry. Each home seems to have been cleared out of any supplies, leaving nothing behind.

"Holy fucking shitballs!" Bri says from around a corner.

I can't tell if it is a good or bad shitballs, so I run to her, ready for anything.

Bri disappears into a fully intact structure that has somehow managed to survive. The door opens up to what was once a bathhouse. The colorful tile walls are muted from a thick layer of dust. The open shower room has three stalls on each wall. She pulls off her clothes and kicks away her shoes. I spin away to avert my gaze. But it's too late. I saw the perfect curve of her back to her ass.

I can't tell if she wants me in there with her or not. I've been so wrapped up in my own thoughts that I have lost track of where she and I stand with each other.

"I'll um...give you some privacy."

"Go. Stay. Whatever. I've got to get this sweat and sand off me."

What does she mean? Does she want me to stay? I need to get my head on straight.

At the doorway, I pause, considering my next move. Go? Stay? I look back and the door to her stall is wide open. Water pours down her head and body. Her eyes are closed, and a slight smile brightens her face. She looks like she's in heaven.

Like any other male in this situation, I put as much distance between myself and the gorgeous naked and wet woman. If she wanted me in there, she would have said something.

Every part of me wants to be near her. It kills me to not know if she feels the same. If everything goes to plan, we will be leaving soon, and I don't know whether we'll be in each other's lives or not.

I drag myself away and head into the neighboring building to distract myself from the battle waging in my head. If I keep my focus on getting home, I won't have time to dwell on our complicated relationship, if you could even call it that.

The desert is doing its best to reclaim the territory. Bri was right. This place is in rough condition. In a few more years, it might be completely buried by sand.

Across the way, a building with an intact roof and solid walls stands out like a beacon.

It takes multiple attempts at slamming my full weight against the door to get it open. The rusted metal hinges fight me every inch of the way. Cabinets line the walls of the square room. I wipe away a layer of grime from the windows, letting enough light in to see what sits in the far corner of the room.

A comms system.

I brush off a thick layer of dust and expose the flat, shiny surface of the control panel. I tap the touch screen to turn it on.

Nothing.

I run my finger along the edge of the flat panel, looking for the reboot switch. I toggle it back and forth a few times. Still nothing.

I pull the access panel loose and set it aside, then lower myself to the floor and slide under the desk. Sand trickles down as I reach up into the exposed wiring and start sorting through the mess.

This is going to take a while.

I picture Bri stepping out of the shower and finding out help is already on the way. That image alone makes me move faster. The work is tedious. Tangled up wires and fragile circuit boards, but I don't mind it. Not for her.

FIFTY

Bri

I shouldn't be disappointed Tai didn't join me in the shower, but I am. I shamelessly got naked and tried my best seductive pose under the water. I ran my hands down the sides of my body. And the guy left without a second look.

How does he know I'm safe in here? I could have been attacked by a giant sand worm or taken hostage by some creepy alien. Apparently, all he cares about is getting off this planet and subsequently away from me.

I should be focused on it as well, but there will be something bittersweet about leaving this place. It's been a crazy adventure from start to finish. And Tai and I have... Well, I don't exactly know what has happened between us, but I'm not particularly fond of the idea of going back to how things were before.

I shake out my dress as best as I can before putting it back on and heading out to find him. Across the way, I hear banging around and cursing.

"You okay out there?" I call out to him.

"Yep. Everything's great!" he calls back, which is followed by a grunt and a crash.

I follow the sounds. Tai's occasional curse and clang guide me to a small building in perfect condition.

Tai's long legs stick out from under some machinery. I spot the unmistakable hologram projector over the flat control panel.

"A comms system?! Holy fuck!"

This machine hasn't been used in decades, but this old, reliable tech could be the miracle we have been looking for! I marvel at the serendipity of it all. My brothers rescued an old system like this from a garbage pile. We spent months getting it working again. We even got a brief signal out to the moon colony before the thing shorted out.

Tai tosses the old motherboard to the side. It lands in a pile of electrical components.

"Just a few adjustments, and we should be back in business," he says. Another piece goes flying across the room.

"Here, let me help," I offer and join him under the unit.

"I got this."

"Do you even know what you're doing? This tech was used on Earth more recently than j'Tilak. Let me take a look." I lie on my back next to him, taking inventory of what we've got to work with.

A thick layer of sand is caked onto hundreds of differently colored cables. Broken wires hang limply around Tai's hands while he works to loosen another part.

"I said, I got this," he says and yanks hard on the green circuit board. It snaps in half with a crack. The tiny noise reverberates through me, dousing my hope for a speedy rescue.

A neat trickle of sand pours from the broken piece right onto his face. The only visible movement is the slow clench of his jaw. He lets go, seeming to accept the sand as his punishment for breaking the only piece of tech that could save us.

"Fuck," Tai mutters.

I grind my teeth together, trying to hold back the string of insults I want to hit him with. "I hope you've got a soldering iron in your pack, because that's what it would take to get this thing working again."

I'm proud of my restraint. He hasn't even flinched. The sand is still all over his face. His chest is the only thing moving, heaving up and down, from him trying to hold back a reaction.

I get up and dust myself off while he lies there and feels sorry for himself. I kick his boots.

"Get up. There's got to be a backup here somewhere." I open and close all the cabinets to find the same thing in each one. Absolutely nothing.

With a growl, Tai pulls himself up off the ground and stalks toward the door.

"I need a minute," he says before leaving me alone with the broken unit.

I'm not in the mood to console him. It's his own damn fault. If he had let me help him, we could have disassembled the thing together. I jump up and sit on the counter, my legs swinging beneath me.

It's quiet in here without him. I hate the silence.

FIFTY-ONE

Tai

I stomp around looking for something to destroy. Apparently breaking the comms system wasn't enough. I need something else to smash. I berate myself with every step to the bathhouse.

"You're such a fucking idiot!" I claw my hands down my face. I didn't want her to fix the system. I wanted to be the one to fix it and have it up and running by the time she got out of the shower. I wanted to surprise her with a hologram of Elowen projected on the screen and help on the way. It would have been perfect.

I'm furious. Furious I'm still on this stupid fucking planet. That every single thing has gone wrong. Furious that Bri looks at me with those eyes and that face that sees right fucking through me. I'm tired of being covered in sand. I've broken the comms panel that could have gotten us off the planet without confronting the presumably psychotic Boraei. There's got to be something else around here that I can fuck up.

The knob to the shower comes apart in my hand when I pull a little too hard on it, and a spray of water hits me in the face from the broken pipe. I take a few long, deep breaths to calm myself before I cause more damage.

The next shower over doesn't get my wrath. I turn on the valve more carefully this time. The water comes out instantly scorching. I stand limply under the scalding stream and let the water soak my clothes, not caring enough to remove them.

Only once I'm all clean and I've washed off the last grain of sand will I be ready for Bri to gloat and tell me, "I told you so." I can picture her smug smile. We both know I fucked us out of our way off this planet.

I deserve it. I deserve for her to yell at me, to call me every possible insult.

I face the shower wall and bend at the waist to let my head rest on the cold tiles. A heavy, dull pain expands across my back. A feeling comes up, one I have repressed and swept aside for six years. It's what's kept me company, the thought that's stayed with me for most of my life: I'm a worthless pile of shit.

"Well, that's one way to do it. But from past experience, it's not the most effective way to shower," a quiet voice says behind me.

I can't bring myself to turn around and look at Bri. She's either angry or disappointed. Anger I can handle. Disappointment might send me over the edge.

"Just say it," I tell her. I want to hear her say what a fuckup I am.

"Tai—" She cuts herself off with a huff. I don't detect anger in her voice or disappointment. Instead, there's a sense of understanding.

I peel my forehead off the wet tile and turn toward her. She's standing within arm's reach. The splatter from the shower dots her dress and face.

"You fucked up. But I'm not mad," she says. She guts me with four words. She should be mad at me.

"You should be. I was in a hurry, and I was careless."

"Yes, you were."

"Finally, we agree on something." My hard laugh bounces off the tiled walls. I can't believe this is what it took for us to see eye to eye.

"Why didn't you let me help? I'm familiar with those kinds of comms systems," she says.

I rake my hand through my wet hair. Of course, she could have repaired it.

"I wanted to be the one to fix this." I brace myself for the full fury of Bri. She probably thinks that I didn't consider her capable, but in reality, it was because I wanted to impress her.

"There is another thing we can agree on," Bri says, "If we are going to get off this awful planet, we need to work together."

Instead of screaming at me, which I deserve, she's given me more kindness and understanding than I have ever received in my miserable life. I don't deserve her.

"Here, let me help you." Bri pulls my shirt off over my head. It hits the ground with a slap. Her dress is soaked now. The peaks of her nipples poke through the wet material.

Her hands are at my belt, pulling the buckle loose. I'm painfully aware of my pants tightening from her touch. I reach down and move her hands away, not wanting her to feel what's happening.

Without missing a beat, she pushes my chest until my back is against the wall.

There goes the possibility of her not noticing my pants tenting. It doesn't matter, because they are pulled off and tossed away.

Her dress joins my shirt on the ground in a wet heap. I gulp down air at the sight of her in front of me. My entire body vibrates with the anticipation of what comes next. I haven't stopped wanting her since the first time I saw her.

"I'm sor—"

"No. No more apologies," she says, cutting me off.

She drops to her knees, and her hands trail up the front of my thighs. She opens her mouth and licks around the throbbing head without breaking eye contact.

I hold myself up against the wall in an effort to stop from grabbing onto her. With her lips around my cock, the glint in her eye completely wrecks me.

Her hands work the base, and she bobs her head, taking me deeper into her mouth. The wet slide of her tongue makes my knees weak.

Every thought flies from my head, every self-loathing thing completely forgotten. All I know is pleasure.

Without stopping her mind-destroying movements, she reaches up, grabs my bionic hand, and places it on the back of her head. It reflexively grabs a handful of her soaking wet hair and moves along with her movements, following her lead.

Her groan vibrates from her tongue to my cock, causing my hand to tighten and take control of the pace. Lost in a rush of ecstasy, I get past the point of no return. I pull her head back. I pop free of her mouth, her lips red and swollen.

Cum rips out of me and pulses onto her chest, dripping down along with the water from the shower. Her hands slow down on my dick until the last drip hangs from the tip. She licks it, sending a whole-body shudder through me.

"Your turn," I say and drop down onto my knees.

She gets down on the shower floor and leans back against the wall. Her knees fall open. My middle two fingers slide into her, wet and ready. My palm pushes against her sensitive clit. I push in and out, greedy for every breath and gasp that comes from her.

I move faster and harder, lost in the moment. Her hips rise off the ground to meet my movement. I can feel the tension building up in her body, and her breathing becomes labored.

With more restraint than I've ever used in my life, I stop before she comes apart. Her eyes fly open, eyebrows pinched together as though she is on the verge of pain from the pause.

I stand up and drag her with me. She opens her mouth to say something, but I silence her with a kiss. I lift her up, and her long, firm legs wrap around me. One step forward and her back is against the shower wall.

I nudge inside her slowly. Excruciating pleasure vibrates through my entire body as I sink deeper into her.

Bri's moans echo against the tiled walls of the shower, and she moves with me, circling her hips as I thrust in and out. My hips move harder and faster, in and out. Her moans turn shaky, and every ounce of blood rushes to my cock.

I grab the shower head for leverage and drive into her.

I come with a roar and yank the showerhead out of the wall. Water spurts everywhere as I fill up Bri's soaking cunt. The broken showerhead hits the floor with a clang. I grab Bri's hips, slowing down and riding out the pleasure with her.

FIFTY-TWO

Bri

Water sprays out from the broken showerhead that Tai ripped straight out of the wall.

He slowly brings us down to the floor, with me placed on his lap. As a taller woman, I've never had the specific pleasure of getting fucked against a wall. The physics never worked in my favor until now.

Tai wipes his face and releases a heavy sigh.

"We need to get out of here," he says.

"Good. I was worried that a shower and a fuck made you change your mind about wanting to leave."

"If memory serves, there are plenty of showers and places to fuck back home," he says earnestly.

"I love your pillow talk." I laugh and rest my head on his shoulder.

"Why would I talk to a pillow? You are the only one I want to fuck."

My entire body shakes with laughter. "I don't mean talking *to* a pillow. It's a saying to mean talking after sex. Saying sweet things to each other," I explain.

"You want sweet words?" His broad smile has me questioning things about myself. I'm usually the first to reach for clothes and an excuse to leave after sex. But I'm curious about what he might say.

"Let's call it morbid curiosity."

"Hm." He thinks for a minute, making a show of his introspection. "There isn't a lot that surprises me anymore. But you are completely unexpected."

His words aren't just sweet; they are genuine and laced with awe. They pierce my chest deeper than any compliment I've ever received.

"More," I tell him.

This time, he doesn't have to think about his words. "You see everything, and under that tough exterior, you care about everyone around you. I've never met anyone like you before."

Oh shit.

He continues, his voice quieter now. "You actually believe it, don't you? That everyone deserves everything. That no one is beneath anyone else." He says it like it's rare, something to be treasured.

My eyes heat, and all of a sudden, it's hard to swallow. The realization that he's seen the inside of my soul leaves me stripped naked and completely vulnerable. This is not where I thought the conversation was going to lead. I thought he was going to compliment my tits and we would go back to the fucking.

I don't know what to say, so I kiss him instead. It's not the passionate, demanding type of kiss. It's sweet and tender. His lips brush against mine, full of assurance and a reverence I didn't think possible.

"Your turn," he whispers against my lips. I take a deep breath. It would be much safer to talk about what a great dick he has. But his words make me feel brave.

"You're real, and honest, and don't waste any time sugarcoating anything. It's refreshing and infuriating," I say. His smile impossibly broadens.

"I thought you hated that about me."

"It might be what I enjoy most. That and your giant cock." I can't resist the urge to guide the conversation back to somewhere less terrifying.

"It's nothing compared to these," he says and gently kisses the space between my breasts.

"I knew it! I knew you were getting around to my tits."

His expression shifts, and I feel the weight of his look. "Bri, you are everything. No words, no language could ever fully capture what you are to me."

The intensity in his face and words cut me to the bone. I don't know how it's possible, but this grumpy-ass alien has wormed his way into my heart.

"You know all the right words, don't you?" I lace my fingers with his.

"Just for you. I'd never say these things to a pillow." He smirks, and my heart fills with immense gratitude for the circumstances that led me to him. I wiggle all the way up against him and turn my back to feel him behind me. I pull his arm around me and sink into the embrace. Safety is being curled up against his body and caged in with his metal arm.

My smile won't fade, even though my eyes are heavy. Tai nuzzles into my neck and my body eases me into sleep.

FIFTY-THREE

Tai

We decide to keep looking through the village. The chances of finding anything are slim, but we need anything we can use that will help us along our journey. Side by side, we overturn blocks and open broken doors and cabinets. There isn't even a stick of broken furniture or any sign of previous life here. Nothing but rubble.

I can't get over the sharp contrast between the broken, empty buildings and the vitality that was here before. The lingering guilt inside me resurfaces. I have to remind myself that no one was killed. Everyone got out and made their homes in other places.

These facts are a poor consolation when I'm staring down the destruction I caused. Leaving home is hard enough. Leaving because of someone else's selfishness must be something else entirely.

I scrub my hand over my face and let out a heavy sigh. It's impossible to act unaffected when I'm elbow deep in the consequences of my bad choices.

"Are you okay?" Bri asks.

"It rips me apart to see this place again."

"Tai, look at me when I tell you this." She grips my shoulders and turns me toward her. "That was a long time ago, and if the Sabaaki have chosen to forgive you, then it's time you did the same."

I can't let it go. Holding onto the guilt helps me prove to myself that I still care. For six years, I tried to pretend like it was all behind me. But I've carried the guilt and shame all these years like a silent passenger. Even though it's weighing me down, the guilt reminds me that I'm different now. If I stop replaying my mistakes, will there still be anything good inside me?

Bri wraps her arms around me and lays her head against my chest. Her steady breathing anchors me.

In, out.

In, out.

In, out.

My thoughts stop circling over my failures. I see myself as Bri does, a flawed kid who didn't know any better.

I'm shaped by what happened, not defined by it.

The space inside me that was occupied by shame feels smaller, slowly being replaced by the compassion I've been freely given.

FIFTY-FOUR

"Have you checked this one?" I ask before stepping into another abandoned home. It's dark inside, and sand has piled up high on every side of the tiny home.

The air around us felt fragile after Tai finally broke down. We stood toe to toe, wrapped up in each other's arms for a while. I felt the shift in him. His muscles loosened, and his breathing evened out. When we finally separated, I knew he had forgiven himself.

Tai pops his head in the door and looks around. "No, not yet."

I go to the back where a kitchen once stood. He flashes me a quick smile before heading off to look for more supplies. His gait is lighter from finally letting go of the lead weight he's been carrying on his shoulders.

The cabinets are all empty. I'm worried there isn't anything else here that will help us get home.

I go to the next house. It's a half wall and a secluded stone arch. I come to a stop, reconsidering whether it's even worth going through this one.

"Don't bother. There's nothing there," Tai says, coming up next to me.

A dark shadow crosses overhead, casting everything in an eerie gray. The ship we've been hunting for blocks out the sun above us.

"The Boraei are here," Tai says.

We run to the house with the empty kitchen cabinets and stand on either side of the doorway, our backs against the wall, breathing hard from adrenaline. Tai peeks out every few minutes while I work to slow my breathing.

A radio squelch is the first warning that someone is on the ground and coming in our direction. Tai puts his finger to his lips. I nod, acknowledging his silent instructions.

Heavy feet approach. I can't tell how many, but it sounds like a lot. A hulking figure with a shiny black helmet and black tactical gear passes the house and continues down the road. I breathe a quiet sigh of relief that they didn't see us.

A herd of h'axom follows not far behind. They press tightly together as they run down the narrow roads. The ground vibrates, and their bellows drown out anything else. When the last h'axom passes by, one final figure dressed in black brings up the rear, holding a long metal baton with two prongs at the end. It looks like a giant cattle prod.

Daisy!

"I have to go find Daisy," I whisper-scream and bolt for the opening.

Tai intercepts me and holds me to his chest. "Hold on. We'll find her. You can't do anything if they catch you," he whispers forcefully. I know he's right.

She's been a good girl. The thought of her getting shocked by one of those prods makes me sick.

The shadow from the freighter passes, and the sky turns bright again. Tai looks out and confirms no one else is around. He sinks down the wall and sits.

After the fear subsides a bit, it hits my nervous system that our ticket home is within reach and I'm pumped full of adrenaline. "Alright. We found the Boraei. Now we get that freighter and go home," I say, infusing my voice with all the optimism I have left.

"We are so incredibly, deeply, and irrevocably fucked," Tai says.

"Why were they herding the h'axom?" I ask, not acknowledging the sentiment I share with Tai.

"They weren't herding them. They are poachers," Tai says and looks me dead in the eye. I don't know how he knows that, but I believe him.

"Poachers?"

"That is a bunch of Yuhlari poachers. This is who is supporting the brethren."

"What the fuck is a Yuhlari?" I ask, getting irritated that I don't know what's going on.

"The most dangerous sort in this galaxy. They control organized crime in this quadrant. They make the brethren look like saints."

Realization dawns on me. "They are killing the h'axom for the gland."

"And I'm sure they are making a ton of credits doing it," Tai says.

"Like hell they are. Get ready, we're blasting our way out," I tell him, deadly serious, "These poaching fucks aren't going to get away with this."

"*Now* you want to blast our way out?!" He looks across the open expanse between us and the poachers.

"Don't tell me the great Tai pt'Alquon is afraid of some Yuhlari and a few tiny blasters."

"I know what you're doing, and I'm not going to fall for it."

"We can't abandon the h'axom. I'll never be able to live with myself," I plead with him.

I don't care if it puts me in danger and breaks my "no blasting" rule. What I do know about the Yuhlari is that they have terrorized the Sabaaki, they needlessly kill h'axom, and they support the dreadful brethren.

Three strikes and you're out.

"I'm not saying we leave them, but we can be smart about this. There's no hurry. We watch and wait for the right time. One that doesn't put us in the middle of a blaster fight."

He's right.

I love us working together. Maybe it's because he likes waving his weapon around, or maybe it's because he hates the idea of these animals suffering. Either way, he's on my side and it feels right.

"Let me think. We need a plan," Tai says. His eyes dart around while he runs through options in his head.

"If you try for one second to tell me to hide back here while you try to be the hero." I try to get ahead of any potential reasoning he could give to not let me play a part in our escape.

"Don't you think I've learned my lesson by now? We're doing this together." He links our hands and I know we can conquer the entire universe.

FIFTY-FIVE

Tai

I should have known the Boraei would be someone like the Yuhlari. There wasn't much time to wonder who "the Others" might be. In my mind, they were just another barrier to me getting home with Bri. But this is different. We have joked multiple times about this planet trying to kill us. Now, we are faced with an opponent that would kill us where we stand without hesitation.

The Yuhlari move around with military precision, weapons always at the ready. Bri and I follow from a safe distance. They arrogantly march down the center of the canyon with the herd of h'axom, so we follow from above. It doesn't take long to figure out who's in charge. While Bri keeps her eye on Daisy, who got swept up in the herd, I study the lead Yuhlari specifically.

The Yuhlari are cold-hearted professionals with credits on the line. I can't count how many briefings I've sat through going through the procedure of what we are supposed to do when we come across them. A full training wasn't necessary. It could have been summed up in one word: run.

Periodically, Bri speeds up and gets closer to the poachers. I hold her back, acutely aware of her proximity to danger. She scowls at me every single time. At least this time she believes me when I tell her how dangerous these people are. It's hard to deny when everything about them is menacing. Every instinct tells me to get her as far away as possible. In comparison, the brethren don't seem all that bad. I could have convinced them to not kill me, probably.

I'm about to suggest we retreat back to the village when a Yuhlari walks along the edge of the herd and shocks each h'axom to get them moving again. Bri stiffens next to me and eyeballs my blaster. I shake my head and motion for us to keep moving.

"We have to wait for the right moment," I whisper, locking eyes with her and not looking away until she nods in agreement.

"We don't leave without setting the h'axom free," she says, gritting her teeth.

"Agreed."

I'm not in complete agreement. Her safety is infinitely more important than these animals. We can always get a message out off planet, and the entire force of the universe will descend on these fuckers.

Across galaxies, there isn't much everyone agrees on—except poaching. Enough planets have been destroyed from the practice that it seems to bring everyone together. Now that we know what's going on here, there is no way it continues. Which makes this even more dangerous. The Yuhlari have every incentive to make sure Bri and I don't succeed in our mission.

By nightfall, we reach a shallow, bowl-shaped valley. It's ringed on every side by low rolling hills. The Yuhlari camp sits dead center, with a handful of battered tents clustered in front of the freighter. Our freighter, after tonight.

Bri and I slide down to a boulder halfway down the hillside and press in behind it. From here, we have a clear line of sight down into the camp. Below us, they direct the h'axom toward a rough enclosure built from stacked rock. The wall is tall enough that once the animals are inside, they disappear completely. No way to see past it from here.

The pen doesn't look like their work. Too crude, no tech, probably something they stumbled onto and decided was good enough to carry out their disgusting plan.

The sound of bells draws our attention to our left.

"You have got to be shitting me." Bri gasps as a group of brethren on h'axom ride straight into the camp.

I recognize Boss and Bug-Eyes right away. They dismount and go straight to the leader of the Yuhlari.

"You were supposed to notify us if anyone landed on Sabaak. That was the deal." The Yuhlari helmet amplifies the mechanical voice.

Boss motions wildly with his arms, not speaking loud enough for us to hear what he's saying.

"I don't care about your goddess, you fools!" the Yuhlari barks.

He doesn't give the brethren a chance to respond. Before the last word is out of his mouth, he raises his weapon and blasts Boss. The rest of the brethren fall to the ground with their hands over their heads.

"Oh fuck, oh fuck, oh fuck," Bri repeats over and over again.

I grab her shoulders and turn her to me.

"Don't look at them, look at me."

"Tai, what are we going to do?"

"Don't panic. I have a plan. We are this close, and we are not giving up." I switch on the military training that's been pounded into me over the last six years.

"I'll climb the wall right there." I point to a place on the wall I feel confident I can climb easily and continue. "Then I'll open the gate and set the h'axom free. When all hell breaks loose, you board the freighter and initiate the pre-takeoff protocol."

"You'll make sure Daisy gets out?" she asks.

"I'll take care of her. You just focus on getting that freighter up and running."

"I don't know how to fly those things!" Bri's voice is laced with panic.

"It's easy. Activate the Automated Support System and tell it to get ready for liftoff," I say calmly, aiming to relax her with my tone.

"A.S.S. Ass? Are you fucking kidding me right now, Tai?" Her eyes are wild and disbelieving.

"It doesn't like being called that. Just use the voice activation, and it should do all the rest."

She wrings her hands, and I can see the gears turning in her head, thinking through the plan.

"How are you going to get to the freighter?" she asks, concern etched across her face.

"Blast my way out." A wide smile stretches my face, and I wait for her to argue. Numbly, she nods with me, mirroring my head movement.

"Just get back to me, okay?" The softness in her voice hits me like a nuclear explosion to the chest. I rest my forehead against hers, savoring the calm before the storm. It's the final stand, and I'm not exactly sure how this is going to go down. Bri getting on that freighter is the only thing that matters. I'll do whatever needs to be done to make sure she gets home in one piece.

A strand of pink hair has worked its way loose from her ponytail, and I tuck it behind her ear. I brush my lips against hers and tell myself it won't be the last time, even though the pit in my stomach says something else.

Unable to resist her, I deepen the kiss, imprinting her on my lips.

FIFTY-SIX

Bri

It's the first time a kiss has given me whiplash. My head is spinning when Tai takes a few steps past the boulder toward the Yuhlari camp. Before running down the sloping hill, he turns and tosses something in the sand near me.

"See you on the other side," he says with a big smile.

Down at my feet lies Tai's blaster. Panic collects in my throat. What the fuck did he do? That was not part of the plan. He's going to need this more than me! I snatch it up and watch Tai run impossibly fast toward the h'axom.

He easily finds handholds on the stacked rocks, climbing faster than I thought possible, all while avoiding detection. When he's half over the wall, he looks back at me with a cocky grin and nods, giving me the signal to stick to the plan. He slings his other leg over and drops to the ground, out of sight.

There is no going back now. Watching the poachers throughout the day, we took inventory of their weapons. They each have long cattle prods strong enough to bring down the massive h'axom with one strike, as well as blasters tucked into holsters at their hips.

We're out-gunned and out-manned. None of that seemed to bother Tai in the slightest. As if our escape was inevitable and everything we have been through was just the cost of survival.

I'm not quite as confident. It doesn't feel right to separate now when we are so close to escaping.

Every cell in my body tells me we should have stayed together. The Yuhlari are terrifying, covered in black head to toe, their reflective helmets obscuring their faces.

I gather up all my remaining courage. Tai's got years of military training to fall back on. My little backpacking trips in the wilderness did not prepare me to fight the intergalactic mafia. Additionally, I have hardly eaten in days. I'm held together by adrenaline and pure spite.

The bad guys do not get to win. Not in my story.

From my vantage point, I have a clear view of the gate Tai is going to open. All I have to do is get past the tents and the Yuhlari between here and the freighter. We are counting on the h'axom to cause enough mayhem for us to get through without being at the business end of cattle prods and blasters.

I run through the plan one more time.

The second the h'axom are out, run as fast as possible to the freighter, find the cockpit, initiate lift-off protocol, wait for Tai, get the fuck out of Dodge.

The gate swings open. Its rusted hinges screech a loud warning. In a rush of noise and chaos, the captured h'axom burst through the open gate and straight toward the tents. I don't know how he did it, but somehow Tai got them to go the right way for maximum impact.

"Get out of here, Daisy," I whisper to myself.

It's not far, but the sand is deep, and my legs are tired from going nonstop for the last 48 hours.

I keep my eyes on the pen, hoping to see him running toward me.

All I can see is the stampeding herd, already destroying one of the tents.

I'm barely aware of yelling as I run through the encampment. The freighter is only a few yards away when I hear the blaster fire.

Don't stop. Don't you dare stop. You're almost there.

I run up the ramp and into the empty cargo bay. I climb the closest flight of stairs, praying the flight deck is close. I get to the landing and fling open every door I come to. A galley, a set of bunks, an engine room, and finally, the cockpit.

FIFTY-SEVEN

Tai

Following the last h'axom out in a cloud of sand, I can't see more than five feet in front of me, but I know what's waiting out there.

I stalk forward. The blaster I gave Bri would have come in handy, but there was no way I was going to leave her unarmed. I step over the bodies of the brethren.

I can't believe I feel bad for them. But I do.

The sand settles enough for me to see Bri on the other side of the camp, running full speed toward the freighter. She moves effortlessly through the tents, making great time. Pride swells in my chest at the sight of her bravery.

The zapping red arc of a cattle prod lights up not far from me. I look for Bri one last time, needing confirmation she made it onboard safely.

She dashes up the ramp. My relief disappears before it can fully settle, because not far behind, a Yuhlari follows her up the ramp.

My vision goes hazy. Colors swirl before my eyes, and I struggle to stay focused. I shake my head to stop the ringing in my ears. I didn't feel an impact, but I could swear an explosion just went off. I'm disoriented and can't think straight.

Power radiates from my chest, down my legs, and to my fingertips. Raw instinct takes over.

Destroy. Protect. Mate.

An unrecognizable hand, my own, claws the restrictive shirt from my chest, ripping it in two. I don't think. I strike. A boulder crumbles beneath my feet into dust. Everything standing between me and my mate won't be there long.

A roar echoes over the frenzy around me.

Pounding. Metal bending. Blaster fire.

My side stings, like something bit me. I brush the pain aside easily and move toward the freighter. My head is jumbled. The only coherent thought is to get to Bri.

I grab a blaster out of the hands of the nearest Yuhlari. The weapon crumples like paper in my hand. I toss it aside. The Yuhlari pulls a telescoping baton from his belt and swings it at me.

The metal stick bends to the shape of my chest. A hit that should have knocked me to the ground felt like nothing. The Yuhlari turns and runs in the opposite direction. I don't follow. I stay on course.

Another sting, this one to my shoulder. I look down and see an empty space where my bionic arm should be. I don't bother to retrieve the missing arm, nothing matters but Bri.

A wall of blaster fire is the only thing that stops my progress. I duck behind the remains of a destroyed tent and look for another path forward. I'm cornered, surrounded by the endless bright pink and purple light of blaster fire.

My mind clears enough to know to stay here. I'll wait until they run out of ammo, then I'll take my turn. The beast inside of me rumbles with anticipation at the thought of ripping them limb from limb. They won't live long enough to regret standing between me and my mate.

FIFTY-EIGHT

Bri

Hieroglyphs light up in every color and shape. I scan the panel, looking for anything to indicate takeoff. Where's the bright red arrow pointing up? Or at least something that goes "boom"?

Tai is down there. Unarmed.

Movement catches my attention. It's Tai making a run for the freighter, for me. Blaster fire follows him until he dives behind a tent for cover.

Only it's not the Tai I know. This one is enormous, in size and presence. Power pulses off him in waves, invisible but undeniable. The air around him ripples like the aftershock of a nuclear blast. I feel it from here, a thrum in my diaphragm.

Raw. Magnetic. Barely contained.

"You've got to be kidding me." I shake my head at the realization.

The Tilak who believed he wasn't worthy of a battleform or a mate now has both. All I feel is pride. He's mine, and apparently every cell in his gigantic body already knew it before he did.

"Come on!" I run my hands along the panel. "Where's the fucking universal language when you need it?"

"Switching to universal language," a robotic voice chirps.

A dark, cold laugh from behind freezes me in place. My hands move instinctively toward the blaster.

"Turn around, slowly," a garbled voice orders.

"Okay. Whatever you say."

Time slows down, everything except my pulse racing in my ears. I pick up the blaster. No hesitation. Just the cold weight of it in my hand. I turn and face my own reflection in the shiny helmet. I fire straight into his chest. Smoke drifts up from his chest as he sinks to the floor.

I step closer and fire another round into their chest. "And that's for underestimating me." I nudge the smoking body with my foot. The lack of response tells me all I need to know. I killed someone. I killed a Yuhlari poacher.

"Tai is going to be so jealous that I got to blast my way out." I spin around and look for him through the smoke and rubble. I don't have time to mourn the space trash I just took out. I need to get to Tai.

Back at the panel, I still don't know what to do. Out of pure desperation, I slam my hand down on the panel. The freighter surges to life and slowly rolls forward.

"Enough of this bullshit." I hit the phaser glyph on the control deck and a lever with a hand grip extends forward out of nowhere. I grab it tightly in my sweaty hand and point it at the ground in front of the poachers. The canon fires off, and a huge explosion of sand and smoke obscures my vision. A handful of Yuhlari bodies go flying from the blast. Still no sign of Tai. I wait for the smoke to clear to take another shot.

When I see the coast is clear and no one is left moving, I run for the cargo bay.

Tai, where are you?

He should already be onboard. Something's not right. The feeling is so visceral it costs me my breath.

Then I'm moving. Down the stairs, through the cargo bay, and my feet hit the ground hard. Through the smoke. Through the wreckage. Through whatever gets in my way. There isn't a single h'axom in sight. Relief hits fast. Daisy made it, but I don't stop moving.

I find Tai against a broken post, half collapsed, his bionic arm gone like it was never there.

"You can't follow the simplest instructions, can you?" he chokes out.

"And you're fucking lucky I can't." I check his pulse at his throat. It's weak.

"Come on, let's get the fuck off this planet," he says and tries to lift himself off the ground. He falls back, unable to get up.

Tai groans when I pull him up. I sling his huge arm over my shoulders. It's almost funny how big he is, leaning down on me for support. But no one is laughing, not at least until we are light-years away from here.

"What is it with your arm and this place?" I ask, trying to get him to focus on me rather than the pain. I can tell he's in shock. I'll get him talking and get him to a medbay.

"I wish I knew."

"We're almost home. Hold on a bit longer," I say breathlessly. He's heavy, and the distance to the freighter feels like it's getting farther away.

We stumble together to the ship, him weighing heavily on my shoulders. With a grimace, he climbs the ramp and collapses in the cargo bay. I slam the button down, raising the ramp and closing us in.

On the floor, Tai's head tips sideways and his eyes roll back into his head until only the whites are visible. I roughly grab his face and pull it toward me.

"Tai, look at me. Stay with me. I'm going to get you home."

"Bri, I need to tell you something. You need to know before we leave," he says struggling for breath.

"No, focus on breathing. You can tell me later."

"No, you need to know."

"No, Tai. It's okay. Whatever it is, it's okay."

His head rolls forward, and his eyes catch mine. "You're so pretty," he says, sounding intoxicated. His only remaining hand cups my face.

"Yes, I'm a goddamn beauty queen. Just hold on, okay?"

Tai laughs. "Everybody loves you." His face scrunches in pain. "But nobody loves you like I do. I would never leave you."

"I know you won't ever leave. I know you won't. I'm worried I will." Tears stream down my face and drop on his torn shirt. My heart is being ripped out of my chest. I touch the side of his face softly. The fact that I love him doesn't change that I'm too much like my father. Too restless, too selfish.

"Look at you over there, pretending you can live without me," he says and hisses sharply between his teeth. He grabs at his empty shoulder, writhing in pain.

"It's nice to see you didn't lose your sense of humor along with your arm." I laugh through sobs, wiping tears away with my dirty hand.

"Never," he says with a painful laugh. "You're a lot tougher than I thought you would be."

"I am my father's daughter," I say absentmindedly as I check his wounds. These are words I've thought often but rarely said out loud.

"No, you're wrong. You're like your brothers. Loyal, hardworking, selfless." He struggles to get each word out, breathing hard between each one.

"I love you." With those final words, he passes out, his body going limp.

"FUCK!" I scream and run to the flight deck.

I snap myself into the harness, not bothering to tighten the straps.

"Assistance Support System!" I shout into the air.

Nothing.

"Activate Support System!" I try again. What were the fucking words?!

Nothing.

"Advanced Systems…" Oh fuck this.

"ASS, turn on the goddamn engines!"

The freighter chimes, and the control panel lights up green. Halle-fucking-lujah. Green means go.

"Automated Support System, Activated."

The engines roar to life, and I'm thrown back into my seat. Nausea rolls through my stomach. I do my best to swallow it back down. The freighter lifts off the ground with a swoop, moving faster than I was prepared for. I'm used to the slow movements of a passenger ship—not a freighter that cares nothing for the comfort of the cargo. We break through the thin atmosphere, and the sight of bright stars against a black sky has never looked so good.

"ASS, link to Hycea 34, Aro pt'Burosa," I instruct the AI system.

"It is preferential to direct the voice activation using the official terminology."

Not in the mood to be lectured by a fucking machine, I hit the mute on the control panel and search for the comms glyph. The link goes through and a small Aro the size of my forearm takes shape under the holoprojector.

"How do I get this thing home?" I ask Aro, skipping all pleasantries.

"You have no idea how happy I am to see you," he says with a smile.

"Aro don't fuck around. I need to get back—now. Tai's hurt."

<hr>

The only thing that matters is getting Tai home. I can't eat. I can't sleep. He was restless at the start, constantly tossing and turning, sweating, and mumbling. The last three or four hours he's been completely still. No movement. I watch his chest slowly rise and fall with his breath, afraid to even blink. The only relief comes from obsessively checking his pulse.

We survived Sabaak together. That's how this story ends. It has to. I fell in love with him while he healed from his past. I didn't know it was possible for someone to change so drastically. All those limiting beliefs fell away right before my eyes. It made me confront some of my own thoughts that hold me back.

I've put myself in the same category as my father my whole life. But Tai is right. I'm like the rest of my family as well. I'm not just one thing.

It took incredible strength to hold himself accountable for what happened here all those years ago. I've never admired someone more.

For too long, I've viewed my strong personality and outspoken nature as a liability. I've felt the energy from those around me, on edge, waiting for me to say or do the wrong thing. I never got that feeling from Tai. It's like he wanted me to step into my strength and not apologize for anything.

I worried love would feel like a cage. I was wrong. It feels like freedom. I'm tired of running. And if I'm going to run, I know Tai will be right there next to me.

FIFTY-NINE

Tai

"I know you're awake. You might as well open your eyes." A deep, familiar voice wakes me up from the best sleep I've had in years.

"It's too early for your shit," I slur. My mouth is not cooperating with me. My tongue feels swollen and sticks to the roof of my mouth. I don't need to open my eyes to know Aro is here. Wherever here is.

"There he is. And you were worried he wouldn't be the same old grumpy bastard," Aro says to someone across the room. I blink my blurry eyes, desperate to see who he's talking to.

Bri comes into focus. She's out of the pretty orange dress I got her and back in the khaki coveralls that I met her in.

Huge windows open to every shade of green dotted with bright flowers. Vines snake up the walls around me. MedBots zoom around the room, silently checking my vitals. I'm under a soft blanket, tucked into a clean bed. The best part is there is no sand. Not a single grain.

Bri hands me a steel canteen, and I gratefully accept the cold, fresh water. Our fingers graze, and it kicks off an immediate response for me to grab her, pull her into me, and never let go.

With Aro and Bri here, the two most important people in my life, standing over me, I know what I have to do. For the last six years, I thought I could forget my past and move on. Instead of dealing with it, I covered it up with the military and avoidance.

"We got you all patched up, brother. You should be ready to get back to work in no time," Aro says.

I fiddle with the canteen, not able to look up, preparing myself to finally explain to Aro who I used to be.

"Aro—"

"How are you feeling?" Bri asks at the same time, saving me from the confession. Her voice is unusually quiet. She looks genuinely concerned about me. I sit up on the hospital bed and puff up my chest. The movement knocks the air out of my lungs. Pain lances through my body. I cover it up with an awkward laugh. I hate that she is worried about me. Bri should be carefree and happy, not concerned about a single thing in the universe.

"I'm okay, really." I roll my shoulder, and for the first time since I landed on Sabaak, it's painful yet it moves without a hitch. A shining new bionic arm gleams up at me. Surprised at the new limb, I rub my hand over it. The sleek metal feels brand new, not a single dent. The joints are smooth, and I can tell the neuro-connector interface is an upgraded model. It's quicker and more precise. There's no delay when I think about moving the arm. It just happens as seamlessly as my own arm.

"I can't wait to hear what happened there," Aro says with a glint in his eye. He's a sucker for a dramatic story, but before he hears about the misadventures on Sabaak, I need to come clean about my past. I need to get this off my chest.

"I need to tell you something," I start to say and look up to Aro finally. I'll just rip the bandage off.

Aro registers the seriousness of my tone and drops down into a seat next to me.

"I grew up on a fueling station. It was rough until I figured out the easiest way to survive. I got with a group of other kids who were in the same situation as me, and we lived off stealing from the travelers who would pass through."

I look over at Bri and try to figure out what she's thinking. She nods, encouraging me to keep going. Aro gets the full story. The crooked mechanic, how I got caught, and hiding out on Sabaak.

I shift uncomfortably, knowing that I'm getting to the part I'm most ashamed of.

Finally, I tell him about how it all went down at the end, how I lost my arm along with any thread of integrity when I chose to save myself.

Aro sits there, his face a blank canvas by the time I'm done. I look over at Bri, and her face is red, the blush spreading to her chest. She looks so angry. But she doesn't direct her anger at me.

Bri turns toward Aro and points her finger at his chest.

"Aro, wait one fucking second. Before you say a word, I've got something to say."

Aro contorts his face in confusion at her. He takes a breath to say something, but Bri beats him to it.

"I don't want to hear a word of judgment out of your mouth. No matter what Tai says, this doesn't change who he is. He's the most loyal, determined, and good person on this planet. He's been nothing but a wonderful best friend to you, and he's saved my ass, on multiple occasions. Fine, he made a mistake, maybe a few. But I don't fault him. He did what he needed to do to survive, and he could have continued down that path, but he didn't. He's proven over and over again who he is, and if you can't deal with that, then you take it up with me. Because I won't let you make him feel bad about his past."

Bri's chest is heaving and she's so red-faced, I fear she might pass out. One hand is clenched into a fist at her side, and the other points angrily up at Aro's face.

I should stop her. I know I should pull her back before she does something we can't take back, but I can't move. I can hardly form a thought. The only thing my mind registers is that she defended me. She defended *me*.

Aro's blank face shifts into anger.

"What I was about to say..." He glares at Bri and then turns toward me. "I already knew all of this. I've known about your past since before we met on our first day in the military. I've always known, and it's never bothered me. And even if I hadn't, you don't owe me any explanation or apology."

He looks back and forth between me and Bri and chuckles. "I think you two have some things to work out. I'll see you tomorrow. Glad you're home, brother." He slaps a hand on my chest and turns to leave. "The signing ceremony is at noon. You should be up and around by then."

He reminds me that I'm expected to re-enlist tomorrow, a plan I've been adamant about. A plan that has been falling apart in my head slowly over time.

The first inkling of a different life took shape when Bri told me about her life. How she grew up and all the sacrifices her family has made for her. Everything they are still doing for her. I realized I might be in a position to help in some small way.

Now that we're alone, I push the blankets back and stand up. The room tilts on its side. I'm still a little woozy from being in bed for who knows how long.

Bri steadies me with her hands on both arms. Holding me up. Anchoring me.

"Did you mean all of that?" I ask, hoping it's the truth about how she feels about me.

"Of course. Every word, and more."

"You've seen the worst parts of me, and you still think all of that?"

"I do. Because it's all true."

She looks up at me, and the redness has faded from her face. Now her eyes shine like the sky and I can't look away. There is still so much more to be said, but I reach down and touch her soft face. It's been washed, no trace of sand or dirt or sweat.

"Should we discuss the whole battleform mate thing?" she asks, her eyes waiting to see my reaction.

"Yes, but let me have this first."

My lips are on hers, and everything feels right. All my concerns about our future melt away. Bri erases all doubt when she pulls me to her and deepens the kiss. She is all hope and brightness. I've finally come home.

SIXTY

Bri

"Finally pulled yourself away from Tai, huh?" Elowen looks over at me with a twinkle in her eye. I wish I could argue against the knowing look she is giving me right now. She saw it first, something there. I denied it at every turn, but there is no denying it now.

"The dude lost his arm for me. It's the least I could do." I drop down onto her comfortable overstuffed sofa and look out over Bihar. Since I miraculously got us back, I've been hovering over Tai in the medbay at the military base.

"Does it count if it was a bionic arm?" she asks, knowing full well it counts, she's feeling sassy.

Of course she is. I teased her and pushed and prodded about Aro, and now it's payback time.

"We both know you'd do the same for Aro."

Elowen stops short, her hands full with a tray of sparkling drinks and colorful snacks. Her wide eyes blink at me, and a smile spreads across her face.

"Did you just say what I think you said?" she asks with a disbelieving laugh.

I take a deep breath and reach for my glass. I'm going to need a lot of this to get through what we went through on Sabaak.

"You might as well sit down."

She plops down next to me and turns, giving me her full attention. The story tumbles out of my mouth, starting with when he showed up on the station to "bring me home." Then there was the argument and the evacuation. The crash-landing on Sabaak and wandering through the desert. She laughs hysterically when I tell her about the brethren and the creepiest cult in the universe. When I express how much I loved Daisy, she declares that she wants a h'axom of her own.

Then I talk through the events that led us home. The little details and shifts between Tai and I pour out. How we both made mistakes and missteps with each other, but somehow it brought us closer. And finally, how he shifted into his battleform when he tried to save me from the Yuhlari.

"You don't seem surprised by any of this," I tell her once I've finally gotten it all out.

"You wanted your big adventure, and you finally got it. I'm just glad it brought you back here. I can't imagine a life here on j'Tilak without you." Her eyes are a little misty when she pulls me into a crushing hug.

"Well, about that," I say reluctantly.

"What? No. You cannot leave! You just got back."

"I need to help my family. My mom and my brothers are back on Earth working themselves to death for me. I can't stay here and live the ideal life knowing what they have done to get me here. I'd never be able to live with myself." I haven't been able to bring myself to call them yet. I'm still processing what happened. But I know the longer I wait to call them, the more pissed they are going to be.

"You can bring them here! Aro can find a home and jobs for them!" she pleads.

"I appreciate the offer, but Elowen, we don't have any money to get them here. They are barely making it as it is."

"I know it's expensive. I'm sure we can figure it out." Her unbridled optimism rubs me the wrong way. I'm tired and not in the mood to explain my family's financial situation.

"Elowen, you have lived a very privileged life. You have traveled all over the universe and never known the struggle of survival on Earth." I make sure to be gentle with my tone. She's still my best friend, but I don't think she'll ever fully understand what my life was before we came here.

"I know life is rough out there. I know people struggle," she says, tears welling up in her eyes. "I'm not naive."

I grab her hands and pull her toward me. "It's different when you've lived it."

That's enough said. I don't want to punish her for not knowing what it's like to grow up like I did. I muster up a smile and redirect the conversation.

"It's time for me to get a grown-up job. I've gotten my education, and now I've had my big adventure. Now it's my turn to help them out." Their generosity and sacrifice have fueled me all this time. A small part of me feels obligated to give back, but mostly I just love and miss them so damn much. I want them to have a beautiful life. One that isn't only work and exploitation.

"You don't have to do this on your own. We can help," Elowen pleads with me.

"We'll figure it out. Let's talk about something else. Anything else," I tell her and force a smile. I don't want her to take on my burdens.

"Are you going to the signing ceremony today?" she asks, bringing the conversation back to Tai.

"Yeah, I'm going to meet him there." Another complicated topic, and my tone conveys my mixed feelings about it.

"What? You don't want him to re-enlist?"

"After everything, he's still trying to prove he's good. The service is how he's chosen to do that. I understand it. Someday he'll realize the job was never the point."

I can do my thing while Tai stays in the military. I'll get back to the genetics lab and figure out how I'm going to raise enough money for the foundation, and someday I'll make my dream come true.

SIXTY-ONE

Tai

There was a time when my unit was all that mattered to me. I lived for these guys. Now they are an obstacle, standing between me and the door I'm waiting for Bri to step through. The seats in the large briefing room have filled up in a blur at the edges of my vision. She's got to come.

My plan doesn't work if she doesn't show up.

We haven't had a chance to talk about anything other than my injuries since I woke up yesterday. The recovery has been brutal. The blaster fire I hardly felt in my battleform is crippling now. The neurolink to my new arm fires off randomly as it calibrates. Bri's been doting on me and neglecting everything else since we arrived. It took a while to convince her that I'm fine, and to go see Elowen today.

In truth, I needed time to get my shit together. I wanted to speak with Aro before the ceremony and make sure we were on the same page with my plans. Not that I needed his approval, because I've made up my mind. I am determined to follow through with my plan.

Finally, I see a pale pink ponytail slip into the room. She's obscured by taller, bluer, and broader bodies. She peeks around for an empty seat when her eyes land on me. They light up, and my breath catches in my chest. I never dreamed I would be so lucky to have her look at me like that. It's more than I ever thought I deserved.

I weave my way through the crowd toward her as Aro and Commander Rialto take the stage.

"Take your seats. We're going to begin," Aro announces with more authority than usual, showing off in front of Elowen.

At the front of the room, a large group of new recruits stand in a line, along with a few re-enlisting. I look over the excited faces of all the new recruits, and the memory of my first day flashes in my head. I didn't look like these Tilaks, all eager and excited for service. I was angry and resentful.

Rather than pushing the thought out of my mind, I observe it with kinder, more forgiving eyes. I've dwelled on all of that long enough. It's time for the next phase of my life. I'm never going to fully let go of what happened, but now it's time to use my past as fuel to make things better for others. This is something I've learned from Bri.

By the time I reach Bri, she has a confused look in her eyes.

"Come with me," I whisper. A ripple of electricity radiates from my hand when I set it on her lower back to guide her out of the crowded room.

"What are you doing? They are about to start!" she whispers back. Her breath touches my ear. How could I have ever thought I could survive without her in my life?

"For once, just follow directions." I've expressed a similar sentiment many times before, mostly out of frustration. Today, all I feel for her is pure devotion. It used to drive me crazy that she didn't follow instructions. I thought her flagrant rule-breaking was a problem. Now it's what I love about her. She doesn't need rules and structure to be good. She is brave and strong and can march out on her own and meet everything head-on.

We step out into the fresh air at the center of the busy military base. The military was a place I believed was keeping me safe from myself, but the walls that provided security are now holding me captive. And I can't wait any longer to tell Bri about my shift in perspective.

She melts against me as we walk. The tension and questions leave her body the farther we get from the building. I take in the beauty of j'Tilak around us. The green looks greener, the blues bluer. Nothing like being trapped on a desert planet to make you appreciate home.

I can't fully enjoy the surroundings because I have a job to do.

Suddenly, the message that was so important to get out dies on my lips, and I'm nervous to tell her. I procrastinate by running my hands up and down her arms. The questioning look is back, and I muster up a little bit of courage to say the words.

"I changed my mind. I'm not re-enlisting," I blurt out.

"I gathered that from the maniacal retreat. What happened? Are you okay?" She scans my body.

"I'm good. No, I'm great. Things have changed for me. You've changed me." I swallow hard and continue before she can reply. "I was scared to leave the military. I was scared that if I were on my own, I would fall back into the life I needed to break free from. Going to Sabaak, and being there with you, I knew I hadn't dealt with my past. I was covering it up with all this." I wave my hand around us. Her eyes are locked on mine.

"You know in the old stories when the hero says that he would destroy the world for love? Well, any idiot can destroy a world for love, but I want to build a better one, with you." My voice cracks with emotion.

Bri watches me, never blinking or breaking eye contact. Everything we've been through seems to flash across her mind, and her eyes fill with tears. A single tear runs down her cheek.

"No, no, not tears. I don't think I can handle tears," I whisper and wipe it away with the pad of my thumb. A soft touch on my strong and resilient mate.

"I want that too," she says with a sniffle.

I pull her up into a hug. Her feet dangle a few inches over the ground. I can't help myself, I spin us around. The sound of her laughter takes me to heights I've never seen before.

"Are you sure? Because there's no going back after this," I tell her and set her back down on her feet.

"There was no going back after you hulked out back on Sabaak," she says without hesitation.

"You always have a choice. You aren't stuck with me, if that's not what you want."

I know Bri well enough by now. There is nothing in the universe that can convince her to do something she doesn't want to do.

"You know, it's not going to be easy. Things with me rarely are."

"I wouldn't expect anything less." I truly mean it.

"So...you're quitting your job to be with me? That's probably not necessary. We could have figured it out if you wanted to stay."

"That's the other thing I figured out. I talked to Aro today, and we came up with a plan. I'm going to work for him. And I'm going to lead the transportation and settlement programs. We're going to find a way to make sure those who need it most can come. Not just the wealthy. Starting with your family."

Sobs wrack her body as she leans into me, soaking my shirt with her tears. Her hands come around my neck, and she pulls me even closer. But never close enough.

"Please tell me these are happy tears," I say.

"They are."

SIXTY-TWO

Bri

Tai's house, our house, is hardly furnished. While we portered here, he kept warning me about how small it was. How he's hardly spent any time here. How we can change whatever I don't like. He was so nervous and adorable.

He wasted all that breath because I love it.

I'll probably get some more furniture and a bigger bed. But it feels like me, like us. Before I even got out of the porter, I knew. The single-story, circular structure wrapped in rounded windows, set on the edge of a forest, instantly felt like home.

Once he saw my smile, he puffed up a little and dragged me around for the grand tour. Which didn't take long.

"And here's our room." He pulls back the door. Inside, it's brightly lit with the late afternoon light pouring in. There isn't a speck of dust or a single thing out of place.

"I think it's time I warned you about my tidiness, or lack thereof," I tell him with an awkward smile. I know myself enough to know it won't be long until my clothes are in a pile on the floor, or a dirty cup or plate gets left on a random table.

He pulls me to him, laughter rumbling in his chest. "There is no chance of things getting boring around here. It's your *Mitchell way* of keeping things exciting."

"You say that now, but you might change your mind when you're rounding up my dirty dishes." I bite my lower lip and look up at him. He groans, throwing his head back.

"I can tolerate a lot, but I draw the line at dirty dishes."

I pull him in the direction I want to go. "I'll find some way of making it up to you." I turn him so he's facing me, and his back is to the bed. I gently push on his chest until the bed hits the back of his knees and he lands on the edge.

A different kind of groan escapes his lips as he runs his hands over the curve of my hips to grab my ass.

"I'd like to hear specifics. How would you make it up to me?" he asks as his fingers flick open the snaps holding my top closed. He pushes his hand under the shirt and pushes it off my shoulders.

"Hm," I hum in the back of my throat. "There are a number of things I could do, all of which will make you forget everything else, except my name."

I catch his hand and set it down next to him on the bed.

"Now that we're home, there isn't anyone who will hear you scream my name when I finally let you come," I tell him. I raise an eyebrow at him. God, I love teasing him. This dynamic we have of seeing who will break first. It's intoxicating.

"Let me?" he asks. "Sunshine, you're going to beg me to fill you up."

Fuck, that did it. I shudder at his words and drop down on my knees between his legs. His pelvis shifts toward me, a small movement that has me ripping at his belt and closures.

His hand in my hair gently pulls my head back so I'm looking at him before I can take him in my mouth.

"Say it," he says, the sexiest command I've ever heard in my life.

I wish I could tease him and make him wait for the words he's so desperate to hear. But my mouth is watering, and I want him screaming my name while he comes undone.

"I'm yours."

I lick up the length of his hard cock and circle the tip with my lips before taking him inside of me. He tastes amazing. And the hiss he lets out makes my thighs shake and my panties soak.

"Yep, that'll do it."

The fact that he's still able to speak and hold a coherent thought is a sign I'm not doing enough.

I suck on him and bob my head up and down, occasionally going down as far as I can, taking more and more of him into my mouth each time. I keep up the fast pace long enough to feel his abs stiffen. His hips rock forward with my movements.

I slow down and ease him back toward the bed. Another hiss, and I reach down between my legs to ease the building pressure. I push my hand under my pants and feel how wet I am. With only the glancing touch, I'm almost ready to come myself.

"Oh no, that's mine," he says and pulls my hand free. I look up at him, and when he licks my fingers clean, I lose all concentration and his dick pops free of my mouth. The purple crown glistens, and the bead of pre-cum gathers at the tip.

With a growl, he lifts me off the ground and plants me down in the center of his bed. My clothes are off before I can gather my thoughts and help him get naked.

With one swift thrust, he's inside me. Filling me. He matches the intense pace I set when I was sucking his cock, driving hard into me. When I don't think I can take any more, my back arches off the bed. His hips jerk when his hot cum pulses inside of me, the sound of my name hoarse on his lips with every last thrust.

SIXTY-THREE

Tai

"Wake up, Sunshine," I yell from the kitchen. I could hardly sleep last night and woke up early to get ready for today. I've been frantically moving around the house, trying to make sure everything is perfect while Bri is sound asleep.

"Breakfast is ready! You better be out here in two minutes or I'm coming to get you!" I hear a sleepy groan come from our room.

"I'm up! I'm up," Bri says and I hear her bare feet hit the floor.

I hit the red icon on the processor to prepare her hot noodles. Usually I make her breakfast, but today we are in a hurry. So, it's noodles, and I already know she'll have plenty of complaints.

She pads her way down the hall toward me. I spin and hold the steaming bowl behind my back so she can't see what I've got.

"Sit down and eat. We can't be late," I order her in the sternest captain's voice I can muster. I've got to be careful when I use that tone with her. Sometimes it sends a shiver of desire down her spine. Other times it has the opposite effect, and I'm at the mercy of her wrath.

"Bossy this morning, are we?"

I plunk the bowl of noodles down in front of her and smile widely.

"Are you kidding me? I'm going back to bed," she says.

"Don't you dare. We have to leave in a few minutes. I know you'll want to be there right when they step off the lander."

When she looks up at me, she tries to scowl, but I catch a hint of a smile on her lips. She shovels into the food with renewed enthusiasm, realizing the time.

The food is gone, and Bri is showered and walking out the door in record time. The porter ride to the base is quiet. She spends most of it with her face plastered to the window, taking in the scenery like she hasn't seen it hundreds of times over the last year.

"It's going to be okay. They'll be here safe and sound," I tell her and squeeze her knee. She looks over at me with a weak smile and worry in her eyes.

"I know. I just hate landing. I hope my mom handles it better than I did," she says.

Her mom and brothers are scheduled to arrive in less than an hour, and I don't think Bri will take a full breath until they are on land with us.

"You've gotten better! You didn't even barf when you brought us back here." I offer support, trying to take her mind off her worries.

"I didn't have any choice! I couldn't puke and land at the same time. If someone had bothered to wake up, they could have landed it for me." She looks over with an accusing stare. It's so fucking cute.

"Wake up? It took two direct hits of blaster fire and losing an arm to bring me down! Trust me, I would much rather not have been injured," I say.

"That sounds like an excuse."

"Don't worry, I'll do all the landings from here on out. As long as you don't get me killed by some psychotic cult members."

That gets a laugh out of her. She shakes her head.

"If I remember correctly, I saved you! I could have left your ass there."

The base comes into view, and I scan the sky looking for any glimpse of the approaching lander carrying Bri's family, my family.

The gates swing open, welcoming us onto the busy military base. Porters and Tilaks hurry in every direction in preparation for the landing today. The same base where I saw Bri for the first time. I was such an asshole that day.

Looking back, it's possible I knew who she would become to me. Maybe part of me recognized her as my mate, but I wasn't ready to accept it. I had a lot of growing and healing to deal with before I was ready for someone as amazing as Bri.

"Hey, I love you," I say when I notice her chewing on her lip. I've noticed she does that when she's worried.

"I love you, too."

I stop the porter in a quiet corner, away from the noise and rush of the rest of the base. Once the engine is off, I hop out and jog to her side. I offer my hand as she steps out. Rather than release her hand, I step toward her, blocking her from moving.

I tilt her chin up, directing her eyes to meet mine.

"I remember the first time I saw you. You stepped off the lander, and the suns hit your pink hair."

I curl a strand of hair around my finger, reveling in the softness.

"I was an asshole and a mess. I was so deep in my own shit, I couldn't see what had come crashing into my life. You barged in and tore down every wall. Once your family is all settled in, I want to do the human marriage ceremony."

"You do?" she asks. "I thought you didn't do human stuff."

"I don't mind it so much anymore." I love teasing her. She smacks me in the abs, and I pretend to be hurt with an "oomph."

"Let's do it. Let's do the human marriage ceremony. By the way, I know that you know it's called a wedding." She pulls me down for a kiss. I slip the small box out of my pocket and slide the tiny ring onto her finger.

Surprised, she looks down at her hand, the blue stone glowing brightly on her skin.

"Tai! What?!" She wiggles her fingers up and down, watching the light dance throughout the stone.

"I told you! I want to do the human thing."

"I love—" She's interrupted by a loud roar above. "They're here!" She grabs my hand and hauls me to the landing pad in the center of the base.

Hand in hand, we run to the landing pad and watch anxiously as the lander slowly descends.

A Tilak steps up next to us, examining his yuriOS. "Your passengers must be important for you to have paid for expedited arrival," he says absently as he swipes through the screens on his yuriOS.

"Tai?" Bri looks over at me. "You did this?"

I pull her into my side and nod at the lander extending its landing gear a few feet off the ground. "Look. They're almost here."

"Don't change the subject. Did you pay for them to come here? I thought it was part of the relocation program." She doesn't look away from me, and I don't want her to miss the landing, so I answer her questions.

"I didn't want you to have to wait. I have credits saved up from my time in the military, and I called in a few favors."

Tears stream down her face. "I can't believe you did that," she yells over the loud engines of the lander.

She shouldn't be surprised. I told her I wanted to build a better world for her.

Hot wind from the propulsion blasts hits us, and she finally turns her attention to the lander. The ground shakes when it comes to a halt. The engines go silent, and the whole world freezes in anticipation until the cargo door whooshes open and Bri is already running for the descending ramp. She crashes into an older woman and wraps her arms around her with a tight squeeze. Her three brothers are close behind. They're all blond, so Bri's pink hair stands in contrast.

They all collide into a group hug, holding each other tight. I've lost sight of Bri. She's in the middle, surrounded by love.

My heart stutters at the sight. I wonder what that's like.

The group untangles, and Bri reaches for me. My feet carry me to her, unable to resist her call. The circle opens and folds me in. I'm suddenly surrounded and held tight with the rest of them.

We stay silent long enough for me to start feeling a little uncomfortable. It's going to take some getting used to, all the affection and people around. We finally pull apart, and I smile at Bri's mom for the first time. They look a lot alike. Bright smile. Big, round blue eyes that match the color of my skin.

"Everyone, this is Tai." Bri laughs and wipes a tear away.

They all turn and look at me with matching smiles. I notice Bri's mom is carrying a puke bag. Without a second of hesitation, I reach for it.

"Here, let me help you with that."

ACKNOWLEDGMENTS

It's magic when an idea turns into a story. Turning that story into a book is something else entirely. That part takes dedication, delusion, and the support of a handful of enablers. The number of my enablers continues to grow, and I am grateful for each one.

Somewhere deep in the internet lurks a small but mighty group of authors. Thank you for the support you've generously given. While juggling life, their own writing projects, and the never-ending quest to beat the algorithm, they have been an amazing source of laughter and strength. Bex, I can't make any promises, but I will attempt to learn where a comma goes (someday).

Rachel, Lauren, M.D., Lyra, Marina, and Warren. It's a vulnerable thing to hand over an incomplete story and ask for feedback. Thank you for helping make Untangled stronger.

Brandon, we have officially reached year 12, the perfect spot in a relationship according to Liz Lemon. Thank you.

And a big-huge-enormous-gigantic thank you to my readers. How did I ever trick you into reading this silly book? Seeing you connect with the story has meant more than you'll ever know.